# FATAL REACTION
## The Beginning

M.A. HOLLSTEIN

ISBN-13: 978-1537150581
ISBN-10: 1537150588

**Book Cover Art by:** SelfPubBookCovers.com/Fantasyart

**Fatal Reaction**
The Beginning
Survival
Battle of the Hunted
Nightfall

**When Darkness Falls**
Awakened
Metamorphosis

**The Niburu Chronicles**
Book of Dreams
Ashes to Diamonds
Hidden Identity

**Ms. Aggie Underhill Mysteries (In Order)**
Deadly Withdrawal
Something's Fishy in Palm Springs
Maid in Heaven
A Hardboiled Murder
One Hell of a Cruise
A Prickly Situation
Vegas or Bust
Dead Ringer
The Case of the Haunted Address
The Mystery of the Beautiful Old Friend
All I Wanted was a Drink
Love is Murder
End of the Rainbow

**A Vienna Rossi Paranormal Mystery**
Awakened Within
Beautiful Beginnings
Cheating Heart
Ghostly Gig, A Vienna Rossi Halloween Short Story

# Chapter 1

Freaking out, Ellie was eyeing her gas gauge, while watching the little red needle steadily drop. Never again would she listen to her stupid GPS. From now on, she'd research the best way to go before relying solely on her phone. She realized that making good time while cutting through the barren desert wasn't worth her sanity. What if she were to break down? Then she'd really be screwed. Ellie glanced at her phone. The damn thing was barely getting any cell service, one bar at the most, and it was intermittent.

After spending the weekend in Las Vegas with some old college friends, Ellie was venturing back home to Oceanside, in San Diego County. Friday, on her way to Vegas, she'd taken crowded, overly populated Southern California highways, and had spent the majority of the afternoon, and evening, sitting in traffic. Therefore, today, she'd programmed her GPS app to avoid highly traveled freeways. She didn't want to sit in traffic with everyone leaving Las Vegas to return home for the work week. That was a *big* mistake! At first, she thought it was great, zipping through the open desert at high speeds with no signs of congestion. Now, she was practically hyperventilating, eyeing her gas gauge like a mad woman, staring at the warning light that'd popped on reminding her that she was running on fumes.

*No duh!* she thought, tapping on the plastic console as if that'd change the situation. *Stop reminding me!*

And, as if that wasn't bad enough, quite a ways back, to conserve gas, she'd turned off her air conditioning. She was sweating to death in the 110 plus heat.

"Oh, thank God," Ellie sighed with relief when she noticed the rundown gas station up ahead.

Running on fumes, Ellie drifted into the dusty, sand covered asphalt lot and maneuvered her car in front of two ancient looking lonesome pumps. She switched off the ignition, swung open her door, and slithered off her sweat soaked seat. Standing in the brilliant sun baking her skin, she shielded her eyes and frowned at the barren building. She didn't like the appearance. The ancient, sun-bleached plaster made it kind of eerie looking. It reminded her of the sort of place you'd see in a horror movie. If she hadn't been in desperate need of gas, she'd never have stopped.

For a moment, she stood there just staring at the building, contemplating on what to do. Not that she had much of a choice. She noticed that there was a vehicle parked on the right side of the building. It was an old, white, Ford pick-up truck that'd seen better days.

Reaching into her car, Ellie grabbed her purse from the passenger seat. Even though the store looked a bit creepy, she was relieved to see the open sign in the window. Thirsty, and also in need of a restroom, she pushed her fears aside.

Pushing open the dusty glass door, the hinges

squeaked, announcing her arrival. Ellie sighed as she was greeted with a heavenly gust of cool air from an old swamp cooler. She made her way up to the counter, tugging at her wet tank top which was clinging to her skin. An older gentleman wearing an old, faded denim baseball cap was sitting in a white plastic chair, watching television on a tiny box TV.

"Have you seen the news?" he asked her, glancing over the thick lenses of his black plastic frames as she approached.

"Um, no. No, I haven't," she said, a bit taken back by his question. "I've been traveling."

"Some sort of epidemic gone viral." He shook his head. "That's why I live here. Stuff like that never affects us desert folk like it does them city folks…"

Not really knowing what the man was talking on about, or caring, Ellie cut him off mid-sentence. "Do you have a bathroom?"

"Right over there," he said, pointing to the other side of the room.

"Oh, and um, I'd like to put this on pump one." She slid two twenty-dollar bills, more than half of her Las Vegas winnings, across the counter.

"Sure enough. It'll be ready for ya."

"Thanks," Ellie said, eyeing the aisle of snacks, and then the refrigerator along the wall, filled with bottled sodas, juices, and water. She'd be sure to grab something on her way out.

She then noticed the grungy door with a blue plastic plaque adhered to it showing that the restroom was for both genders.

*Oh, well,* she thought. *When you gotta go, you gotta go.* She'd be careful not to touch anything. Her biggest concern right now was trying to get her sweaty shorts down and then back up again. She tugged again at the back of her wet tank top that was glued to her skin before entering the small restroom. To her surprise, the bathroom wasn't as bad as she'd expected. It was clean, just old.

After washing her hands, and splashing cold water on her face, Ellie felt rejuvenated and reentered the little store. She went straight to the refrigerator section and grabbed the largest bottle of spring water she could find. She then made her way to the snack aisle. She grabbed a bag of potato chips and a couple of candy bars. She was debating on what flavor gum she wanted when the front door crashed open. She heard a woman weeping.

"Are you alright, Miss?" the old man behind the counter asked.

Ellie peeked over the candy aisle and glanced at the counter. A woman in denim cut-off shorts and a pink T-shirt shuffled over to it, moaning.

"You don't look so well," he said. "Need me to call an ambulance?"

The woman let out a horrific moan and doubled over while clutching her stomach.

"Miss?" he asked. "You okay? Miss?"

Curious, Ellie walked over to the counter with her snacks and water in hand.

"I'm gonna call for help," the man said, picking up the receiver of an old rotary phone. Ellie didn't even know that rotary phones still existed. "Mind you, it might take a while," he explained while dialing. "Bein' we're out in…"

"Aurghhh…" The woman collapsed to her knees.

"Oh my God!" Ellie shrieked. She set her purse and things on the counter and kneeled next to the woman. She gently patted her back. Extreme heat radiated through the thin cotton fabric. The woman was burning up. "Are you okay? What happened?"

"Uhhh…" the woman groaned. She lifted her head. Ellie gasped, quickly hopping to her feet. The woman's face was puffy and swollen, covered in what resembled hives, distorting her facial features. What terrified Ellie the most was the woman's eyes. They shined a bright golden yellow. Red, broken, blood vessels spider-webbed around a yellow center.

"Maybe she's having an allergic reaction." Ellie glanced at the old man, who was still fussing with the phone. She wasn't a doctor, she was an administrative assistant, but she'd had several allergic reactions in her time. If that's what was happening, the woman needed steroids and Benadryl.

*But her eyes…* Ellie thought. *What'd do that to her eyes?*

"Yes, okay," the man hung up the phone. "Paramedics are on their way. Might take a while, though."

"Benadryl," Ellie said, in a rush. "Do you have any?"

"Um, yes… I think so." The man finished putting Ellie's snacks in a bag and then shuffled around the counter. "It's over here."

The woman clutched her stomach again, bellowed out in pain, and then buried her face in her hands.

Ellie followed the man. He stopped in front of a shelf with over-the-counter products and scratched his head. "This might work," she said, grabbing a box of generic antihistamines next to a bottle of aspirin. She also grabbed a dusty box containing a bottle of the children's liquid allergy medicine in case the woman's throat was too swollen to swallow pills. She prayed that this would help, or at least keep the woman stable until the paramedics arrived. She remembered when she had a near-death experience due to an allergic reaction caused by Penicillin and how horrible it was. She'd been scared to death.

Ripping open the box, Ellie thought she'd start with the liquid. The woman didn't appear well enough to swallow pills. "Here," she said, kneeling next to the sobbing woman. "Try to drink some of this, okay? I think you're having an allergic reaction."

The woman didn't respond.

Ellie pursed her lips. She gently patted the woman's back, amazed by the amount of body heat she was generating and held the open bottle in her other hand. She decided not even to bother measuring the liquid. Any amount of antihistamine would be better than none. She just hoped the woman could swallow it.

"This is just like on TV," the old man said, standing behind her, watching. "Be careful. They say it's contagious. Nothin' like this ever happens out here…"

Ellie had no clue what the man was going on about. "Please, try to take a sip. It's okay. I'm trying to help you… please…"

The woman lifted her head. A deep rumbling resonated from her chest.

Ellie held the bottle to the woman's white lips. "I think you're having an allergic reaction," she repeated. "It's okay. This'll help. I promise."

The woman lifted her hand. Ellie thought she was going to take the bottle from her, but instead, she smacked the bottle out of her hand. Grape flavored syrup spilled onto the floor. Before Ellie could even comprehend what was happening, the woman shoved her. Caught off guard, Ellie toppled backward and landed hard on her bottom. Scrambling to her feet, she couldn't believe her eyes. She watched, horrified as if in slow motion the young woman lunged at the old man. The woman's shrieking was bloodcurdling. She and the man crashed down into a row of chips and crackers. Boxes and bags flew off the shelves, scattering all over the floor.

It took Ellie a moment for her brain to register what she was witnessing. She wasn't sure what to do. She grabbed the first thing she saw that could be used as a weapon, a bottle of cheap wine. The man screamed as the woman clawed at him, digging her nails deep into his flesh. Giving into the fight or flight instinct, gripping the neck of the bottle with both hands, Ellie smashed the bottle against the back of the woman's blonde head. Glass crunched, shattering everywhere as it collided with the base of the woman's skull.

"Get off him!" Ellie screeched. "Get off him!"

Dazed, the infected woman got to her feet and stumbled backward, far enough away from the old man for Ellie to get a glimpse of what was left of him. Blood poured from his nose, and he had deep gashes from the woman's nails across his neck. His eyes were closed. Ellie couldn't tell if he was still breathing. The crazed woman spun around and snarled. Her golden yellow eyes fixated on her new target.

*Shit!* Ellie still clutched what was left of the wine bottle in her hand. The end was sharp and jagged. "Stay away from me!" she yelled jabbing the air with the bottle. "I mean it! I swear… don't even come near me!"

Tilting her blonde head to the side, her silky locks slid forward, covering half her face. The woman lifted her puffy upper lip and bared her blood-stained teeth.

Taking tiny backward steps, not daring to look behind her, Ellie's back hit the counter, startling her. She jumped, dropping the bottle. The woman sneered, hunching her shoulders and bending her knees as if she were some wild animal ready to pounce.

"I'm warning you!" Ellie's voice squeaked, heart drumming in her ears.

"Crrrrlllaauhhh…" the woman gargled. A disgusting mixture of drool and blood dripped from her swollen mouth.

"Run!" the old man yelled, staggering toward the infected woman.

Ellie's brown eyes grew large. She hadn't even noticed the old man get up off the floor. He and the woman crashed into the opposite side of the aisle, taking down several shelves.

*What was he doing? She couldn't just leave him.*

The old man screamed out in agony. The crazed woman was now on top of him, mauling him. Within seconds, the woman buried her teeth into the man's neck, ripping out a chunk of his flesh. The man's eyes rolled back in his head, and he stopped squirming. Blood gushed from the wound and pooled on the floor. The woman continued to emit a series of guttural grunts as if she were some sort of wild animal, gnawing on her prey.

Frightened, not knowing what else to do, Ellie took this chance to escape. She ran toward the counter, near the door. With a one-armed swoop, she grabbed her purse. Heart racing, she ran straight to her car. Clutching the handle, she yanked open the door and jumped inside. With trembling fingers, she searched her purse for her car keys.

"Come on, come on…" she fretted. She kept looking up and staring at the glass door while groping around in her purse. Frustrated, she dumped the contents onto the passenger seat. Spotting the keys, she grabbed them and started up the car. She threw it in reverse when the engine sputtered.

"Come on!" she yelled, staring at the red light of doom. Her gas tank was still empty.

She glanced at the door. The rabid woman was still inside. She had two options; option one, she could make a run for it and follow the road. Eventually, someone would find her. The paramedics had been called. Surely, they'd be there soon. Her second option would be to start pumping gas. After all, the pump was primed and ready for her.

Not happy with either option, Ellie reached for her latch to open the tank. With a snap, she heard the little door pop open. Still staring at the glass door, heart racing, she took a deep breath and prayed. Careful not to make too much noise, Ellie opened the car door and slid back out of the driver's seat. Taking another deep breath, not even aware of the fact that she'd been holding it, she made a dash for the nozzle. She turned and stared again at the door.

Still closed.

*So far, so good.*

Grabbing the nozzle, she shoved it into the gas tank. She pushed down the little latch on the handle to keep the gasoline flowing, but it was broken. She wanted to wait in the safety of her car while the pump did its thing. Unfortunately, she'd have to stand there, holding the trigger down.

"Damn it!" she muttered, under her breath. "Come on! Come on!"

She glanced at the door.

Still nothing.

She then glanced at the numbers slowly rolling on the pump. *Tick, tick, tick…* They seemed to be moving in slow motion as the gas trickled into the tank.

"You've got to be kidding me." Her heart thudded while her stomach rose into her throat. "Hurry up." She tapped her foot impatiently. "*Hurry!*"

Just then, a crash alerted her. Ellie looked up to see the woman stumbling out of the building. Blood drenched the front of her pink T-shirt and was smeared across her distorted face. For a second, Ellie froze. So did the woman. When the yellow eyes made contact with hers, Ellie let go of the nozzle and raced for the safety of her car. Her fingers fumbled with the handle.

Once inside, she slammed the door shut and twisted her key in the ignition. Immediately, she tapped on the door lock button several times, praying that all the doors were secure. The woman lunged at the hood. *Thump!* Her body thudded against the windshield. Her face was pressed against the glass. The sight of the old man's blood smearing across the windshield made Ellie feel sick.

Making a snap decision, Ellie threw the car into reverse. It hesitated for a second as if something was holding it. Then there was a loud metallic clanging noise. Ellie realized it was the nozzle wrenching free from her gas tank. The snarling woman clung to her windshield. Ellie thrust the vehicle into drive, lurching forward, and then slammed on her brakes, hoping to dislodge the rabid woman. Unfortunately, she was still clinging to the windshield wipers, eyes locked onto Ellie's. Determined to be rid of this woman, Ellie stomped on the gas. The woman's body shifted, sliding sideways across the hood. Unable to see around her, Ellie swerved blindly onto the main road, praying there were no other vehicles. She couldn't see what the hell she was doing and the last thing she needed was to be sideswiped. She floored it. Frightened, tears escaped her eyes, rolling down her cheeks as the snarling woman lifted an arm to claw at the windshield with bloody fingertips.

*Fwop!* Losing her grip on the wipers, the woman rolled and flew off the car. Ellie glanced in her rearview mirror at the crumpled body in the middle of the road. It wasn't moving. She wasn't sure if she should stop and wait for the paramedics to arrive or to keep driving. She began to slow down. Sirens sounded. An ambulance, followed by a Sheriff's car, was headed in her direction. Ellie slowed down, and then pulled over, relieved to see help. The sirens of the oncoming vehicles whirled in a blaring surreal sort of way as they passed by her.

# Chapter 2

Amanda wasn't sure what to do. Her boyfriend was in pain, doubled over, and moaning. Filled to the brim with nervous energy, she paced back and forth on the other side of the door. There was nothing she could do for him, short of taking him to the hospital, but he refused to go. He was so freaking stubborn. *Why won't he just go to the hospital?* She knew why, but still, she wondered if he'd rather die than take a chance of possibly going to jail. Glancing over at the TV, she shook her head. All day, reports of a dangerous epidemic had been broadcasted. Since it's considered extremely contagious, people were warned to stay indoors. *What good would it do to be trapped indoors if my boyfriend is infected?* For all she knew, at this very moment, he was spreading the goddamn disease to her. *Enough was enough!*

Flinging open the bedroom door, she glared at Jasper. He was clutching his stomach. "That's it!" she said, hands on hips. "I'm taking you to the hospital."

"No!" he moaned. "It's just the flu, baby."

"Just the flu?" she said, stomping a foot down. "Have you seen the news? People are dying! You wanna die?"

Jasper groaned.

"Come on," she said. "Let's go."

Jasper looked up at her. His forehead had broken out in a sweat. "I swear, it feels like food poisoning."

"That's why you need to get to the hospital, you moron. Get up!"

"Don't call me a moron, *bitch*!"

"Get up!"

"There'll be police... I can't."

"I think the police have got their hands full. They ain't gonna be lookin' for a small timer like you. Now get up!" Amanda kneeled, slid her arm around his waist, and tried to heave him to his feet.

"Who you callin' small timer?" he groaned. "Ugh... Fine," he said, pushing her away from him. "Let's go. My head hurts, and I feel like I'm gonna puke."

"Don't you get sick in my car," she said, sliding open a dresser drawer to snatch Jasper's gun before leaving the bedroom and entering the living room. "Where's my purse?"

Jasper leaned against the wall for support. Amanda spotted her purse on the kitchen counter and slipped the gun inside of it. She grabbed her keys from a hook on the wall. "Okay. I'm ready."

Jasper wrinkled up his brow and spat at her, "They won't let you in with a frickin' gun! What are you? Crazy? You wanna put us both in jail? Leave the gun here!"

Frowning, Amanda glanced at the gun in her purse and then made a snap decision. "I don't care." She shook her head. "It's going with us. You've seen the news. I'm not taking any chances. I'll take the heat for the gun. We need protection."

Jasper glanced at the TV. People were rioting; buildings were on fire, the usual panic when something major happened. "Yeah… okay… just leave it in the car. Ugh!" He doubled over in pain. "We need to get there… quick!"

"No, duh," Amanda said, grabbing hold of his arm and guiding him out of the apartment building and over to her older model blue Toyota.

They made it to the car fairly quickly, even with Amanda balancing in her new four-inch gold strappy heels. She clutched the handle and opened the passenger side door so that Jasper could get in. She was relieved when he easily slid into the seat. She closed his door and looked around. The neighborhood was quiet except for the sound of ambulances and police sirens.

Amanda found it hard to believe that according to the news, people were rioting, and the city was going straight to hell, not too far from there. Unfortunately, the hospital she wanted to go to was located smack in the middle of all the mayhem, and she was a nervous driver. Southern California traffic always frightened her. Nevertheless, she didn't have much of a choice. Jasper needed her.

Amanda took a deep breath to steady her nerves and got into the car. "Here goes nothing," she said, starting it up. They weren't even four blocks away when Jasper started fussing and yelling at her.

Amanda did her best to keep her temper. She kept telling herself that he was sick and to ignore the name-calling.

"Oh, God," Jasper groaned, clutching his middle again. "Hurry it up, will you!"

"I'm trying! Just hold your horses!"

"You drive like a frickin' granny!"

"If you'd listened to me earlier, we'd already be there by now!" she spat back, turning right at the streetlight that'd lead her into town. She hopped onto the freeway, drove a few miles, and got off at the exit leading to the hospital. Her heart sank as she hit a sudden wall of traffic.

"I think I'm gonna puke!"

"We'll be there soon."

"I…uh…I don't think, I…" Jasper began to cough, bile rising in his throat.

"Roll your window down!" Her eyes darted from car to car. No one was moving. Up ahead, she watched as the light turned green. Still, no one was moving. Several angry drivers were laying on their horns.

"Uhnnn!" Jasper moaned. Amanda was about to tell him again to roll down his window, but because he looked so miserable, she decided not to say anything. She'd never seen him ill before.

Rolling down her window, Amanda unlatched her seatbelt and stuck her head out. "Hey!" she yelled at no one in particular. "What's the holdup? Move it!" Not knowing what else to do, she blew off some frustration by joining in on the chorus of horn honking. Jasper's moaning was getting louder. Listening to him was driving her crazy. She needed to get him to the hospital right away. The damn traffic wasn't even moving. Suddenly, Jasper threw open his door.

"What are you doing?" she asked in a panic, tucking her long blonde hair behind her ears. "You okay?"

Jasper leaned over and heaved his guts out onto the asphalt. Amanda watched as the stoplight changed from green to yellow to red. Not one of the cars had made it through the light. They were still at a standstill.

"You've gotta be kidding me!" She slammed her hands down on the steering wheel. "That's it!" she yelled, flinging her door open and getting out of the car. She leaned in and grabbed her purse from the floorboard, keeping her gun with her. "Screw it! We're walking!"

She marched around to the other side of the car; Jasper's side. His door was still open and his head between his legs.

"What are you doing?" he asked, his voice barely a whisper.

"I'm gonna get you to the hospital. Come on." She did her best to step over the puke-spattered ground; she didn't want to get it in her sexy sandals while helping Jasper out of the car. She was genuinely worried about him. His face was so pale that he no longer looked African American. His skin was almost as pale as her own. She'd never seen him sick like this before. He'd always been so strong and healthy. "It's only a couple blocks away. Walking will be faster than driving."

"What about your car?"

"We don't need it."

Jasper didn't argue with her. He was too weak.

Amanda looked over her shoulder to see a man in the car behind her shaking his fist at her. She rolled her eyes, flipped him the bird, and then helped Jasper weave through the traffic over to the sidewalk. He was dragging one of his legs, slowing them down.

"You okay?" she asked, looking at him. For the first time, she noticed what looked like a set of claw marks on his neck. The redness stood out amongst his pallor. Jasper didn't answer. She could hear him gasping for breath as she practically pulled him along. She wanted to ask him about the marks. *How'd he get them?* They looked like a set of women's fingernails made them and she was worried she already knew the answer. She wasn't sure she wanted to know. If he told her that he'd been fighting with his ex-wife again, she'd lose it. She'd dump his ass right there in the street. Jasper's relationship with his ex drove her freaking nuts. If it was over, it should be over. There shouldn't be a reason for them even to talk, let alone see each other, or argue. It's not like they had kids together or even owned anything together.

Amanda wondered why she continued to put up with his sorry ass. It was beyond her comprehension as to why she continued to see him. All he ever did was walk all over her. Half the time he wasn't even nice to her. And she knew something was still going on with him and his ex. She wouldn't at all be surprised if she were to learn that he was cheating on her. She knew he was no good, yet she kept dating him, anyway.

*Why? Why was she allowing this to happen?* She was an attractive woman with long blonde hair, green eyes, and was in pretty decent physical shape. She could easily rate a man that'd at least treat her with respect. *So why did she put herself through this?* Maybe she was attracted to the bad boy image. Or maybe she wanted to fix someone who was more messed up than she was. Heck, maybe she was just afraid to be alone. Whatever the reason, she just kept on dealing with him and all of his crap. *At least he's better than my ex-husband,* she thought. Not that that was saying much. Her ex-husband was nothing but a piece of...

"Uhn," Jasper groaned. His legs were barely moving.

"Keep going. You can do this. We're almost there," Amanda lied, trying to stay positive. She was lying just as much for her own sake as she was for his. "We'll be there soon."

A sudden, ear-shattering scream practically made Amanda trip over her stilettos. "What the..." Jasper leaned into her for support and groaned some more.

"Let's keep walking. It's nothing. Just walk," she said, trying to keep up the motivation. "We're almost there..." She was thankful that Jasper's legs began to move a little faster.

The scream rang out again over the loud honking of car horns. From the corner of her eye, Amanda spied a woman in a black and red dress running down the middle of the street dodging cars. A dark-haired man was chasing after her, snarling. He pounced on one of the cars, landing on the roof while reaching over the side, trying to get to her.

"Oh my God! Faster!" Amanda urged, practically pulling Jasper along. His weight was slowing her down, and his right leg was barely moving. "Come on, baby! You can do this!"

The woman's screams pierced Amanda's ears. Other screams joined in and rang out all around her.

People were opening their car doors to see what was happening. Amanda didn't look back. She pushed on. The sidewalk was becoming crowded. Frantic people were running about, screaming.

A man in a black coat and sunglasses bumped hard into Amanda's shoulder. "Watch it!" she snapped. The man didn't apologize or even bother to acknowledge her. Crowds of people were closing in on them. Some were screaming, some crying, most were looking frightened and confused. "Move it!" Amanda yelled, pushing people along. "He's sick! Move it! Get out of the way!"

People continued to swarm around them. None were paying her any attention. Through the throngs of people, she could hear more blood-curdling screams coming from the street. A mother with two children rushed past her, and one of the kids flew into her leg. Amanda stumbled, losing her grip on Jasper and he collapsed to the ground.

# Chapter 3

Spotting Ellie's blood splattered windshield and front hood, and then the body crumpled on the side of the road, the ambulance slowed down. The Sheriff's car slowed too and pulled over. The Deputy jumped out of the car; gun drawn. Ellie got out of her car and watched as the Sheriff, gun pointed, cautiously walked toward the dead woman. He nudged the woman's shoulder with the toe of his boot. He turned and nodded at two paramedics walking up behind him.

"She's dead!" Ellie heard him say.

The paramedics pulled on thick black rubber gloves.

Ellie's legs felt like Jell-O. Her knees were weak, and she could feel her body trembling the closer she got to the dead woman. At any moment, she expected the woman to jump up and attack.

The sheriff turned around. Eying Ellie, he raised his gun again. She stopped dead in her tracks. Not knowing what else to do, she raised her hands just like she'd seen people do in the movies. "She attacked a man at the gas station," Ellie said, thinking the Sheriff was extremely good-looking, except for the way he was aiming his gun at her. That was a turn-off. "I was there."

"Did she touch you?" he asked.

Ellie stared at him and wondered why he'd ask such a question. Did he think she murdered this woman? Ellie kept her hands up and took a couple of steps closer. Maybe he couldn't hear her. "She *attacked* someone!" Ellie said loudly. "She went all crazy!"

"Stay back! Don't you move any closer!" he warned. "Did she *touch* you?"

Ellie couldn't remember. *Maybe. No. She didn't think so. Would that make her a murderer if the woman hadn't touched her first? She didn't understand the question.*

"No," she said, finally. "I don't think so. She *killed* a man. I saw the whole thing. And then she came after me."

"You positive?"

"Of course, I'm positive!" Ellie couldn't believe it. Why wouldn't he listen to her? And why the hell was he still pointing a gun at her? She was obviously unarmed. Where would she hide a gun anyway? In the back of her shorts? She was frickin' harmless. "I watched her attack him!" Ellie raised her voice as if that'd make him understand. "It looked like she was having some kind of allergic reaction and then went all crazy like."

"I *meant*, are you positive she didn't touch *you*," he repeated. "You know, did she scratch you or bite you or anything?"

"Um, no," Ellie said, watching the paramedics carefully flip over the body.

"Good," the Sheriff lowered his gun.

"We've got another one!" one of the paramedics yelled.

"Yup! Infected!" the other confirmed, examining the body.

The Sheriff shook his head. He walked over to Ellie.

"What do they mean by infected?" Ellie asked, her voice barely a whisper. "What does she have?"

"We're not sure, but it's spreading like wildfire," the Sheriff answered. "The man she attacked; is *he* dead?"

"Um, yeah, I think so." Ellie crossed her arms protectively over her chest. She felt chilled even though she was standing outside in the broiling desert sun. She worried about the talk of infection. She remembered patting the woman on the back. Surely, that wouldn't be enough to spread it to her.

"You *think* so… You're not positive he's dead?" He frowned at her. "This happened at the gas station?"

"Yeah." Ellie nodded. "I'm pretty sure he's dead." The image of the rabid woman gnawing a chunk out of his neck flashed before her eyes. She quickly pushed the disturbing thought from her mind. In order to think clearly, she needed to keep her emotions in check.

"Guess I'd better go check." He turned to walk away. "We don't need any surprises."

"Wait!" Ellie called after him. "Is that it?"

"Yeah, you're free to go."

She watched as the paramedics wrapped the body in what looked like a thick plastic tarp.

"Don't you need me to make a statement or something?" Ellie followed the Sheriff, practically running to catch up.

"Nope," he said, not turning around. "Go

home!"

"But…" Ellie tried her hardest to keep up. The Sheriff was headed for the gas station, gun drawn. "What *is* this infection?"

To Ellie's surprise, the Sheriff stopped walking and spun around on the heel of his boot. He scrunched up his forehead. If circumstances had been different, and she hadn't known he was getting aggravated with her, she'd have thought he was pretty darn cute. He raised an eyebrow at her. "Where the *hell* have you been? Haven't you been listening to the news?"

"I was in Las Vegas for the weekend," she said, "with friends. I'm on my way home."

"Guess it hadn't hit Vegas yet. Lucky you. Where's home?"

"Oceanside, California."

"Oceanside." The Sheriff shook his head. "Los Angeles was hit first. Bet San Diego County ain't much better right about now." He reached into his pocket and slid out a business card. "My advice to you is that you get in your vehicle and drive straight home unless you need provisions. Get them now. And once you get there, stay inside until this thing is contained. Understand?"

Ellie took his card. She glanced at his name, Sheriff Michael Wilson. She studied the seriousness in his hazel eyes. "Until *what* is contained?"

"We don't know." He shook his head. "The news is downplaying it. Hopefully, it won't last long. Call me, and I'll get a statement from you later. Right now, I'm up to my ears in calls like this. They're all the same."

"All right." Ellie frowned. "Thanks for

23

nothing," she muttered just out of earshot, shoving the Sheriff's business card into her back pocket. She turned to walk back to her vehicle. Her hands were trembling. She hugged them to her chest. She wondered what in the world was going on. Her stomach lurched at the thought of what she'd seen. Were people really getting sick, going crazy, and attacking each other?

The paramedics were lifting the plastic wrapped body into the back of the ambulance. To her horror, she noticed several other bodies wrapped in the same fashion already stacked in the back. One of the paramedics hopped down, a grave look plastered across his face. "I've never seen anything like it," he muttered, shaking his head. He walked right past her as if she wasn't even there.

"We've got another one!" yelled a paramedic standing by the open passenger side door. "Hurry it up!"

"I think the Sheriff has another body in the gas station," he replied. "It'll need to be taken care of."

"Well, you stay here, and I'll circle back. Take a tarp."

Ellie hurried to her car. Maybe the sheriff wasn't exaggerating. She thought of her bare cupboards and empty fridge at home. If things were as bad as the sheriff was saying, she loathed the thought of dropping by a grocery store. Maybe he'd let her buy a few things from the gas station.

Hopping into her car, Ellie started it up, did a three-point turn and went back to the gas station. She figured she might as well finish filling up the tank. She'd need the gas to get home without stopping. Plus, her windshield could use a good scrubbing so she could see. The scolding sun was baking the blood smears into the glass. And the thought of having to look at the blood the entire drive home turned her stomach. She needed to get that stuff off as soon as possible.

She parked in front of the gas pump and watched the paramedic walking with his bag of goodies, and a roll of thick plastic under his arm. She sucked in a deep breath. She didn't want to re-enter the store, and she figured the sheriff wouldn't be too happy about it either, but she'd much rather be near him than alone in some other store full of possibly infected strangers.

"I thought I told you to go home," Sheriff Wilson said when Ellie entered the store. He and the paramedic were hunched over what was left of the old man's body.

"I need gas," she said, turning away from the repulsive sight. "That's why I was here. Is he, um, is he dead?"

"Yeah," Sheriff Wilson replied. "He's dead."

"Doesn't look to be infected," the paramedic said, examining the body. "Poor guy, sure took a beating though."

Sheriff Wilson glared at Ellie. "What are you still doing here? I thought I made myself clear! Get your gas and go home!"

"Um, that's the problem. You said I'd need provisions and, um, my apartment is, well… and I have a two-hour drive still…"

The sheriff sighed. "You know, you're a real pain in my backside." He grabbed his phone from his belt that was buzzing with an incoming call and frowned while staring at the screen. "Get what you need." He then pushed a button answering his phone, "Wilson, here."

"I'll pay. I'll leave money on the counter." Ellie grabbed a grungy blue plastic basket and began grabbing supplies. She quickly grabbed what she could, filling it up. She brought it to the counter and then snatched a second basket, which she filled with items from the fridge. She hoped that she was grabbing enough to last at least a few days, maybe more.

"You okay here?" she heard the sheriff ask the paramedic. "Got another 911 call."

"Yup. They're swinging back by soon. All I gotta do is wrap the body."

"Okay."

Ellie eyed the sheriff as he walked by. "I only have a twenty on me... but, I have my credit card."

The sheriff shook his head. "I ain't seen a thing," he said. "Just get the hell home and stay put."

Ellie dropped her twenty on the counter and nodded.

# Chapter 4

Amanda knelt next to Jasper. "Get up, baby!" she grabbed his hands and yanked. They were hot to the touch. He was burning up.

Jasper let out a terrible groan. His face was breaking out in huge welts, distorting his features.

"Oh my God!" Amanda shrieked, pulling on his hands. "Get up!"

"He's infected!" someone screamed. "Don't touch him!" The panicked crowd widened around them.

"Get up, or I'm gonna leave your ass here!" Amanda yelled. Not that she'd ever leave him there. She didn't know what else to do. It was evident that no one was going to help her, and she couldn't lift him. *How do you motivate a man of his magnitude?* Jasper was a good-sized man, over six feet tall and had the stature of a linebacker. She was surprised she'd been able to help him as much as she had without collapsing beneath his weight.

"You gotta get up," she begged, tears flooding her eyes. She let go of his hands and tucked her long thick locks behind her ears. "Please, baby, I don't know what else to do."

To her surprise, Jasper forced himself to his feet. His lips were puffing up and turning white.

Amanda slid her arm around his waist and helped him limp forward. People moved out of the way, not wanting to be too close to him. She could hear people yelling about him being infected. She thought maybe that was a good thing since no one wanted to be near them. It was as if the crowd was parting just for them.

"Keep going, baby," she coaxed. "We're almost there." The hospital was only a couple blocks away. She was determined to get him there. Screams and yells were coming at her from all directions, but she kept her mind on her goal. She was going to get Jasper to the hospital if it was the last thing she did. Nothing was going to stop her.

They'd somehow managed to push their way down the street. They had only one block left. She'd been to this hospital once before. She knew they were close. The crowd of people became thicker. She pushed and shoved, not caring what anyone thought. Couldn't they see she was helping a sick man? *What was wrong with these people? Get out of the way!*

"Move it!" she barked, trying to push toward the building. She elbowed a few people in the process. They were almost there. "Move! He's sick!"

A man in a brown leather jacket turned around and spat at her. "Who isn't?" He had one hand pressed to his middle. Large welts were forming on his cheeks as he glared at her.

For a second, Amanda stared at him in shock. She suddenly realized that these mobs of people were all trying to get into the hospital. They were *all* sick. There were so many people surrounding her that she couldn't even see the hospital doors which she knew were straight ahead.

"Come on, baby," she said, yanking on Jasper's arm. Jasper wasn't moving. "We're almost there. We just need to get through this crowd."

"Uhnnn!" Jasper clutched hold of his stomach, doubling over. He began to throw up, but not much was coming out since he'd emptied the contents of his stomach earlier.

Amanda let go of him. She looked around nervously. "I'll go get us some help."

Jasper looked up at her and Amanda's stomach lurched. His eyes were turning yellow. She remembered the news reports mentioning yellow eyes. He leaned back over and began to dry heave.

"I'll be back, promise." Amanda worked her way through the crowd until she reached the steps to the front door. Two security guards stood in front of them. Just past them, Amanda could see inside through the glass. It looked like there were just as many people inside as there were outside.

"Please," a woman sobbed, cradling a child wrapped in a blanket in her arms. "He's burning up."

"I can't let you in," one of the security guards answered.

"You can't deprive us of medical help!" stated a sharp dressed man standing next to her. "We've got insurance!"

"I don't care what you've got," the security guard

said. "You've gotta wait your turn just like everyone else. Someone will be out shortly."

"You said that hours ago!" someone in the crowd barked.

"Yeah!"

"What's going on?" Amanda asked, pushing her way through the onlookers. "Why won't you let us in?"

"There are too many people inside and not enough staff," the other guard said. "I can't let you in! The hospital is over capacity!"

"I don't give a damn!" said the sharp-dressed man, tugging on his power tie. "We're going in!"

"Yeah!" shouted a few people from behind Amanda.

"I wouldn't do that if I were you!" challenged the first security guard. He was short, stout, balding man with a thick black mustache. He pulled a baton from his belt to show he was serious. "Keep back!"

Amanda looked over her shoulder. There were so many people crowded around her that she could no longer see Jasper. Just then, several individuals stormed the entrance. The rest of the crowd followed suit. The two security guards began fighting back the horde. Amanda tried to go against the pack to get back to Jasper. She'd take him to another entrance.

"Jasper!" she called out, frantic. She couldn't see him anywhere. Too many people were crowding her, pushing her. "Jasper!"

Amanda spun around, confused as to which direction she was facing, there were too many people in her way. The front doors to the hospital swung open. Screams penetrated her ears. "Jasper!" she called out. "Jasper!"

An infected person wearing a hospital gown came leaping out of the hospital with superhuman speed. More people screamed.

"What the hell?" Amanda froze. The crowds began to push and shove in all directions trying to get away. The infected woman had golden yellow eyes, matching the color of her greasy, straw-like hair, staring out of a puffy white face. She was working her way through the crowd, as people pushed and shoved to get away. A streak of crimson smudged her pale, swollen face. A guttural animal type of sound resonated from within her.

Amanda was too frightened to move. She just stood there, mesmerized by this horrible thing that was making its way toward her. It was as if she were in one of those horror movies that Jasper loved to watch. All she could do was stare. Her eyes locked onto the infected woman's eyes. They were so yellow...

*Crack!* A baton smashed the side of the infected woman's head. Her neck snapped to the side. She'd only been a mere few inches away from Amanda when the security guard hit her. The woman's knees gave way, and she collapsed. Amanda stared down at the woman's lifeless body on the ground in front of her. Her eyes then focused on the baton gripped tightly in the security guard's hand. His hand was swollen and red. There was a human-sized bite mark embedded in his skin.

"Run!" he yelled at her, as several snarling infected people escaped from the hospital and began attacking the crowd. Screams rang out all around her, breaking her from her horror-induced daze.

Eyes wide open, Amanda spun around and

searched the crowd for Jasper. He was nowhere to be seen. She didn't know what else to do. She'd have to leave him. She didn't want to, but she had no choice. Pushing her way through the horde of screaming people, she ran down the street. From the corner of her eye, she saw a man running next to her. He suddenly fell to the ground as an infected person pounced on him, taking him down. She could hear him bellowing in agony.

Scared out of her mind, Amanda ducked down an alley. The sky was growing dark. She found an old blue dumpster and crouched down behind it, praying that no one would find her there.

# Chapter 5

Growing impatient, Ellie tapped on her steering wheel. The sky was growing dark, and she was just sitting there. She'd been waiting in line for nearly an hour to get over the border from Nevada to California. Many of the vehicles around her had switched off their engines and rolled down their windows. Some had just given up, turned around and went back the way they'd come.

Ellie had turned her engine off a couple of times, but when the interior of her car would grow too uncomfortable, she'd switch it on again just to blow the fan. Right now, it was off. She rolled down her windows. A gentle breeze had picked up. Staring at the sky that was quickly growing dusk, she sighed. At this rate, she wouldn't return home until late. But she was happy that with the sun going down, the desert was finally cooling off.

*So much for cutting through the desert to save time,* she thought.

Her mind kept going back to the crazy woman who'd attacked that man right in front of her. She still couldn't believe that'd happened. It was as if she'd dreamt it. It wasn't real. Was it as bad as that sheriff had made things out to be? She couldn't imagine. But what if it was? She was sure it had something to do with why she'd been sitting at the state border for so long. They'd taken the time to construct a barrier that no one could pass. She was positive that it had something to do with them trying to contain the so-called virus. What if they didn't let her go home? The sheriff had mentioned something about it being bad in Southern California.

Ellie tried not to look at the dried blood at the bottom corners of her windshield. She hadn't cleaned it as good as she should have. Her hands had been shaking, and she'd just wanted to get the hell out of there. As soon as she'd left the gas station, she'd noticed there was still blood on her windshield and had turned the wipers on. All that did was push the blood into the corners.

Switching off her iPod and turning on the stereo, Ellie searched for news stations. She figured while she waited, she might as well see what was on the news. Maybe she'd learn more about what was going on instead of just speculating. Ellie found a station that was coming in pretty clear, just a little static, and sighed. They were discussing riots going on in all the major cities due to the widespread epidemic, of what they were describing as a deadly virus.

Frowning, Ellie wondered what Oceanside was like. She prayed that she'd be able to get home safely. Hopefully, there weren't any riots going on. She made a mental note to make a doctor's appointment tomorrow to be checked out. She prayed she hadn't been infected by that crazy woman at the gas station. After all, she *did* touch her. Would that be enough to spread it? She hoped not.

Finally, the cars in front inched up in line. Ellie turned the key in the ignition, and the engine turned over. "Thank God," she muttered, thinking it was about time they started letting people cross the state line back into California.

When she finally made it to the front of the line, with only one car ahead of her, Ellie felt relieved. She glanced at the time on her stereo. She should be able to make it home in time to get a few hours of sleep before work tomorrow. She watched the silver SUV in front of her and anxiously awaited her turn.

Two border patrol officers, dressed in black shirts, black slacks, and black baseball hats, shined flashlights into the windows of the vehicle. She watched as one of the officers tapped on the window with his flashlight, motioning for it to be rolled down. She wondered what it was they were looking for. She hoped the food she'd purchased at the gas station wouldn't be an issue. Surely, they only cared about fresh fruit, right? That's what they typically checked for.

The officer seemed agitated. Ellie watched as he knocked again. Then he leaped backward as the passenger door flung open just missing him. Someone stumbled out of the vehicle. Ellie watched as the other officer, that'd been standing near the driver's side of the SUV shook his head and held up his hands, palms out at her. He then motioned for the driver of the SUV to pull over to the side. He walked over to the guy with the dark blonde hair that'd emerged from the SUV and shined his flashlight into his eyes. The man's shoulders slumped over. He then clutched his middle and began to vomit all over the asphalt. The border patrol officer jumped backward and then checked his boots to see if they'd gotten away clean. The other officer ran to his side while talking animatedly into a walkie-talkie.

"Oh God," Ellie gasped. She hoped the guy was just hungover from a wild night in Vegas, but deep in her gut, she knew what it was. He was infected.

With her window down, she could hear the guy groaning. The border patrol was trying to usher him to the side of the road next to the SUV, but the man wasn't moving.

Another man, this one a highway patrol officer, whom Ellie hadn't noticed until now, walked up to her window. He shined a flashlight in her eyes.

"Ow," she said, blinking hard against the bright light. "Geez…"

The man ignored her complaint. "How are you feeling?"

"A little agitated," she said. "I've been waiting for nearly an hour, just wanting to get home. How's that guy doing?"

The officer glanced over his shoulder. The sick guy was now curled up on the ground in the fetal position with the two border patrolmen looking frazzled. One of them nudged the guy with the toe of his boot. "We've got a call in for an ambulance. We're just trying to move the guy."

"Yeah…um…" Ellie's stomach churned. "Is he…"

"We don't know. Best to keep…"

The pickup truck behind her impatiently blasted

its horn. The officer glared at them. "We all wanna go home, buddy," he barked. "Hold your friggin' horses!"

"Has there been a lot of sick people?" Ellie asked.

"This is the first I've seen at the border. I was just given the okay to start lettin' people go."

"Oh, thank God," she said, hoping that meant the virus was being contained. "So… did I pass your test? Can I go home?"

"Yeah," he said. "You're free to…"

Startled, Ellie shrieked. In a quick blur, the officer was suddenly taken down. He screamed out in agony.

Ellie's heart raced. She could feel the blood instantly drain from her face. It took her a moment to comprehend what happened. "Oh my God!" she shrieked, again, leaning out her window.

The officer was on the ground, struggling beneath the infected man from the SUV who was snarling like a wild animal. The officer was fighting to get him off. Ellie noticed him putting his arms up to shield his face. His uniform was soaked with red sticky blood gushing from a chunk of gooey flesh ripped from his forearm. Everything was happening so quickly.

"Get off him!" Ellie screamed, unlocking her door and swinging it open as hard as she could, bashing the crazy man in the head. Taken by surprise, the man lost his balance and rolled onto his side. Ellie noticed the officer wasn't trying to get up. His body convulsed as blood gushed from what was left of his throat pooling on the asphalt. Within seconds, he went still. Ellie's eyes widened.

Grabbing her door, she slammed it shut as the infected man crouched, and then leaped to his feet. "What the hell?" she gasped, watching him move. It was as if he'd been transformed into a rabid beast. His movements were far from human. His head tilted and his golden yellow gaze zeroed in on her. There was no mistaking that she was his next target.

"Oh, shit!" She panicked and glanced in her rearview mirror. She needed to get the hell out of there, and her car was boxed in.

Suddenly, the black pickup truck behind her flew into reverse, bashing into the vehicle behind it. Ellie jumped at the horrific sound of crunching metal.

"Oh no!" she screeched as the truck flew forward, smashing hard into the rear-end of her sedan, causing her to lurch forward. Her car skidded sideways, hitting the infected man and knocking him down. Stunned by the force of the crash, it took Ellie a moment to realize that her windows were still down. Breathing heavily, she looked around in a panic while still clutching her steering wheel. Her eyes landed on the window. Bloody fingers gripped her door over the rolled down glass. The man was using her window to pull himself up. Frantic, Ellie tried to roll it up with one hand while putting her car into drive with the other hand.

*Bam!* Ellie flew forward again. This time her chest hit the steering wheel, temporarily knocking the wind out of her. She looked up and glanced in her rearview mirror. The black truck had rammed her again in a desperate attempt to flee the border. It was now flying into reverse. Ellie tried to regain her breath. This time the truck had crashed into her with such force that her car skidded to the left. She was now facing the side of the silver SUV that'd been in front of her. The man in the driver's seat flung open his door and stumbled out. He, too, looked ill. He wiped at his pale forehead with the bottom of his white T-shirt and staggered into the street. People in the vehicles all around her were beginning to panic. Cars, trucks, and SUVs were bashing into one another as they desperately tried to turn around or tried to run straight through the barricade to escape Nevada into California. Cars on the opposite side of the road that were trying to enter Nevada from California began to freak out as well.

"Roll up, roll up!" Ellie screamed, now focusing on her window and the bloody fingers still clinging to it. How the hell was he still holding onto her car? Emerging into view was the top of his dark blonde head. Within seconds, red, bloodshot eyes with golden centers stared at her with a swollen face as he lifted himself up to snarl at her. Blood dripped from the infected man's lips. Lifting the top corner of his upper lip, he growled, giving her full view of red blood-stained teeth. Ellie freaked out and held down the button on her door, forcing the window up. It seemed like it was taking an eternity to close. The man was now on his feet. She ducked to the side as he shoved a hand in at her, trying to grab her hair. The window stopped moving. The glass had clamped down on his wrist. Leaning to the side, still trying to avoid his clawing fingers, Ellie kept her index finger on the window button. She was afraid that if she were to let it go, he'd somehow be able to force it open.

"Shit! Shit! Shit!" she cried. All other words eluded her.

Doing the only thing that came to mind, Ellie stomped her foot down on the gas pedal, lurching her car forward, and then quickly slammed on the brakes before crashing into the parked SUV. She kept leaning to the side while practically lying across the passenger seat. She quickly threw her car into reverse. She couldn't see behind her because she couldn't lift her head to look in the rearview mirror without the possibility of being grabbed. Regardless, she knew she couldn't get very far without crashing. There were too many vehicles blocking her in.

The infected man growled and continued to claw, trying to reach her. Blood leaked from his wrist, dripping down the window. Skin peeled back as he forced his arm into her car. Ellie reached for one of the plastic bags of groceries on the floorboard of the passenger side. Her finger hooked a handle. She yanked the bag toward her and reached inside. The first hard item her hand grasped was a can of soup. She clutched hold of it, and with all her strength, struck the hand with it. The man bellowed at she smashed his hand repeatedly. She felt the crunching of bones with each blow. Again, she threw her car into reverse and then slammed it into drive. The man's wrist finally dislodged from her window leaving behind a bloody mess.

She tapped the window button, rolling it the rest of the way up. Without thinking, she forced her car over the divider and into the opposite lanes of traffic. There were too many crashed vehicles and people running in complete disorder around her to venture home. And if she veered into the sand, she was afraid she'd get stuck and end up being on foot. Going the way she came was the better choice since there wasn't any danger of oncoming traffic with the barrier up between the two states.

People were screaming, running amuck, and climbing out of their vehicles. Infected people seemed to be appearing from out of nowhere and attacking whomever they could. Ellie watched as an older woman standing next to a baby blue Buick was attacked on the opposite side of the road. Tears stung her eyes. She wanted to stop to help her but knew there wasn't anything she could do. It was too late. If she stopped, she too, would either die or become infected. She wondered how many of these people, waiting to cross the border to go home had known they were infected or that their loved ones were.

"God damn it!" Ellie cussed, pounding a fist against the steering wheel. She didn't know what the hell she was going to do. Tears flooded her eyes and streamed down her cheeks. She could no longer control her emotions. She forced her car forward, driving in the same direction she'd just come from. Her car thumped along making all kinds of odd noises. Her back bumper dragged on the asphalt. Her poor car wasn't in the best of shape since it'd been rammed several times, but she floored the gas pedal regardless. She wanted to put distance between herself and the border.

Even though she was trapped in Nevada, and couldn't go home, she was thankful to be alive. But where the hell was she going to go now? She'd tried calling her parents and her sister in Florida while she'd been waiting at the border. Neither had answered her calls. She'd left several messages wanting to make sure everyone was okay. Her parents, she could see not checking their answering machine. Half the time they were oblivious to new messages. But not her sister. Being a teenager, Claire's phone was practically glued to her ear. She prayed that whatever the heck this virus thing was it hadn't affected the east coast. She'd also left voicemails for both of her girlfriends whom she'd met in Las Vegas for the weekend. She hadn't expected a reply from either one, knowing that they were currently up in the air, flying back home.

Heart pounding, Ellie drove farther into the Nevada desert, the sun was now completely gone. When she felt she was far enough away from the pile-up at the border, she pulled over to the side of the road. She was frightened to stop moving but needed a moment to stop and think. She grabbed her cell phone and dialed 911. A recording played announcing that all the lines were currently busy. Frowning, Ellie ended the call and glared at her phone. *How the hell can 911 be busy?* She tried several more times to get through. She was no longer getting a recording. The phone would just ring. Frustrated, she finally gave up. She needed to think. *What in the world am I going to do?*

She leaned her head back on the backrest and stared out the windshield into the darkness. She then glanced at her window, thankful that the darkness of the night hid the blood dried on the glass. On the verge of fresh tears, she had an idea. She reached into the back pocket of her denim shorts and did the only thing that came to mind. She pulled out the business card and dialed Sheriff Michael Wilson to report what had happened.

# Chapter 6

Amanda shivered. She wasn't cold but chilled to the bone with fright. She stayed huddled in the dark by the dumpster until she could no longer hear the agonizing screams of the people in the street. She could only picture in her mind the carnage that was going on out there.

She hadn't a clue what she should do.

Should she try to go back to her car? She was doubtful that it'd just be waiting there in the street for her. And if it was, would she be able to go anywhere? It'd probably still be blocked in with traffic.

Her mind drifted to Jasper. She'd never found him. Was he now one of those *things*? One of those horrible *things* she'd seen on TV, and at the hospital, that were attacking innocent people? She hated to think of him that way. A part of her wanted to venture back to the hospital to look for him, to make sure he wasn't lying there on the ground sick, but the other part of her warned against it. She'd just have to pray he was okay. Maybe he was in the hospital and being treated.

*Stop being such a wuss!* she told herself. *Do*

*something!* It'd been quiet for over an hour, maybe even two hours now. She would've checked her phone but had somehow lost her purse in the throngs of people at the hospital. She listened. She didn't hear any more screams or shouts. There were no sirens, no gunshots, nothing. Everything was quiet. The quiet scared her even more than the noise. At least when there was noise, she knew there was still stuff going on.

Should she try walking back to the hospital? Things should be better by now. Right? Maybe the police had everything under control. Surely Jasper was there. She was sure of it. She had to do the right thing and at least make sure he was okay. She'd never be able to live with herself not knowing what'd happened to him. Besides, she needed to see if she could find her purse. Not that she really expected to. She figured it would be long gone by now. However, getting her hands on her cell phone and some cab money would be nice. And if not, maybe the hospital would be able to help her out with that. The least they could do was to let her use the phone. And hell, she'd forgotten all about the fricking gun. She wished she had Jasper's gun. It was in her purse. Not that she knew how to use it, but she was sure she'd be able to figure it out pretty damn quick. If only she'd paid more attention, she wouldn't have somehow lost her purse. She didn't even remember losing it. Everything had been happening so quickly. Maybe Jasper had it. Maybe she dropped her purse when he'd collapsed. That's probably what happened. She had dropped her purse when he went down. The straps must have slid off her shoulder as she tried to lift him up. That meant that he had the gun to protect himself. The thought made her feel a little better. If Jasper had his gun, then it wasn't like she'd abandoned him without protection. He'd be okay. He would've been able to fight off the infected and get himself checked into the hospital.

Trying to talk herself into getting up, Amanda's legs refused to move. She'd been huddled in a crouching position next to the dumpster for so long, that they'd gone numb. She sunk down until her rear-end was flat on the ground and she could feel the coldness of the pavement seep in through the thick fabric of her jeans. She'd been so frightened; she hadn't even realized that the entire time she'd been in hiding, she'd been crouching there in her gold high heels. For the first time, she realized how bad her feet hurt in those stupid ass shoes. Heck, *all* of her hurt. What the hell was she thinking when she'd bought them? For one, she'd never believed she'd be running for her life in them. Next time, though, if there were a next time, she'd make sure to buy a more sensible pair of shoes. A pair she could run in.

Amanda leaned her back against the brick building and closed her eyes as she waited for the blood flow to return to her legs. They were now sticking straight out in front of her. Her feet were just past the edge of the dumpster. She felt a little more exposed sitting this way, but she was pretty sure no one would notice her feet if they looked down the alley from the street, unless they were looking for them.

Rubbing her thighs, Amanda braced herself against the uncomfortable feeling of pins and needles as the blood began to flow again. She rubbed at her legs and then froze. *What was that?*

"Shhhh…tchhhh…"

She heard something. Something scraping. Scuffling. This was the first noise she'd heard in a while. She held still and listened.

"Shhhh…tchhhh…"

Amanda's nerves were on end. The little hairs on the back of her neck stood up. She held her breath, afraid to breathe. Whatever it was that'd made the scuffling sound was close by. It was in the alley. She could hear it on the other side of the dumpster. She braced herself, pushing her back against the wall.

"Shhh…tchhh…"

The sound was growing closer. She wanted to pull her legs up, pull her knees up to her chest. Try to melt into the shadows. She was too frightened to move for fear of being heard. She prayed that her feet wouldn't be seen. Maybe if she held still enough, they'd blend in. Her hazel eyes, large with fright, darted from side to side. She searched for something within arm's length that could be used as a weapon. *Nothing!* There was absolutely nothing! Just some flattened cardboard boxes and a stack of old newspapers but she knew that already. She'd had hours to think about it when all the carnage was going on in the street. All she'd been able to think about was what she could use as a weapon. And she still had no answers. There was nothing but frigging boxes and paper. Thank the heavens no one had entered the alley. No one until now.

Then she saw it. From the corner of her eye, something moved. It scurried around the bottom of the dumpster and stopped by her foot. There was just enough light filtering into the alley from a streetlamp near the sidewalk so she could see it. A pale-yellow glow lit up a large gray rat. It stopped near her foot, hunched onto its hind legs, and twitched its long wiry whiskers.

Amanda let out an exasperated sigh, and her shoulders slumped with relief. She closed her eyes and said a thank you prayer. Typically, a rat would've sent her over the edge, but not tonight. She was so grateful to see that it wasn't someone or something else. She was so relieved; she had the sudden urge to want to kiss the furry varmint. Well, *almost* that relieved. Rats still gave her the heebie-jeebies. Not that she was complaining. Amanda concentrated on her breathing while trying to steady her racing pulse. It had been a rat.

"Squeeee…!" A high-pitched squeal tore through the alley, shattering the silence.

Amanda's eyes popped open just in time to see a hand snatching the rat around the middle and squeezing. Without thinking, she pulled her legs in and jumped to her feet. A man in a long tan trench coat was on all fours near the front corner of the dumpster. Like a wild animal, he shoved the rat, headfirst, into his mouth and bit down. Blood spurted from his lips, and the rat's body went limp. He'd been so preoccupied with the rat that he hadn't noticed her watching him.

Doing the first thing that came to mind, Amanda slipped off her heels, feeling the cold pavement beneath her feet and held them protectively in her hands. The first words Jasper had spoken to her when she'd come home with them after a full day of shopping, rang in her ears. *"Damn, baby! You could use those heels as weapons!"* And that's exactly what she was going to do.

Making the first move, Amanda flew out of her hiding place from within the shadows. The man was still on the ground, chomping down on the rat with blood dripping from his chin and hands, and stared up at her with golden eyes.

"Stay back!" she warned, clutching her shoes tighter.

A snarl escaped his lips.

Amanda gasped. The only way out of the alley was to run past him. She knew she had to act fast. There was no going back to hiding in the shadows. She glanced over her shoulder. The other direction led to a dead end.

Amanda went to dart past him, when the man tossed what was left of the rat carcass to the ground and leaped to his feet with quickened reflexes. A hand grasped her long blonde hair as she ran, yanking her back. Screaming, she reacted without thinking, swinging the point of her spiked golden heels behind her without looking. The man bellowed as one of the spikes made contact with his eye and his grip released, freeing her hair. Dropping her shoes, she ran barefoot down the deserted sidewalk, sprinting in the direction of the hospital.

# Chapter 7

Sheriff Mike Wilson nudged the body of a little girl, no older than five years of age, with his boot in case she tried to attack him. He'd made a near fatal mistake a couple of hours earlier and could've ended up either dead or infected himself. She didn't move. He closed his eyes and said a silent prayer. There was nothing more heartbreaking than seeing a dead child. He then walked around the living room of the small two-bedroom house. The next-door neighbor was the one that'd made the 911 call when she'd heard screaming. Mike sighed. The mother's lifeless body was draped over the couch, gnawed on, and mutilated. His guess was the little girl had somehow become infected and then changed as they all seemed to do. That change had led to the attack on her own mother, killing her in the process.

He walked over to the tiny eat-in kitchen, peeked into the pantry that'd been left wide open. Next, he headed for the dark hallway. The bathroom door was ajar, and so was the door leading to the master bedroom. The house was old and rundown. The carpet was filthy and in desperate need of changing. Mike stood at the entrance to the bathroom. There was nothing of interest in there. He then pushed the door open to the master bedroom with his foot and carefully let himself inside. Patting the wall next to the door, his hand made contact with the light switch, turning on the overhead light to the ceiling fan above a queen-sized bed. He made his way around the bed, exploring the somewhat messy room. There was a large pile of dirty laundry stacked against the wall beneath the window. He nudged it with his foot.

The neighbor had mentioned that two young children were living in the house with their mother. He wanted to make sure that the other child wasn't there hiding somewhere. He hoped that only one child had been home when this atrocity occurred.

Kneeling, Mike lifted the blue plaid comforter, that'd slid down over the side of the bed and peeked underneath. It was dark. A couple of pairs of shoes and a stack of magazines obstructed his view. He carefully pushed them aside.

A yowl caused him to jump to his feet as a cat raced out from beneath the bed, startling him. Mike chuckled, pressing his hand over his heart. "Damn cat," he muttered, shaking his head. Normally, something like that wouldn't have affected him, but after today's turn of events, his nerves were on edge.

"You all right in there?" a fellow Sheriff asked, he stood in the doorway looking in. Somehow, they'd both been called out to the same location even though law enforcement was spread thin.

"Yeah, fine. Just a cat," Sheriff Michael Wilson replied, shaking his head.

"The whole world's gone to hell," the other

sheriff said. "Last I heard this thing had spread worldwide."

"You've gotta be kidding me…" Mike sighed. He'd been so busy the last couple of hours that he hadn't kept up with the news. "Are you being serious?" he asked, taking off his hat and running his fingers through his wavy brown hair. "This thing… is everywhere?"

Sheriff Jimmy Arnold nodded. "It's all over the news. They're now calling it a worldwide epidemic."

"That's just great… *Christ*! I was hoping this thing was going to burn itself out. I don't think I can handle another day like this."

"I'm not sure you noticed, but dispatch is down. Haven't been able to get through since this last call. All lines are busy."

Mike slid his phone from his belt. He hadn't been paying much attention to his phone, his mind preoccupied since he'd stepped foot into the house. He checked the screen. No missed calls. No new messages. His phone had been ringing all day since this so-called epidemic, or whatever the hell it was, broke out. He should've realized that his phone had been quiet for the first time. To test it out he dialed the office and got a busy signal. Frowning, he disconnected.

"Try the 911 line," Jimmy suggested. "It's out, too."

The 911 line wasn't one that Mike normally dialed but tested it regardless. A prerecorded message played. He then tried a few other numbers. Jimmy was right. They were all down. "What the…"

"Yeah, brother," he said. "I haven't been past the office in a while, but I think we're on our own."

"What do you mean by that?" Mike retorted, checking the walk-in closet before stepping out into the hallway.

"I mean, the world's gone to shit, and we're all gonna die."

"You serious?" Mike stopped walking. He turned to face Jimmy, his back to the other bedroom. He shook his head. "Don't tell me you're one of those doomsday prophets, glass half empty type of guy."

"Don't tell me you can't see it, man." Jimmy extracted his gun from its harness. "It's the end. Are you frickin' blind? That little girl over there," he waved his gun in the direction of the living room, "killed her *own* mother! A little, freakin' girl! Did you see the bite marks all over that woman's body? She ripped her own mother to shreds! What kind of monster does that? I'll tell you what kind… I've been to calls like this all day! Don't tell me you don't see it! The devil is here! He's walkin' this planet. He possessed that little girl!"

Mike took a deep breath. He'd been seeing nonstop carnage all day, too. And he still didn't believe it was the end of the world. And he *definitely* didn't believe in the devil. He believed in bad people that chose to do bad things, and he believed in bad luck. And this epidemic was most certainly bad luck. How it started and where it came from, he'd probably never know. He wouldn't be surprised if it'd been created by a bad man, if it wasn't some sort of mutated freak of nature. But one thing he knew for sure, was that it wasn't created by some imaginary, horned creature running around in a red suit.

Again, Sheriff Mike Wilson shook his head. He

hated to see a person, especially law enforcement, lose it. Because when they snapped, they usually snapped in a big way, harming innocent people in their path. Warily, Mike eyed Sheriff Jimmy Arnold. He hoped he wouldn't have to physically disarm him. There was nothing worse than having to disarm a fellow Sheriff, but he didn't like the way he was waving his piece about. Jimmy Arnold wasn't someone he generally worked with. So he didn't know the man's usual temperament, but right now he was worried the man was about to do something rash. He hoped, for his sake, he'd pull it all together. Quickly.

"Hey," Mike said, putting his hands up palms out. "Take it easy."

"Take it easy?" Jimmy bellowed, waving his gun around. "Are you friggin' nuts? The entire world is falling apart, and you're gonna tell me to take it easy!"

"Everything will work its way out," Mike said, calmly. "It always does. Okay?"

"I just tried calling my parents in Tennessee. They're not answering their phone. All I can do is picture them in my head, lying in a pool of blood, after one of them changed into some sickly crazed psycho and murdered the other one. And you're telling me to *take* it easy!"

"I'm sorry," Mike said, hands still up in a non-threatening manner. He eyed Jimmy's gun. He'd give him one more chance to calm down and holster that puppy. "I got family, too," he lied, being a product of the foster system. He just wanted to settle the guy down. Give them something in common. "I haven't tried to call them yet."

Jimmy laughed. He shook his head and then followed Mike's gaze to his gun. "I'm not gonna shoot you," he said, sliding his gun into the holster. "I was just voicing my concern."

Relieved, Mike's shoulders relaxed. He didn't want to have to take a fellow officer into custody.

Jimmy patted him on the shoulder. "You're one of the good guys. We gotta stick together, especially in times like these. Guess we should try to call in a coroner. Oh yeah, can't," he said sarcastically, throwing his hands up in the air while chuckling. "Not sure what the hell to do. Just leave them, I guess."

"We might have to." Mike scratched his brow. "Let me check this last room. Make sure there aren't any other kids."

Jimmy bowed, extending his arm out toward the closed door. "Be my guest."

Mike grasped the doorknob and turned it. The door creaked open. There was a nightlight on, plugged into the far corner of the room. A crib was against the opposite wall and a twin bed near the door. He figured the twin bed belonged to the little girl.

Without turning on the light, since there was just enough to see with the nightlight, Mike slowly walked over to the crib. It looked as if a toddler might be in there. If there was, he didn't want to chance frightening him or her. When his eyes finally adjusted to the dim light, he realized that there *was* a child in there, sitting in a blue Onesie with his back to him.

"Hey, buddy," Mike said, softly, not wanting to startle him as he approached. "You okay, buddy?"

He had his hand out to pat the small boy's shoulder. The poor kid had no idea his mother and sister were gone. He felt bad for him. Now he'd be put into the system, a system he personally knew all too well, unless there was another family member around to take him in. Such a shame. Poor kid. He hated the thought of it.

"Don't be scared." Mike gently patted the boy's shoulder. Heat radiated through the boy's pajamas.

The boy rolled and jerked his body onto all fours. Mike pulled his hand away, having never before seen a toddler move so fast. It took him a second to comprehend what was happening. An animal-like growl rumbled from deep within the child's chest.

Mike took a step back and stared at the boy. Just then, the lamp on the dresser next to the crib lit up the room as Sheriff Arnold entered. "I was wondering what was taking you so long... What the hell!"

In a flash of blue jammies, the boy jumped to his feet and clutched the rails of his crib with chubby little hands while snarling. Mike jumped back, out of the boys reach. He then noticed the dried brown blood on the boy's chin and smeared across his right cheek. His face was so swollen with hives; his eyes were practically swollen shut. From what he could see, he only had a couple of teeth, but it was obviously enough to inflict damage and spread this thing. Studying him, he realized the boy was even younger than he'd initially thought. He then looked over at the twin bed with the pink blankets tossed to the side. There were blood droplets on the flower printed pastel sheets. He frowned at the realization of what had happened here. The baby had become infected first and bit his sister, spreading it to her. The mother probably put the baby in the crib, not knowing what else to do while she took care of the little girl.

The sound of a gun sliding out of its holster made him turn around. Sheriff Arnold was sighting his gun on the baby. Mike put his hand up. "Whoa! What are you doing? Put it down."

"It's infected."

"It's a baby."

"Yeah, so! Look at it! It's rabid!"

Mike looked at the snarling baby. "I don't care. Have some compassion! What if there's a cure?"

"There ain't no cure!" Sheriff Arnold snapped, cocking his gun. "He's gonna infect others if he ain't done so already. I need to put him down."

"Killing a baby is a chargeable offense! I can't let you do that."

"And you're gonna stop me?"

"Yes." Mike stood in front of the crib, shielding the child. He made sure to stay out of arms' reach. The baby growled more fiercely at his close proximity.

Jimmy laughed, shaking his head in disbelief, and lowered his gun. "You truly are a dying breed. What ya gonna do with him then?"

"I'm not sure," he said. "Paramedics should be on their way. They should've received the call when we did. I'll leave this one up to them. Maybe they know how to handle something like this."

"*If* they got the call."

Mike nodded, following Sheriff Arnold from the room, leaving the child in his crib. Then his phone rang. Maybe dispatch was up and running. He looked at the screen, not recognizing the number on his caller ID. "Yes," he answered.

A frantic woman cried on the other end of the

line. Her voice shook, "Is this Sheriff Michael Wilson? My name's Ellie Thomas. I don't know if you remember me. We met at the gas station earlier today."

"Yes, Ellie. I remember."

"Please, I need your help. I don't know what to do."

# Chapter 8

Ending the call, Ellie felt better knowing that she'd gotten through to someone and had reported the incident of what was happening at the state line to Sheriff Wilson. He then recommended a motel for her to stay in for the night that wasn't far from her current location.

Tucking her hair behind her ears, Ellie took a deep breath and stared at the reflection of her hazel eyes in the rearview mirror. According to Sheriff Wilson, the motel was a few miles up the highway. She'd get off at the first exit and then make a right. The motel would be about a quarter mile down the road. He said she wouldn't be able to see it from the highway, but it'll be easy enough to find once she takes the exit.

"Here goes nothing," Ellie said, turning the key in the ignition. She was a little worried about arriving at the motel. *What if there were infected people around?* But then again, she knew that once she got a room, she'd feel much safer. She'd make sure to lock the door and stay inside. It'd be much safer than sitting in her car on the side of the road for the night.

"*Ch...tch...tch...*" The engine didn't want to

start. Ellie frowned and tried again. This time it didn't even try to start. Nothing happened.

"You've got to be kidding me!" Ellie gnawed on her bottom lip and tried again. Still nothing. The damage to her car must've been more extensive than she'd realized. She was kicking herself for having been so stupid, shutting off the engine to conserve gas while she sat on the side of the road to think. "Damn it!" she cursed. "Urrr! Now, what am I going to do? This is just my luck!"

Staring out into the dark of night, she wondered if she should stay put until morning. *No,* she thought, *that wouldn't be safe.* Then again, neither would be hoofing it to the motel. *How long would it take me to walk three miles?* She figured at least half an hour, maybe longer. She hadn't a clue. Maybe she should try a tow truck. And on top of everything, she really had to go to the bathroom. If only she hadn't drunk all that water while waiting in that stupid line at the border.

She looked at the deserted highway. A couple of times, she'd seen a vehicle heading toward the California border. She wanted to warn them not to go there but didn't have the guts to get out of the car. She figured once they'd gotten there, if they were smart, they'd turn around and head back this way. So far, no one had returned. It had been a little while since she'd been parked on the side of the road. Maybe everything was under control now. Maybe the border was open.

Ellie pictured the crazy infected people, attacking the motorists at the border. She couldn't imagine that things were now under control. Not with all the carnage going on. She was fooling herself into thinking things weren't as bad as they really were.

Closing her eyes, Ellie concentrated on her choices, and there were only two. She could either walk or stay put. Grabbing her phone, Ellie did a quick *Google* search for tow trucks in the area. She'd try that first before making any kind of rash decision. She dialed the first number. The line was busy. She returned to the previous screen and dialed the next number. It rang, igniting a spark of hope. Then the line continued to ring and ring. No one picked up. After trying a third and a fourth number, Ellie gave up. She obviously wasn't going to find a tow truck. Again, she turned the key in the ignition. This time there was a clicking sound at least. She tried pumping the gas as if it might help, even though she knew it wouldn't. Nope. Nothing.

Ellie decided to try dialing Sheriff Wilson one more time. Unfortunately, her call went straight to voicemail.

"Hi, Sheriff Wilson. This is Ellie Thomas. I'm sorry to bother you again. I know you have your hands full. I'm stranded on the side of the road. I can't get hold of a tow truck. I may have to walk to the…" Just then, Ellie heard a click and then silence. "Hello?" she said, wondering if the call had been picked up somehow, but then she realized it was the opposite. She'd been disconnected. Ellie pulled her phone away from her ear and stared at the screen. Maybe the battery died. She hoped not. She had been conscientious enough at making sure it'd been charging the entire time she'd been in the car. She tapped on the screen. The battery level was full. She then tried to redial.

"What?" she asked puzzled. "No cell service? I

just had service! What the…!" She stared into the dark desert and shivered. She hoped that the sheriff had at least received her message and would be able to send a tow truck her way. Sucking in a deep breath, she decided that she needed to use the bathroom and couldn't wait any longer. She'd have to squat down on the other side of her car, in the sand away from the highway. Not that anyone would see her. Not very many people had been driving past anyway.

Opening her door, Ellie slid out of the driver's seat and stepped out into the night. The air was warm and comfortable. She looked both ways down the highway. Not a car or person in sight. She walked around the front of her car until she reached the passenger side. She hated the fact that she'd have to go to the bathroom outdoors, but she'd already been holding it for well over an hour and couldn't manage for much longer. She told herself to bolster courage. *I'll make it quick and be back in the car before anything happens. No need to be afraid.* Besides, if Sheriff Wilson happened to send someone to help her, she didn't want to be caught in the act.

Ellie undid her shorts and hastily took care of business near some scrub brush about ten feet away from the car. It was the closest plant life that would shield her from the street. When she finished, she stood up to zip and button her shorts. She was about to walk back to her car when she heard it. *Footsteps.* It was the unmistakable sound of gravel and sand crunching beneath heavily booted feet.

Quickly, Ellie bent forward and then crouched down, while trying to stay hidden the best she could behind the prickly desert brush. She stared at her car,

trying to get a better look. Her heart raced. Someone
was standing next to the driver's side. She watched as
the man tried the handle and opened the door.

Ellie's hands began to tremble. *Should I let the
man know I'm here?* She wanted to yell at him to get
away from her car. Her wallet, phone, luggage and
the food from the gas station were all inside. She
clenched her hands into tight fists and bit her tongue.
She had no idea what the man would do to her if she
confronted him. Best-case scenario, he'd run; worst
case scenario, he'd rape and murder her. Being that
there was only one man, she hoped he'd just run off.

"Hey!" the man suddenly called out.

Ellie's pulse quickened. *Was he talking to her?
Had he spotted her?* She stayed in a crouching position,
holding completely still.

"Yeah?" another man's voice answered as he
came running across the street. "What ya got?"

*Not good!* Ellie thought, not liking the odds. *Now
there are two of them.*

"I think I found us a car," he said, "and it's
stocked full of crap."

"Yeah, buddy!" the other guy said, smacking him
on the back when he reached the car.

*Oh my God! Oh my God!* Ellie chanted in her
head. She didn't know what to do. She couldn't let
them steal her stuff. She needed her wallet, clothes,
and food. Heck, she needed her car even if it wasn't
running. What was she going to do?

"Doesn't look to belong to anyone," he said,
sliding into the driver's seat, tapping on the steering
wheel.

"Guess it's ours," the other guy laughed and
pulled on the handle of the passenger's side. "Hey,

idiot, unlock the door. Let me in." Ellie watched as the other guy leaned over, reaching across the car to the passenger door, letting him in.

*Click, click…* Ellie listened as they tried to start the vehicle. She could hear the men's voices as they cussed from within her car. They tried again and again. Finally, the passenger door flew open. "It's probably the damn starter! Grab the food. Don't forget the wallet. Any cash in it?"

"Nope….nada."

"Friggin' figures! Just take whatever cards are in it."

"Hey, look. A phone."

"Grab it! I'm sure we'll find another car. Maybe even something better than this piece of shit!"

Ellie tried her best not to make a sound, but her foot slipped a bit, and her tennis shoe crunched on the brittle desert foliage. She held her breath hoping they hadn't heard her.

"What was that?" asked the big guy, nearest her.

The skinny guy was now digging through her luggage in the backseat. "What?" he asked.

"I heard somethin'."

"Probably just a coyote. They're everywhere out here. Need some panties?" The skinny guy teased. "Ain't nothin' worth takin' in here."

The big guy kept staring in Ellie's direction. She prayed he couldn't see her through the shrubbery. She knew if he looked hard enough, he could.

"Nope," he snapped, shaking his head. "Not a coyote. They ain't that dumb." He stepped off the asphalt and into the sand. He took a few steps toward Ellie, his shoes crunching on the dried sagebrush. "I think we're being spied on."

The thin man emerged from the car, plastic grocery bags in his arms. "What? Where?"

"In these here bushes," he said, taking a couple more steps, getting closer to Ellie.

She sucked in a breath.

"So?" the other guy said. "Who cares? Let's go find us a car. This one ain't no good."

"I don't like people who spy…" the big guy said. "Need to teach this hombre a lesson…nosy son of a…"

"Come on," the other guy said. "Just leave it. Whoever it is, they're stuck out here just like us. Who gives a crap if they're spying on us?"

The man chuckled. "I need to take out some of my frustrations; otherwise, I'm a gonna snap. You want me to snap on you? Huh?"

"Well, then, hurry it up already," the skinny guy said, impatiently. "Do what you have to do. These grocery bags are heavy."

Petrified, Ellie jumped to her feet. The man was getting too close. He stopped. Moonlight highlighted the left side of his face. His expression frightened the hell out of her. She didn't like that he seemed amused. "Well, well, well," he chanted. "What do we have here? This is much better than I expected."

"Please," Ellie said, taking several small steps back. "Don't hurt me. Take whatever you want from my car. It's yours. You can have it all."

The man chuckled again. He licked his lips, his hungry eyes looking her up and down. "I'll for damn sure take what I want."

"Aaagghhh!" Unexpectedly, the skinny man over by the car let out a horrific scream.

"What the…!" The large man turned to look over his shoulder. His friend was being assaulted in the street. "Carl? Carl!"

Ellie immediately recognized the growling and shrieks. It was the sound of someone being attacked by one of the infected. Unfortunately, the sounds were becoming all too familiar. The animalistic guttural sounds made her skin crawl.

Not waiting to see what was happening, Ellie took this opportunity to get away. She ran in the direction she had planned on traveling to the motel. She was never a good runner, and the sand seemed to be slowing her down, but she forced her legs to move as fast as possible. She wanted to look back but was too afraid. *What if the man is chasing me? What if there are more infected people around? What if I'm attacked next?*

More screams, yells, and growling traveled on the still night's air. Ellie kept running, refusing to look back.

# Chapter 9

Amanda ran in the direction of the hospital. To her relief, but also her horror, no one was around. Cars were left abandoned in the street. A few dead bodies littered the sidewalk. She tried her best to dodge them, praying that thing wasn't still chasing her. Several cop cars with their lights still flashing, and a fire truck, were parked in front of the hospital, abandoned.

*Where is everyone?* she wondered. She ran up the steps leading to the front doors of the hospital. She grabbed hold of the door and shook it. Even though the lights were on, the doors were locked. She peered through the glass doors. Scattered papers were strewn about the entrance hall. She glanced in the direction of the waiting room. There were several people seated in the chairs.

Looking behind her, she made sure she hadn't been followed. No one was there. She shook the door. Hospitals didn't have closing times, did they? Maybe they did. She probably needed to go around the building in search of the ER. The Emergency Room was surely open. She bet they'd be able to tell her whether or not Jasper had been admitted. Then she'd see if she could use their phone. She'd call her friend Tina and ask for a ride. Well, if Tina could even get to her. Worst-case scenario, she'd at least be able to take refuge in the ER waiting room until morning.

Amanda knocked on the glass to see if she could attract the attention of one of the people sitting in the waiting room before running around the building in search of the Emergency room entrance. She didn't like the thought of running around in the dark with infected people lurking about. Her mind returned to the man in the alley. She looked over her shoulder in the direction she'd come from and shivered. The street was abnormally quiet. At least she hadn't been followed. Or at least she hoped not. Again, she wondered where the police officers and firefighters went. She pushed the thought from her mind. She didn't want to acknowledge their disappearance and what it meant. Right now, she clung to the hope of the hospital giving her refuge even with what'd happened earlier. She was sure it was just a fluke thing, some of the infected people escaping and going all crazy. She was sure the hospital would have things under control now and know how to help people, people like her Jasper. They'd be able to treat him.

Amanda turned her attention to the waiting room and knocked on the glass hoping to get the attention of one of the few people sitting there. No one moved. She wondered if it was loud enough. Her knock sounded a bit weak. Balling up her hand into a fist, she pounded on the glass leaving marks, smudging it with the oils of her skin. She then grabbed the door and shook again, trying to make it rattle.

"Oh, come on," she said, banging again on the door. This time she banged so hard her hand felt as if it were bruising. The people in the waiting room had to have heard her. There was no way they didn't. She then pounded again. *Are they ignoring me?*

Finally, to her relief, she noticed someone wearing scrubs walking down a hallway to the right.

"Hey!" she yelled into the doors, now using both hands to bang on the glass. "Hello? Please! Can you hear me?"

The man in the scrubs stopped walking.

"Oh, thank God," she muttered. Someone had heard her. She couldn't wait to get inside. It was getting chilly outside, being so close to the ocean, with the breeze kicking up over the water and blowing inland. And obviously, she had deeper concerns than just the weather that was causing her to feel chilled. The entire spread of infection, or whatever it was, was totally creeping her out. She wondered again if a hospital full of sick people would be a wise place to take refuge for the night, especially with what had happened earlier. Not that she had many choices right about now.

She could still picture in her mind that infected woman escaping the hospital and then attacking the security guard right in front of her. She looked over her shoulder again at the street littered with vacant vehicles. She shrugged, not knowing what else to do. She hoped that whatever had taken place there earlier was now under control since everything seemed quiet. No one was running around screaming. No infected people were attacking people. Even though she told herself that everything was under control, deep in her gut, she knew it wasn't. She just didn't want to believe it. Cops and firefighters don't just leave their vehicles abandoned on the streets.

Amanda returned her attention back to the inside of the hospital. She was desperate to get inside. Standing out in the open was making her more nervous by the minute. The man in scrubs was still standing there in the hall. She wondered if maybe he hadn't heard her after all. *What was he doing?*

"Hey!" Amanda called while making a fist and pounding on the glass door. "Hello? Can you hear me?"

The man's head snapped to the side. Amanda watched as he turned around. It looked as if he was trying to figure out the source of all the noise.

"Out here!" she said, shaking the door. "My boyfriend is inside. Can you let me in?"

The man lifted his head and stared in her direction. Amanda waved at him. He began to sprint down the hall toward the door. It took Amanda a second to realize what was happening. The man leaped over a row of chairs in the waiting room with animalistic movements. As he grew nearer, she could see the puffed-up distortion of what used to be his face. She took a step back away from the door as the man ran into it. His hands curled and clawed at her, his face snarling, pushed up against the glass. Hot breath steamed up the smooth cold surface. Amanda screamed, jumping backward as his yellow eyes made contact with hers. Next to him, another snarling man in a police officer's uniform pushed his face to the glass too. Drool and steam from hot breath spread across the door as he snarled, biting threateningly at her. More infected people began to crowd around on the other side of the glass doors. Either they were locked inside the building, or they didn't know how to open the doors. Either way, Amanda wasn't planning on hanging around to find out.

Quickly glancing over her shoulder, she stumbled and grabbed hold of the railing next to her. Thankfully, she caught herself before falling down the cement steps. She wasn't sure what she should do next. She'd have to find somewhere else to go, and quickly. She wasn't sure how long the doors would hold them as more and more people appeared.

Afraid to go very far in the dark, Amanda eyed the abandoned police car not far from the hospital and had an idea. She wasn't sure if it was a good one, but it was the only thought that came to mind.

# Chapter 10

Mike raced down the freeway toward the state line. He tried to call it in to dispatch, but the lines were still tied up. Several attempts later, his phone completely cut out. Nothing was working. Not even his scanner. He had no means of communication with anyone, whatsoever. Regardless, he took it upon himself to continue in that direction. The state line wasn't too far from his current location.

As he drove, he wondered if he'd done the right thing leaving that infected child with Jimmy to watch over until the paramedics arrived. He would've stayed with the kid himself if he hadn't received the distress call from that girl, Ellie. God, he hoped he'd done the right thing.

Mike floored the accelerator, picking up speed. From what Ellie was telling him, the border patrol was being overrun with the infected. *What in the world was going on?* His mind drifted to Jimmy's words; *the world's gone to shit, and we're all gonna die.* He shook his head. *Could this really be the end? Has the whole world gone to hell?* He didn't like the thought of that and pushed it from his mind. He wasn't going to let Jimmy's negativity sink in.

*Bad things happen all the time,* he told himself. In his line of work, he'd seen it all. *This too shall pass.* He then wondered if Ellie had ever made it to the motel he'd suggested. She seemed like a nice enough girl. He'd hate for anything bad to happen to her. And the way things were progressing with this so-called epidemic, the chances were pretty high that something bad could happen.

Swerving into the left lane, up ahead, Mike noticed a car parked on the opposite side of the highway. As he passed by it, he thought he recognized it.

"What do you know?" he muttered, slowing down and making a sudden U-turn, skidding through the sandy divider. As he slowly drove up behind it, he realized he was correct. He did recognize it. It was Ellie's car. He could see the driver's side door had been left open and the dome light was on. As he pulled up closer, he stopped suddenly when he noticed a body, or what was left of a body, in the middle of the highway.

Mike turned on his hazard lights and hopped out of his car, gun ready. "What the hell?" he cussed while cautiously approaching the body. He eyed Ellie's car, and then the dark desert. He stopped walking and stood still for a moment, listening, before deciding it was all right to take a few more steps forward. Once he felt he was close enough, he nudged the body with the toe of his boot. Nothing happened. He switched on his flashlight to get a better look without getting too close to the body. He wasn't going to take the chance of feeling for a pulse. Normally, he'd kneel and get a better look, but since this epidemic broke out, he'd become more cautious.

The last thing he needed was to be attacked if this guy wasn't dead. He shined his light on the man's face. Well, what was left of his face. It'd been mauled pretty badly. But the good news was that it didn't look distorted. That was a good sign. It meant that this guy was just battered and probably not contagious. The asphalt around him was slick with blood. A large chunk of flesh had been ripped from the man's throat having caused him to bleed to death.

To be on the safe side, Mike nudged the guy again. He lifted the victim's shoulder with the toe of his boot and let it fall back to the ground. He waited. Nothing happened. Almost positive that this man wasn't going to jump up to attack him as soon as he turned around, Mike cautiously headed over to Ellie's car. He stuck his head in the door and glanced inside. Keys were still in the ignition. He then glanced down at the ground. Something caught his eye. He shined his light on it. A can of instant soup was near his foot. He then spotted two plastic grocery bags and food items scattered on the road. His stomach clenched as he derived at a conclusion.

He shut the door and walked around to the other side of the automobile. He looked out at the vast, quiet desert and stepped off the asphalt into the sand. Again, his stomach clenched, and he hoped that Ellie was all right. He wondered if she had been smart enough to head toward the motel on foot. He stared in the direction of the motel and shined his flashlight on the sand, looking for footprints. He frowned. It looked like several sets of footprints. Not that he was a tracker but at least two sets, maybe more. He looked up at the moon and then back at the street where he'd left his car. He figured he should take a drive over to the motel he'd recommended and check on her. He bet she was there or at least headed over there. Poor girl. She must be frightened out of her wits. Hell, any sane person would be.

*Shit! I gotta get to the border,* Mike thought. But then again, he figured that there probably had been many distress calls before the phone lines went down. He was positive they'd have lots of help over there by now. They wouldn't really need him. He'd check on Ellie, and once he knew she was safe, he'd then swing back around. He could do both. Hell, he wasn't even supposed to be on duty still. Therefore, it wasn't like he'd get in trouble. It wasn't as if he had anyone to report to. He'd been cut off from dispatch. All he could do was wing it. He wouldn't be able to live with himself if something happened to the girl because he didn't check on her. He'd feel like shit if he didn't at least try to help her.

Mike spotted the nearby shrubbery and decided to do a quick search. He shined his flashlight over the bristly shrubs and sagebrush to make sure Ellie wasn't lying there injured. He walked farther into the desert. He was now several feet away from the asphalt. Dried plants crunched under his feet. He was relieved not to see any bodies as his flashlight swept the surrounding area. Once satisfied, he switched off the light. The moon lent more than enough light for the walk back to his car. He headed toward the asphalt when something gripped his ankle, startling him. Chills raced up his spine.

"What the…!" Mike hollered, jerking his steel-toed boot. The heel smashed into something hard. A loud howling shriek shattered the silence around him. Mike's stomach jumped into his chest. Fumbling with the flashlight, Mike quickly switched it back on. In the light, he was surprised to see a burly, dark-haired man with wild yellow eyes staring up at him from the ground. He wasn't sure how he'd managed to miss him when he'd swept the area in search of Ellie. Unnerved, Mike stumbled back aiming his gun at the yellow eyes. He shined his light over the man's body inspecting him. The man tried to lift himself up from the sand. It was apparent that the heel of Mike's boot had made contact with the man's face. Thick, dark blood gushed from his nose.

"Stay back!" Mike warned, glaring into the other man's golden eyes. "I don't wanna have to shoot you."

The man tried to lift himself again and then sunk back into the sand. He raised his head and squinted at the brightness of the flashlight.

"Do you know who you are?" Mike asked. He was aware that once someone was infected, they grew delirious as the fever increased.

The man growled. Struggling, he pulled himself up into a sitting position.

Mike took another backward step.

The man groaned, clutched his stomach and doubled over. He heaved into the bushes. Mike cringed. He'd seen this too many times today. He knew all of the symptoms leading up to the change. There was no doubt about it. This man was infected. He was in the middle of changing into whatever the hell it was that people were turning into; sick, deranged, dangerous lunatics. Soon this man would lose all self-control and begin to attack.

"Shit!" Mike swore. He hated dealing with this crap. There was no paramedic to call. So,there was no way for him to help this man. Yet, he couldn't shoot him without reason. Morally, he couldn't do it. The man would have to try to attack him. However, if he didn't shoot this guy and left him on the side of the road, the man would either spread the infection to other people he came in contact with, or he'd brutally rip them to shreds.

Mike took a couple of backward steps in the direction of his patrol car while keeping his eye on the infected man. He wanted to keep a safe enough distance between them. Coughing and sputtering, the man continued to clutch his stomach and moan in misery.

"Did you see the woman driving this car?" Mike asked, close enough to Ellie's sedan to pat the side panel. He knew it was probably useless questioning this guy but did it anyway. He hoped the man was still coherent enough to understand. "Hey!" Mike barked, trying to get the man's attention. "The *woman*… the one driving this car… Did you see her? Is she okay?"

"Arrrr…!" the man bellowed, lifting his head. He coughed violently; phlegm hung from his thick bottom lip. His golden eyes glared. Mike could see the man's face puffing up around them. "Bitchhh!" he snarled. "F'n bitch….!"

"I'll take that as a *yes*!" Mike said, his stomach lurched again as he envisioned the groceries scattered on the highway. *Did this man harm Ellie?* The thought of having to shoot him wasn't quite as bothersome now.

"Urrrr!" the man snarled. His eyes glanced in the direction Ellie would've headed to get to the motel. He then leaned forward and dry heaved some more.

"Thanks. That's all I need to know."

Mike scowled. He decided to leave the man to his change. Even though he was tempted, he couldn't kill him unless he was provoked. It just wasn't in his nature. He grabbed the door handle to his car when he heard the quick crunching of footsteps on the desert foliage behind him. Mike spun around and fired, right as the man leaped to attack. His large body crashed to the asphalt as a bullet lodged into his chest. The man bellowed, and Mike shot again, making sure the infected man was down. Once his body was still, Mike shook his head with pity and slid into the driver's seat. He didn't bother to take a closer look. As the engine roared to life, Mike made a mental note to call the incident in as soon as the phone lines were back up, if they came back up. He hated to think that way. But as the night progressed, he was having a hard time staying positive. Maybe Sheriff Arnold was correct. Maybe this was the end. Frowning, Mike floored the accelerator and headed in the direction of the motel.

# Chapter 11

Breathless, Ellie clutched her side and leaned forward. She never knew she'd had it in her to run for so long. But then again, she'd never been running for her life before. Now that Ellie had stopped to catch her breath, she realized how tired she was. Running was never her thing. Heck, she didn't even like to jog. Not willing to give in to her fatigue, Ellie forced legs to continue forward, now at a snail's pace. She cursed at herself for being so physically out of shape. Her muscles felt like Jell-O, and each step was becoming a major challenge.

Glancing over her shoulder, she looked behind her. From what she could see, no one was following her, and there didn't seem to be anyone else around. "Thank God," she whispered. It'd been awhile since she'd heard any other sounds over her labored breathing and the beating of her heart that was pounding in her ears. She wondered how much farther it was to reach the motel. She prayed she was headed in the right direction. As far as she knew, she was. She'd moved more inland, away from the highway, because she'd felt it might be safer to be in the desert.

A part of her wanted to travel along the highway so that she knew she was heading in the right direction. The other reason was so that someone might see her walking and stop to help her. Though, that was also the problem. She didn't know if she wanted to take that chance. *What if whoever stopped had good intentions, but was infected? What if I ran into men with bad intentions? Men like the ones trying to take my car.* Goosebumps covered her arms at the thought. She'd never forget the look on that man's face. She knew exactly what he'd planned on doing to her.

Sick to her stomach, Ellie pushed the thought from her head. She tried to think positive. Soon she'd be running into the road that turns off from the main highway, the road with the motel that Officer Wilson told her about.

*Officer Wilson…* Ellie's mind drifted to her phone conversation with him. She held onto the hope that he'd be on his way to the state line right about now. And maybe, just maybe, he'd see her car stranded on the side of the road. He'd help her. She could trust him. Unless, of course, he too was infected. She tried not to think about him being infected. She needed to focus on something positive. He'd help her. She was sure of it. Not really believing the story she was telling herself about Officer Wilson coming to her rescue, she glanced in the direction she thought the highway was in. She prayed she hadn't gotten turned around. The miles and miles of desert surrounding her all looked the same. Scrub brush and prickly dried up plants were everywhere. It all looked the same. Maybe she should head toward where she thought the highway was and walk along it so that

Officer Wilson could see her.

*No,* Ellie told herself. *Officer Wilson coming to my rescue is wishful thinking. I'm on my own. Besides, it's safer to stay away from the highway.*

Just then, Ellie thought she saw something. A light. She squinted to get a better look. She *did* see a light. Up ahead and over to her right, there was a slight twinkling. She bet the turn off from the highway was right up there. She looked toward the twinkling lights to her right. She bet they belonged to the motel. If she cut diagonally through the desert, taking her farther away from the highway, she bet she could get there pretty quick.

As fast as her legs would allow, which didn't seem so fast anymore, Ellie headed through the desert. Scratchy plants tore at her skin. The plant life seemed to grow thicker and denser the farther she wandered from the highway. She cursed herself for not having worn jeans.

Trying to be a bit more careful, Ellie headed forward with the hopes of a nice motel room that she could lock herself away in until this virus epidemic thing was either contained, or she could find a way home.

***

Amanda slid into the driver's seat of the patrol car and shut the door. She let out an exasperated sigh. She furiously fumbled with the door, trying to find the lock. It took her awhile to figure it out. Eventually, her trembling fingers found the latch, and she was able to lock the doors manually. She then searched for keys. Nothing.

"Damn!" she cursed, staring wearily out the passenger window across from her. Gnawing on her bottom lip, she slunk down into the seat as low as she could while still being able to keep an eye on the hospital. From what she could see, the horde of infected people seemed to be thinning out and moving away from the doors. "Thank God," she whispered. The last thing she needed was for them to break through the doors and come after her. Her shoulders began to relax as the tension eased. The streets seemed baron. It was eerie to be sitting in downtown San Diego and not see anyone about. Well, not anyone who wasn't infected anyway. *What am I going to do?*

Amanda took in a deep breath, held it for a moment and then exhaled. Her eyelids were suddenly feeling heavy. She hadn't realized how exhausted she was until now that she was somewhere hidden. Somewhere safe. Well, hopefully, safe enough. Being locked up in a cop car sure beat kneeling next to a dumpster all night. She figured she'd probably stick it out until morning, using the car for shelter. She wasn't quite sure what else to do. And she wasn't about to wander the streets shoeless and in the dark with creepy infected people.

Amanda glanced again at the hospital. She wondered why that was. *Why was it that the people infected were attacking people? And why weren't they attacking one another?* They'd been clambering all over the door trying to get at her, but none of them bothered fighting each other. So odd. Everything was so odd.

Looking at the dash, Amanda tapped some of the buttons. She grabbed a walkie-talkie, or whatever it was called, she wasn't sure, and pushed the button. Nothing happened. If only she had the key, she could start up the car and call for help. Then she remembered the cop inside the hospital that'd been salivating on the door, chomping his teeth at her. *Was there any help? Would someone come to my aid?* This patrol car had been abandoned, same as the fire truck parked behind it. *How often did you see that?* "Never," she whispered, answering her own question. It felt as if her heart dropped into the depths of her stomach at the thought. No one would be coming to her rescue.

In a warped sort of way, she thought life was ironic. She'd spent a good portion of her youth hiding from the cops. She generally had been up to no good. In fact, she'd taken quite a few rides locked up in the backseat of a patrol car similar to this one. She ran her fingertips over the steering wheel. It was kind of an odd feeling sitting in the front seat, let alone the driver's seat. Now, of all things, she wished to be able to call out to the police for help.

Amanda slunk farther down in the seat trying to hide. She wished she could recline it, but couldn't. The car obviously wasn't made for comfort. She felt safer, not being so visible through the windows. She leaned her head toward the center console and made herself as comfortable as possible. Her eyelids were growing heavy again. She wasn't sure she could keep them open for much longer. She told herself that she'd let herself get a couple of hours of sleep. Then, hopefully, when the sun came up, the world would look different. She prayed that when she awoke, everything would be back to normal.

## Chapter 12

"Shhh…," Joanna hushed her husband. "I just got him to sleep. You're gonna wake him."

"Fever come down?" Bill asked, peeking worriedly over his wife's shoulder into their son's room. Benjamin was tucked in between his sheets, and his navy blue blanket was tucked under his chin. His favorite teddy bear with the flattened stuffing and matted fur was lying next to him. He'd carried his teddy around everywhere when he was a toddler. Now he was seven, and his buddy was more of a security blanket. He cuddled with it to keep away nightmares at night. Bill frowned. He hoped that the teddy bear also protected against nightmares during the day.

"No." Joanna shook her head, trying not to cry. She'd seen the news reports. They'd both been watching up until the cable went out. "Not yet. I'm sure the Tylenol will work… always does… We just need to give it more time."

"What time did you give it to him?"

"I just gave him another dose," she shrugged. "Maybe a half hour ago."

"But the first dose didn't work."

Frowning, Joanna shook her head again. Tylenol

always worked for him. In the past, it'd been the miracle of all miracles whenever Benjamin had the flu.

Bill didn't want to bring it up. He hated to even think of it, but he had to. The reality was that he could have it. "You don't think…"

"No!" she snapped, her voice wavering. "No! Benji's fine!"

"You sure?"

"Of course I'm sure!" she whispered harshly, firmly shutting the door behind her. "He's not one of those... things. He's *not* infected! So, don't even think it!"

"Okay," Bill said, knowing how upset his wife was. Her bloodshot eyes stared daggers at him. He knew she blamed him for their son's condition. He should've never taken Benjamin with him to the corner store to grab some food. He should've gone alone. He didn't believe that there was much to worry about. Well, he believed it enough to know he wanted to stock up on some snacks in case this so-called epidemic were for real, and they were trapped inside for a few days. Joanna had been upset about it. She didn't think it was safe to bring Benjamin with him and he'd yelled at her. He'd called her paranoid. Man, if only he could tell her he was sorry. If only he'd have listened to her, then none of this would've happened. That little girl in the store, she just went berserk and bit him, right before his eyes. Benjamin screamed and next thing he knew, people were running, screaming, and panicking. They began to trample each other and started grabbing food off the shelves and running. And his boy had a set of teeth marks on the back of his leg. Thank God he was wearing jeans. Somehow though, the girl had managed to nick his skin. He hadn't thought it was enough to spread it. And even though he didn't want to believe it, he was positive that Benji had been infected because an hour or so later, he started feeling sick, feverish. *What else could it be?* He prayed that it could be something else, anything else.

Sighing, Bill headed for the small living room. "I'm gonna check the news," he said. "See if things have settled down some."

Joanna walked right past him, not even acknowledging him. She headed for the kitchen. Bill knew she was worried about Benjamin and decided not to push her. He'd give her some space. Leaning forward and grabbing the remote from the beat-up walnut and glass coffee table, Bill pushed the 'On' button. The old projection screen, which took up half the space in the little room, lit up a bright turquoise blue.

"Huh," he said, clicking on the cable channels. Nothing happened. The channels were changing, but the screen stayed blue. Bill directed the remote to the cable box and turned it off and on, thinking that maybe he needed to reset it. Still, nothing happened. The screen was still blue. "Figures," he groaned, getting up from the couch. He manually pushed the button on the cable box, switching it off and on. He then checked the connection of the cable to make sure it wasn't loose. Everything was fine. Frowning, he pulled open the little panel on the front of the TV and tried changing the input. That didn't work either.

Bill wandered to the kitchen where his wife was washing dishes and sniffling. He came up behind her and lovingly placed a hand on her shoulder. "It'll be all right, you know." He could feel Joanna tense beneath his touch. She stared out the kitchen window in the direction of the swing set in the backyard. "Ben's gonna be fine."

Joanna nodded and returned to washing the dishes without saying a word.

"Cable's out," he said, picking up the phone off the kitchen counter next to a pile of junk mail and bills. That corner of the counter was always cluttered with mail. Sorting through the bills and junk mail was a never-ending battle in their household. "Do you know the number?"

Joanna sniffled and shook her head. "On the counter," she cleared her throat. "I paid it a couple of days ago."

Bill shuffled through the mail, searching for the cable bill. When he found it, he picked up the phone and dialed the number. Nothing happened. "What the…" Bill pushed the 'Talk' button. He pressed the phone to his ear. No dial tone. "Was the phone left off the hook again?"

Joanna shrugged and then closed the dishwasher.

Bill hit the redial button. The phone redialed the number. The little battery symbol on the screen showed full power. He again pressed the phone to his ear. Nothing.

"Phone lines must be down," he muttered. "Where's your cell?" He'd accidentally left his at work and had been too lazy to turn around on Friday to get it. He'd been halfway home at the time when he'd realized he'd forgotten it.

"In my purse," she said. Wiping tears from her eyes with the back of her hand.

Bill snatched Joanna's purse from one of the chairs at the small kitchen table where she always put it. He reached inside and found it beneath her wallet. Her battery was almost dead. He'd probably have to plug it in while talking to the cable company. This could take hours. He hated having to call them. It never was a fast and easy process. He'd more than likely get a hold of someone overseas at a help desk in India. Then he'd be put on hold several times until he'd be able to either get someone to help him or schedule an appointment to have a technician come out. Hopefully, that wouldn't be the case. Hopefully, they'd be able to fix the problem over the cable lines.

Typing in the phone number on the touchscreen, Bill pushed *Send* when he heard a loud crash coming from the other room.

Joanna's eyes grew large. "Benji!" she shrieked. "I'll check..."

Ready to race from the room, Joanna held her hand up at Bill. "I'll check on him!" she snapped. "You've done enough already! Call the damn cable company!"

Bill frowned, the phone felt heavy in his hand.

Joanna fled from the kitchen. Bill heard another loud crashing sound. This time he knew it was coming from Benjamin's room. He wanted to chase after Joanna but knew better. She blamed him for Benji's being sick. He'd try calling the cable people again, and then he'd peek his head in Benjamin's room.

Bill redialed the number and pressed the cell phone to his ear. Nothing.

"Are you kidding me?" He looked at the screen. The battery level was at 6%, and the little icon at the top of the screen was red. Maybe the low battery was keeping him from dialing out. He found the charger connected to the wall next to the home phone and hooked up the cell. He put the phone on speaker and tried again. Still nothing.

"What the hell?" he cursed, losing his temper. He slammed a fist on the counter. At the same moment, the lights went out, bathing him in darkness. The room grew eerily silent as the refrigerator, air conditioning, and all the rest of the noises that were a usual constant came to a halt. Bill turned on the cell phone, using the glow to light up the kitchen counter. He worked his way over to the junk drawer where he kept an emergency flashlight when he heard a bloodcurdling scream and another loud crash.

"Joanna!" he yelled, wrenching open the junk drawer so hard that it crashed to the floor. Frantically, he flipped the drawer over and rummaged through the contents until he found the small black metal flashlight. Another scream rang out through the otherwise silent house. Tossing the phone onto the counter, Bill ran to Benjamin's room. "Joanna?" he yelled, grabbing hold of the doorknob to Benji's door and yanking it open. "Ben!"

He shined the high-powered beam of light into the room. The beam swooped through the darkness until it landed on his son's face. Bill took a step back, his breath catching in his throat. Benjamin was standing next to his bed, face distorted and puffy, with what looked like blood, dripping from his lips. He could hear his wife sobbing.

"Joanna?" Bill quickly scanned the room. "Ben, where's your mother?" Benjamin didn't answer. He just stood there, staring at him.

Bill rushed toward the sound of his wife's muffled sobs. Finally, the beam of light landed on

Joanna's back. She was curled up on the floor near a toppled over bookshelf. Books were scattered around her. She was clutching her neck, and blood oozed from beneath her fingers.

"Oh my God!" Bill rushed to her side.

"Get out!" she screamed. "Get out!"

"We need to get you to a hospital." Bill tried to lift her from the floor when he heard a growl behind him. He aimed his flashlight at his eight-year-old son. His eyes gleamed a golden yellow, and his lips curled as he snarled. Keeping his eye on him, Bill crouched down and slid an arm around his wife. "Let's get you up."

Joanna wouldn't budge. Her breathing became labored causing her to cough and wheeze. "Leave me… take Benji to the hospital…"

Bill yanked at her again, trying to get her up. "I need to get *you* to the hospital… both of you."

Benjamin spun around, snarling. He turned his back to them and began to bang his fists hard against the wall. Bill wondered what was going through his son's head. He'd seen so many infected people on the news today attacking people for no apparent reason. The news people described it as being delirious with fever. Bill wondered what would make people snap that way. He could understand the delirious part due to a high fever, but to attack people? To attack family? Loved ones? It didn't make sense. Was Benjamin trying to control his need to attack by mauling at the wall instead? Bill wasn't sure. He never in a million years would've thought he'd be afraid of his son, his flesh in blood. But right now, he was beyond frightened. He was mortified.

"Come on," Bill whispered to Joanna, as he

carefully watched his son beat on the wall with what seemed like a tremendous amount of strength. He remembered the news crew discussing that too. Again, wouldn't a fever diminish your strength? Something evil was happening. And now it was infecting his son. A tear of despair escaped one of Bill's pale blue eyes and rolled down his cheek. Sadness and fright gripped his soul as one of Benjamin's small fists suddenly broke through the drywall with a crack startling him into action. He needed to get Joanna out of the bedroom and lock Benjamin inside until he could figure out what to do with him.

Within his arms, Joanna's body suddenly went limp, and he was having a hard time holding her up. Her hand dropped from her neck. Her wound was much worse than he'd realized. Blood soaked her gray t-shirt and the beige carpeting beneath her.

Nervous, Bill shined the light at his son whose banging quickly turned into clawing. He was now pulling and ripping chunks of drywall from the bedroom wall while snarling wildly. Blood dripped from his mangled fingers and smudged the light blue paint of his wall in disgusting streaks of dark red.

"Joanna?" Bill shook her shoulder and gently set her back down on the floor. "Joanna…" He shined the flashlight on his wife's face and then down her body to the carpet. He knew she had lost a lot of blood, but he hadn't been aware of how much. He leaned in, kissed her cheek, and listened for breathing. He heard none. Fresh tears flooded his eyes. "No," he cried, his voice barely audible and rose until he yelled out. "No… no… no!" His hands shook, his body trembled, racked with a mixture of intense emotions. Remorse, rage, and guilt pumped through his veins.

His son, their precious baby, killed his *own* mother... killed *his* wife... and it was *his* fault that Benjamin had transformed into some kind of monster. In reality, he'd killed Joanna. He was to blame for this! If only he'd left Benjamin at home. If he'd just listened to Joanna and not have been so God damn stubborn. None of this would be happening.

Bill's cries of agony at the loss of his wife caught Benjamin's attention, drawing him away from his clawing at the wall. Benjamin's gaze landed on his next victim. His father. There was a deep rumbling coming from his chest as if he were growling. Bill swiped at the tears in his eyes with the back of his hand and shined his flashlight at his son staring at the gleaming golden eyes.

Bill's mind flashed to the lockbox in his closet where he kept his gun. Joanna had been against him purchasing it but only agreed to it if he promised to keep it locked up. Her worst fear was that Benjamin would get a hold of it. And now, he was contemplating killing his own flesh and blood with it. Bill eyed the door. He'd have to walk past his son who looked as if he were preparing to attack. The growls were getting deeper and more guttural.

Frantically glancing around, Bill snatched up a decent-sized remote control, gas powered jeep that was sitting on the floor near his feet. He'd given this jeep to his son last Christmas. They'd built it together.

Without thinking twice, he grabbed the jeep, and with all of his strength, lobbed it at his son as he ran for the door. Once through, he slammed the door shut, hearing his son's body thud against the wooden door behind him. He gripped hold of the doorknob and held it tight. After a few minutes, he realized that his son wasn't trying to turn the knob. Instead, it sounded like he was scraping at the door with his fingernails.

Bill wondered if the infection, or whatever the heck it was, affected the brain's capacity to think. Obviously, his son knew how to open a door, but Benjamin wasn't even trying to turn the knob. A couple of times he heard him bump against the knob, jerking it. It was almost as if he'd been transformed into some sort of wild animal. Bill felt the handle press deeper into his hand before realizing how hard he was squeezing the metal to keep his son contained. He stared at the handle, waiting for it to turn. It didn't. He then glanced down the hall in the direction of his room. An image of his gun box flashed again before his eyes. And then his wife flashed before his eyes, poor Joanna. Another round of tears squeezed out and trickled down his cheeks. He knew what he had to do. He didn't have a choice.

Even though Ben hadn't yet opened the door, Bill figured it was only a matter of time before he crashed through the door, or accidentally turned the knob while mauling at the wood. Sucking in a deep breath, he let go of the handle and sprinted down the hall. When he entered the bedroom, Bill shut the door behind him and locked it. He wasn't going to take any chances. Sliding open the closet door, Bill removed a stack of baseball hats and tossed them to the floor. On his toes, he reached as far back as he could on the top shelf that ran the length of the closet. The shelf was deep. Perfect for storing their comforters, blankets and other household items that weren't used every day. The tips of his fingers brushed the cold metal of the gun box. He reached a bit farther until his thumb and fingers could grasp the corner of the box and tug it in his direction. After a couple of tries, he'd slid it close enough to the edge of the shelf, so that he could grab ahold of it. He lifted the cold steel in his hands and tossed the box onto his bed.

A new round of banging noises started up down the hall. It sounded as if Ben was back to beating on the walls. Bill quickly rounded the bed and yanked open the top drawer of his nightstand. He patted around the back of the drawer until his fingers felt the small key. Next, he yanked open the bottom drawer where he kept the bullets in a small box under his magazines. It took a few tries to unlock the gun box, his fingers were so unsteady, and he kept fumbling about.

"What the hell!" he mumbled, then finally the lock sprung open. Bill stared at the gun.

# Chapter 13

With tires squealing, Mike Wilson's car screeched to a halt. Two people had darted out into the street, one chasing after the other. He'd just turned off at the exit that'd take him to the little motel he'd recommended to Ellie. Unlatching his seatbelt, he threw open his door, hopped out of the car and chased after the man that was pursuing the woman down the street. The woman was screaming at the top of her lungs.

"Sheriff!" Mike yelled. "Stop where you are!" The couple kept running. The woman quickly glanced over her shoulder, long hair flying in her face, but didn't stop running.

Mike sprinted after them. He grabbed the handle of his gun and withdrew it from the holster. "This is a warning!" he yelled. "Stop, or I'll fire!"

They didn't listen, just kept running.

Winded, he stopped running. Feeling the weight of his gun in his hand, he wondered if he should fire a round into the air to get their attention. *What if the man was infected?* He wouldn't be surprised. After today, nothing would surprise him. He'd soon know for sure. Maybe he should aim to kill. Get it done and over with.

Just then, the woman changed course and took off into the desert. The man leaped, cat-like, over a heap of sagebrush along the side of the road and continued to chase after her.

"Crap!" The last thing Mike wanted to do was run through the sand and cacti. He took off at a diagonal sprint into the desert. He'd never seen anyone leap like that before. Well, not until today. Today, he'd seen all kinds of strange things. He was now fairly sure that the man was one of the infected. There was no other explanation for the way he had leaped. It was very animalistic. Suddenly, the woman screamed out again. Higher this time. Her voice pierced the air. She stumbled and fell to the ground. Mike could no longer see her. It was too dark.

"Hey!" he yelled when an idea struck him. He needed to draw the man away from her. Give him some fresh prey. Someone else to pursue. "Leave her alone!" His arm reached for the stars as he fired a round straight into the sky. The shot rang out in the otherwise silent surroundings. The infected man stopped moving. With his back to Mike, he stood completely still. Mike waited for him to turn around, to charge at him, but he didn't. Mike walked briskly, yet carefully, toward the man. His heart pounding in his chest.

"You!" he yelled, addressing the man. The man didn't react. "Yeah, you!" Mike tried again to get his attention. "Turn around!"

Still no reaction.

*What the hell?* Mike thought. *Why is he just standing there? Is he infected or not?* The others that he'd encountered that'd been infected didn't seem to have the capacity to think. It was as if the fever destroyed the reasoning part of the brain, causing the infected to go insane. This guy was thinking. Or at least it seemed like it. Was he debating on whether or not he should turn around? Maybe he wasn't infected at all. Maybe he was a wife beater teaching his so-called property a lesson. Mike scowled at the thought. He'd rather shoot a wife beater on the spot. He had no empathy for wife beaters *or* child molesters. But, of course, he couldn't just kill the bastard, even though he'd get much more satisfaction putting a bullet in the head of someone that deserved it, instead of these freaking infected people. He felt a pang of sorrow for the infected. What if there was a cure? His mind conjured up an image of that toddler in his crib. Did he even stand a chance of recovering? Deep down, Mike knew the answer. More than likely, the boy was already dead.

*If the guy wasn't infected,* he thought while staring at his backside; *then he had one hell of a leap.* Mike took a few slow, cautious steps toward him. The closer he got, the louder the woman's sobs grew. "Sheriff!" Mike repeated, softer this time. "Put your hands up and slowly turn around."

Unexpectedly, the man spun around. His face was dark within the shadows. Mike still couldn't tell whether or not he was infected. "Hands up!" he repeated, voice gruffer, his gun aimed at the man. "Don't make me do something rash. I don't wanna shoot you!"

A deep guttural growl resonated from deep within the man's chest. Mike sucked in a sharp breath. He'd heard that eerie sound way too many times today. He felt the hairs on his arms rise as goose bumps emerged. The growling was something he knew he'd never get used to.

"Don't shoot him!" the woman called out

through the gargled sound of tears. "Please…"
Behind the infected man, the woman got to her feet
and stumbled toward them. "My husband is sick…
he's…" But before she could finish her sentence, the
woman's husband turned and grabbed hold of her by
the hair. She screamed as he mauled her.

Without thinking twice, Mike fired at the man,
hitting him in the shoulder. He would've aimed for
the head, but didn't want to risk shooting the woman.
The woman screeched. The infected man stumbled,
letting go of his prey and spun around again to face
Mike. He growled and charged at him. Mike fired
without hesitation. He could hear the woman
screaming at him. The bullet connected with the
man's face. He crashed to the ground with a loud
thump, a few feet from the toes of Mike's boots.
Adrenaline pumping, Mike's heart was drumming in
his ears.

The woman ran to her husband who was face
down in the sand. She sobbed uncontrollably,
kneeling over his body.

"Are you hurt?' Mike asked her.

The woman didn't answer. She continued to cry
hysterically. Her body shook, wracked with grief.

"Did he hurt you?" Mike tried, again. He took a
few steps closer and nudged the man's body with the
toe of his boot. The man didn't move. Blood seeped
into the sand. Mike had gotten so used to doing that
as a precaution that he'd forgotten how callous it
must look to the woman mourning the sudden death
of her husband. A man he'd just shot dead. And
here he was, nudging him with his boot. The woman
was now staring up at Mike. The moonlight
highlighted her face just enough so that he could see

the anger that was now morphing her features.

"He was sick!" she spat, her thick red hair falling forward covering one of her eyes. "You killed him!"

"I'm sorry," Mike said, kneeling on the other side of the man so that he was eye level with the woman. "I truly am. But he was infected. He was going to kill you."

The woman looked down at her husband. A fresh wave of tears struck her. She leaned forward and hugged her husband's back. Her body heaving.

Mike had the sudden urge to pat her back. He wanted to comfort her. Guilt for killing this woman's husband tugged at his heartstrings, but he hadn't had a choice. It was either killing this man or letting him kill his wife. He had to do it.

Watching the woman cry while hugging her husband's lifeless body made him feel a bit voyeuristic like he shouldn't be there. However, at the same time, he couldn't leave. He couldn't leave this woman alone in the middle of the desert, mourning her husband. He had an obligation to make sure she made it home safe and sound. He needed to talk her into leaving with him. Maybe she lived nearby. Maybe he could get her home with the promise of sending someone to move her husband's body. He knew she wasn't going to want to leave him there. The coyotes would probably feed on his remains.

The woman turned and buried her head in her husband's back. After a while, her sobs became quieter, and her shaking began to subside. She had her husband's blood seeping all over her shirt. Mike hoped the infection, or virus, or whatever the hell it was, couldn't be spread through contact with the blood. Then he thought of the ambulance crew he'd been working with earlier in the day. None of them seemed to have been affected by it, and he had been working with them for the better portion of the day.

"Hey," he said, quietly. "Let me give you a ride home?"

The woman didn't answer. She barely sniffled. Her ear was pressed against her husband's back with her face away from him.

"Miss?" he said, trying again. "Do you have friends or family nearby? Is there anyone that could help you? A neighbor, maybe?"

The woman still didn't answer. Mike got up and walked around the husband's body. He stood next to the woman when he noticed it. Her hair had slid to the side, and the moonlight was hitting her just right. Fresh blood. Not all the blood on her clothing belonged to her husband. There was no mistaking the large set of teeth marks on the upper fleshy part of her arm.

"Damn," he whispered. He'd hoped that what he was seeing wasn't real. He closed his eyes for a second and then gazed again at the woman's arm. "Hey," he said gently. "Are you okay?"

The woman didn't answer him. He leaned forward and gently touched her shoulder. "Are you feeling okay?"

The woman's head snapped to the side in an unnatural way. Mike jumped back, almost tripping over his own feet. Thankfully, he caught his balance before going down. The woman began to cough, turned her head, and then clutched her stomach, groaning.

Mike breathed in, taking another step backward, and he drew his gun.

# Chapter 14

Out of breath, Ellie was happy to see the small stucco motel. She'd come up around the side of it. She walked past a dumpster and then headed to the front of the building. There were no more than maybe, ten rooms. She wasn't really paying attention. Her mind was reeling, her heart pounding. Her adrenalin had kept her moving, but now fatigue was beginning to set in. She noticed there was only one car parked in the parking lot. It probably belonged to whoever was working the desk.

Sucking in a deep breath, Ellie tried to compose herself while dreaming up something to say to the person working there. She had no wallet, so no credit cards and absolutely no cash. Heck, she didn't even have her ID on her. Everything was in the car. Damn, what would she say? Would they give her a room? She doubted it. Maybe she'd be able to convince them to let her use the phone. If she could call her parents, they could give them a credit card number over the phone. That is if her parents answered their phone. She prayed they were okay. Her sister. She'd try her sister again. Her chances of getting ahold of her sister were better than her parents. *Or,* she thought, *I could call Officer Wilson.*

Pushing open the glass front door, a string of bells tied to the handle jingled. Ellie was thankful the door was unlocked. She looked around the dimly lit front room. She walked over to a small wooden oak rack on the wall near the built-in desk and counter which was filled with travel brochures. Being that the motel was near the border between California and Nevada, there was a mixture of brochures advertising casinos, specialty shows like the *Blue Man Group* and *Cirque du Soleil* and site seeing in Las Vegas; as well as advertisements for California including *Disneyland*, *Sea World*, and *Whale Watching*. Ellie spied the small beige couch against the wall across from the counter. She was so beyond tired. A part of her thought she should sit down and rest for a moment until the person working the desk came back. The other part of her warned against it. The last thing she wanted was to fall asleep. Not here. She needed to get a room. Maybe, if she could reach her parents, she could also have them rent a car for her.

Ellie walked up to the counter and leaned against it. She glanced around. There was a dark hallway to the right. She wondered if there was possibly a staff break room down there. Ellie propped her elbows on the counter and spied the clock on the wall. It was going on ten o'clock. It seemed so much later than it was. Ellie stared down at the two black ballpoint pens and the chewed up yellow #2 pencil next to the keyboard of the small flat screen computer. She then eyed the telephone when she heard a loud thud. It was coming from somewhere down the hall.

"Hello?" she called, again, hoping that she'd be heard. Maybe the motel clerk hadn't heard the jingling of the bells when she'd entered. The motel was kind of tucked away. Maybe they weren't used to getting much business especially this late at night. She glanced up and down the counter in search of a bell. *Didn't motels usually have a bell? In movies, they always had a bell.* "Hello!" Ellie tried louder this time. "Anyone here?" She waited a moment, listening.

Silence.

Ellie wondered if she should go in search of someone working there. She studied the dark hall to the right, in the back of the tiny office. She heard another thudding sound. It was quieter this time, but it still made her jump. Ellie turned and glanced out the glass front door into the night and chills raced down her spine. She had no desire to go back outside. Not in the dark.

Doing the only thing that came to mind, Ellie walked around the counter and headed toward the hallway. She stopped at the entryway. "Anyone here?" She stood there for a moment, hand on the doorway, steadying herself. Her legs didn't want to move. "I'd like a room, please…"

Standing near the opening of the hallway, it took her a moment to gather her courage. She wasn't one to walk down dark hallways in strange places, but she needed a room, and she was tired. She knew someone was there. A car was parked out front, and she'd heard those noises. She waited for a few seconds for an answer. Still nothing.

Ellie began to wander down the hall. There was a dingy yellow bucket on wheels with a mop against the wall. A tiny stream of light was seeping into the hall from the front office. There were two closed doors. The mop was next to one of them. She figured it was probably the storage room. The other door was at the end of the hall, and she could see a sliver of light seeping out from the doorjamb.

Ellie quietly crept nearer the door. Then she thought better of being so quiet. She didn't want to startle anyone. "Hello?" she said again. "Anyone here? I'd like a room…"

There was a shuffling sound on the other side of the door. She could hear footsteps. The person had to hear her. "I'll wait in the front office," she said, louder. "I just wanted you to know I'm here!" There were more shuffling and scraping sounds. Ellie waited, but the door didn't open. She nervously gnawed on her bottom lip. *I'll wait up front,* she thought, turning around. "Oh," she said, almost forgetting to ask. "Do you mind if I use your phone? My car broke down."

No answer. More scraping.

The door began to shake but didn't open.

Ellie spun back around and eyed the door. It was too dark to see it. She lightly pressed her fingertips to it. "Are you okay?" she asked, having the sudden thought that maybe something was wrong with the door. Maybe the person inside couldn't get out. "Are you locked in?"

Against her better judgment, Ellie pushed down on the handle. She carefully pushed the door open, and it hit against something. She tried again and suddenly realized she was bumping someone with it. "Oh, sorry," she said. "I didn't mean to…"

The person shuffled to the side, and Ellie opened the door a bit more. An elderly man stood there. His foot was blocking the door from opening all the way. "I hope I hadn't startled you," she said. "No one was up front."

The man reached for her and snatched a lock of her long hair. Ellie screamed as he yanked. A golden eye gleamed at her through swollen puffed up skin. Instant flashbacks of the infected woman at the gas station and the man at the border popped into her head.

Pulling her head back, she screamed some more. The man's hand was tangled deep in her long hair. Her scalp burned something fierce. With his other hand, the man reached for her, clawing, snarling. His gnarled fingers were close to her face. Ellie still had a hold of the door handle. She pulled it toward her, trying to yank it shut. She managed to slam the heavy door on the man's arm, hoping he'd release her. His grip didn't loosen. Instead, he began to growl.

"Let go!" Ellie shrieked, pulling hard on the handle and leaning back with her full body weight. She clutched it with both hands and prayed it didn't slip out of her grasp. Tears streamed down her cheeks. Her scalp felt like it was on fire. She pulled with all of her might. *Eventually, he'll let go,* she thought. The door was heavy. She pulled again, leaning hard. Her hands were becoming sweaty. Pursing her lips, she focused on her grip. She heard crunching. The bones in the old man's wrist were shattering. His growls became deeper with the struggle.

"Let go!" she hollered. "Let go of me!" She reached for the man's gnarled hand trying to free it from her hair while continuing to pull the door closed with the other hand.

Suddenly, his fingers released, the door slammed shut, and she stumbled backward, slamming her back against the wall across from her. Regaining her footing, she sprinted down the dark hall to the dimly lit front office. She'd expected the old man to be snarling behind her, yet the door didn't open. She wasn't sure if it'd somehow locked when it closed or what had happened. Fingernails scraped down the other side of the door.

Ellie spied keycards sitting on the counter. She grabbed the stack and raced out of the office. She wanted to use the phone to call for help but didn't want to take a chance on the old man getting loose.

*What the hell kind of virus was this?* she wondered, not for the first time that day.

Shivering, Ellie stepped into the shadows. Her heart was still racing. She was as terrified of being outside as she was inside the motel. She had no idea what, or who could be lurking around in the dark. Feeling the keycards in her hands gave her a small glimmer of hope, a false sense of security. She decided to try the keycards on each of the motel room doors. She hoped to get lucky and be able to take refuge inside one of the rooms. Then she'd lock herself inside. By morning, everything should be better.

\*\*\*

A soft scraping sound penetrated her sleep and worked its way into her dreams. Amanda was trying to ignore the sound but couldn't. Her eyelids flickered open and a sharp pain radiated through her neck. She reached up and massaged the knot in her muscles. Everything was dark. She'd been sleeping in a strange position, and it took a second for her to remember where she was. Shivering, she crossed her arms over her chest and turned onto her side, even though she was practically sitting up since the damn seat wouldn't recline. She closed her heavy eyelids and began to doze some more when the scratching sound started up again. It went on for a minute or two. It wasn't until the scratching was accompanied by moaning, that Amanda's eyes snapped open. She stared out the window across from her. She was in the driver's seat of the patrol car, facing the passenger window with the driver's side window to her back. It was dark.

"Uhhhh…" *Scratch, scratch… scrape…scratch…*

The sound was coming from behind her.

Spinning around, Amanda faced the driver's side window. A woman's face was pressed against the glass. Hot breath fogged it up. Long slender fingers curled and scraped, as pink manicured nails clawed at her.

Amanda let out a scream.

This seemed to provoke the woman. She pawed at the glass, trying to get inside. One of her acrylic fingernails snapped beneath the pressure of the incessant clawing. Blood oozed from her index finger as her scraping became more manic. Near perfect teeth bit hungrily at the smooth surface of the window, leaving a smear of disgusting drool beneath collagen-enhanced lips.

Panicked and wide-eyed, Amanda double-checked the door lock. She fumbled with it. As far as she could tell, it was locked, but didn't know for sure. She scooted her body over the center console and into the passenger seat; all the while keeping her eyes trained on the infected woman, whom at one time was probably very beautiful and refined. Now she'd been transformed into some kind of crazed zombie-like creature that was desperately trying to force her way into the car.

No longer drowsy, Amanda was wide-awake, shaking, and scared out of her freaking mind. Should she flee the car? Make a run for it? Unable to get herself to do anything, she pushed her back against the passenger door. She wanted to get as far away as she possibly could from the snarling bimbo.

*Thump!*

Amanda's breath caught in her throat. Unable to move, her body seized up.

*Thump! Thump!*

Something hard banged against the door behind her. *Bam!* She spun around in her seat. A man was staring at her. Breathing heavily, she grabbed for the passenger side door and fumbled around until she found the lock. Her nails kept missing the latch. She cursed herself for having such long nails. As much as she loved her French manicure, it didn't come in handy when you needed to use your fingers. She continued to grope around the door handle. Finally, her nails scraped over the buttons. *Was it locked?* She couldn't tell. Being that there were no keys and with everything being electric, she just couldn't tell. *Was there a way to manually lock a door in a newer model car? Shit!* she thought. And for the first time ever, she wished to be trapped in Jasper's ancient piece of rusting crap with the old school manual locks and windows. At least then, she'd know for a fact that the friggin' doors were locked.

"Oh my God," she breathed, "Oh my God. This is not good... oh my...g..."

The man leaned in and pushed his bearded face closer to the glass. There was just enough light shining from the street lamp above that she could see a hint of his gold to his eyes as his gaze zeroed in on her. She held his stare for a moment while trying to hold down the bile that crept up her throat. She refused to let herself throw up. Not now. She needed to stay strong and alert. She quickly glanced at the blonde woman, still clawing at the passenger side window. In her desperate effort to get inside, more fingernails had snapped off. Blood was smeared all over the glass.

Amanda's eyes shifted back to the bearded man. He was large, overweight, and wearing a plaid shirt that barely fit over his beer gut. He placed a meaty hand on the glass. She winced, moving away from the window. She worried about the amount of weight behind him. He'd be more capable of tearing his way into the police car than the woman.

*Bam! Bam!* The man slammed the roof of the car with his fist. A bolt of fear shot straight down Amanda's spine.

Quickly glancing over her shoulder, she wished she could get into the backseat, but there was a barrier. Her eyes drifted to the glove box. In movies, cops kept guns in their glove box. Or was that mobsters? She wasn't sure. Leaning forward she tried to open it. Locked.

"Damn it!" she shrieked. Again, the man banged down on the roof of the car. "Go away!" she yelled at the window. "Leave me alone!"

Her screaming riled the man up. He then began pounding on the roof with both of his fists. *Bam! Bam! Bam!*

Amanda could also hear the woman. She was now banging on the glass.

"Oh shit!" Amanda screamed when she noticed

an extra set of hands on the passenger side window. The car began to rock.

She then watched as a young man in a Metallica T-shirt, and tattoo-sleeved arms, crawled up onto the hood of the police car and began to yank at the windshield wipers.

"Go away!" she screamed, moving away from the windows. She was now sitting on the center console with her back pressed against the barrier that kept her from being able to hide in the backseat.

"Leave me alone!" Tears streamed down her cheeks. "Leave me alone! Leave me alone..."

More people surrounded the car, drawn to the commotion. There were so many of them that their bodies were blocking out the street lamps, leaving Amanda in the dark. She pulled her knees up to her chest, hugging her legs.

Amanda's heart fluttered at a new sound. It was the sound of a handle being pulled. Someone was trying to open one of the doors. It was a distinct sound. *Which door?* Her body was trembling, but she forced herself to hold still and focus on which door the sound was coming from. She forced herself to focus her senses. Her eyes shifted from side to side. It was too dark to see anything. She concentrated on separating the sounds.

Then she heard it again. *Click, click...* The handle lifted and was then let go of. It was hard to tell which door was trying to be opened over the loud snarling, growling, and banging.

*Click, click...* Her ears perked as she pinpointed the direction of the sound.

*The passenger side door.*

The handle lifted again. She flung herself to the

passenger seat, ready to grab the door from the inside, if someone were to open it. She clutched the door and held her breath. The handle lifted… and released… lifted… and released. She then heard tugging. She let out her breath. Nothing happened. The door was locked.

Melting like butter, Amanda slithered onto the floor by the glove box. Her knees were pressed to her chest. There was nowhere to hide from the monsters outside. She tried her best to make herself invisible. Squeezing her eyes shut, she remembered the last time she'd played hide and seek with her nephew. He was three. She'd pretended to be looking all over the apartment for him as he giggled, standing in the corner of the room, with his eyes closed. She remembered how funny that was. He'd actually thought she couldn't see him because he couldn't see her.

Amanda heard another bang on the glass rousing her from the comforting thoughts of playing hide and seek with her nephew. At the time, she'd felt put out because she hadn't wanted to babysit. She'd had plans to go out with Jasper and had to cancel at the last minute. Right now, she'd give anything to be home babysitting Johnny. She wondered how her sister was doing. Were she and Johnny okay? Were they with mom? She hadn't spoken to her sister or her mother since that night. Amanda had begrudgingly taken care of Johnny because she'd felt she had to, and then later she'd let her sister have it, when she returned home. At the time, she'd felt her sister had purposely signed up for extra hours at work, just to keep her from going out with Jasper. It was no secret how much her sister and mother hated

Jasper. They believed he was the same as her ex-husband, if not worse. *But he wasn't,* Amanda thought. *He wasn't nearly as bad. He actually loved me.*

This time the banging sound was louder than any of the previous hits. She prayed that the glass of the windows stayed intact. Once the glass was broken, she'd be in trouble. As soon as the thought entered her mind, she heard the shattering of glass. She looked up from her hiding place on the floor. The back windshield had given way. She was now thankful for the barrier between the front and back seats.

Closing her eyes, she pretended she was invisible, just like Johnny had done. If she made it out of the police car alive, she'd call her family. It'd been over six months since she'd last spoken to any of them.

Amanda focused on keeping her eyes squeezed shut. She hoped that after a while the infected would forget she was in there and wander off after some other unfortunate soul. That was when her mind drifted to Jasper. *Was he out there wandering the streets, attacking innocent people? Was he amongst the infected banging on the car?* She hated to think of him like that. It tore her up inside. Amanda began to cry.

# Chapter 15

He couldn't do it. He couldn't. Bill stared at his son who was thrashing about, wrestling against the restraints. It tore at his heartstrings to see his little body bound. Nevertheless, for being so small, restraining him had been a challenge. It took a while, but he'd finally managed to do it. He had had to wrestle Benjamin to the ground while being careful not to get bit. Then he snapped on a set of handcuffs that'd been, until then, used for a fun fantasy of cops and robbers that he and his wife had played. He tried not to think of his Joanna's lifeless body still lying in a pool of blood on the floor of his son's room.

Bill opened the coat closet where he'd stashed his son, trying to settle him down, while he thought things over. Benjamin was both handcuffed and gagged, leaning in the corner.

For the last two hours, Benjamin bashed his small body against the door and the walls of the closet while Bill had sat on the sofa, gun in his hands, trying to figure out what to do. He couldn't kill his son. He couldn't. Even though he hadn't much hope after everything he'd seen on the news earlier, he just couldn't get himself to do it. What the hell was he going to do? He'd already lost Joanna. He couldn't lose Benjamin, too. No. He had to do something, but what? What would Joanna want him to do? She'd want him to take care of their son. She gave her life trying to take care of him.

That thought made up his mind. He'd do what Joanne would've wanted him to do. He wanted to honor his wife's last wish. She gave her life taking care of their son. She would want him to do whatever he could in his power to save Benjamin.

"Hey, buddy," Bill said, staring into the small closet. Jackets and hangers were piled on the floor around Benjamin's feet from all of his thrashing about.

Benjamin's eyelids flickered open at the sound of his father's voice. The boy's face was so puffy that Bill could barely see the yellow of his eyes. If he hadn't known it was his son, he wouldn't have recognized him.

"How ya feelin'?" Anxiety grew in the pit of stomach, tearing away at the lining. He could feel his ulcer acting up.

A grumbling noise rumbled in Benjamin's small chest. Staring at him, Bill thought how little his son looked. How weak, and tiny. His baby boy had blood smeared across one of his cheeks and a dab on his forehead. Most of the blood was on his upper lip and soaked into the front of his pajamas. His nose was swollen, reddish purple, and crusted over. Bill frowned. With all of the thrashing, Benjamin had bashed his nose in pretty good. Bill hoped it wasn't broken. However, he knew that a broken nose was an easy fix in comparison to whatever the hell this outbreak was that'd infected him.

"I'm gonna take you to the hospital," he explained softly. "Okay, Buddy? We're gonna go get you some help… make you all better…"

Benjamin continued to growl, but he didn't move. He stayed in one spot, leaning against the wall. Blood streaked the white paint behind him. Bill spied the boys' fingerprints within the bloody mess. He must've been grasping at the wall through his constraints. His stomach ached.

Frightened, yet feeling odd about being afraid of his own son, Bill stepped into the closet and put his hand on Benjamin's arm. Heat radiated through the thin material of his blue and red Superhero pajamas. He was burning up.

"Come on, son." He gently tugged at his arm to try to get him to walk. Benjamin didn't move. "Let's get you to the hospital." Bill now pulled at his son's arm. The growling deepened, and Benjamin threw his weight at his father, lunging at him. Not expecting the reaction, even though he felt he should have, Bill stumbled, almost tripping over his own two feet. He caught himself before hitting the ground. Ben snarled while gnawing at the fabric of the thick gag, unable to attack, trying to bite into his father's side. Bill grabbed hold of his son around the waist, tossed his slight body over his shoulder like a sack of potatoes, and rushed out the front door to the car. He was having a difficult time holding onto the wiggling, snarling, hot body. He was worried he'd drop him. Once he got to the car, he reached for the handle to open the back door. It was locked.

"Shit!" he swore. The keys were in his pocket. He set the boy on the ground in the driveway next to the car as he plunged his hand into his pocket. He grabbed the keys as Benjamin tried again to attack. His mouth was biting furiously at the thick cloth.

Bill pushed the button on the alarm, disarming the car. He forced his son into the backseat, pushing hard against his chest to keep him still enough to seatbelt him in. "I'm doing this for your own good," Bill said. He pressed his wrist against his son's forehead. Ben's skin was so hot that it felt as if it were on fire. "I love you, son. You're gonna be okay. Promise. I'm gonna run inside and get a few things. Be right back." Bill shut the door, locking his son inside. He sprinted back into the house to grab his wallet and Benjamin's favorite teddy bear. Not thinking straight, he forgot the gun.

***

Mike walked back to his car, leaving the bodies behind in the desert. He tried not to think about it. He did what he had to do. The woman was infected. Just as her husband had been. He hadn't had much of a choice. It was best to put her out of her misery. And at the same time, he'd prevented another human from being attacked or infected or both. Shaking his head, Mike stared straight ahead. Life had suddenly thrown him a curve ball. Hell, it'd thrown everyone a curveball. When he woke this morning, this was the last thing he'd ever expected to happen. If someone had predicted this widespread outbreak, he'd have never believed it. This was like something straight out of a horror movie.

With his gun in hand, Mike kept his ears and eyes open. His senses were on high alert. Never in his life had he ever been this on edge. And he'd been in some extremely precarious positions. Nothing could have or would have ever prepared him for something like this. He thanked his lucky stars to have a gun and that he was an expert marksman. Before becoming a sheriff, Mike was in the Marine Corps. After he'd put in his four years, and two deployments, one being to Iraq, he'd decided to get out. Not sure of what he wanted to do with his life, but knew he didn't want to be a lifer in the military, he'd decided to put his expert shooting skills to work in a different profession. He had decided to go into law enforcement.

When he'd left Camp Pendleton, his last duty station in San Diego County, he'd gone to the sheriff academy in Los Angeles. He'd put in a couple of years in the city, before moving to a small town just outside of Las Vegas. Enjoying Nevada, hoping to get a little closer to the glitz and glamour of Las Vegas, he'd applied for a job. After a while of trying, he'd eventually been offered a job. Unfortunately, he didn't work in Las Vegas, as he'd once hoped, but worked the stretch of acreage between the Nevada and the California border.

Mike pushed his way through the desert shrubbery and stepped up onto the asphalt. He could barely make out his car in the distance. He hadn't realized how far he'd followed the couple. A rustling noise out in the distance caught his attention, and Mike stopped walking. Turning toward the desert, he stood and listened. After a few moments, he heard some yipping. Coyotes.

The odd sounds of the surreal yipping and yapping that the coyotes made at night were something he'd never been able to get used to. Even after the three years of living in the middle of the desert, the sounds they made still unnerved him. Pushing forward, he headed for his patrol car. He hoped Ellie had made it to the motel. His next stop was to check in on her.

***

With tears in her eyes, Ellie was two doors away from the end of the building. The motel was small, and she was running out of options. The longer she stood out in the open, the more frightened she became.

"Come on," she begged, trying to open the door with the first of the three cards she had in hand. The lock wouldn't accept the keycard. Fumbling, because her hands were shaky with nerves, Ellie dropped the cards. They fell onto the pavement, and a tear rolled down her cheek.

*Don't lose it now,* she told herself. *Keep it together.*

She wondered if it'd be hard to break into one of the rooms. Maybe she could pry open one of the windows. She looked around at the darkness surrounding her. With what? What could she use to pry open a window? It wasn't like there would be a crowbar just lying around. Would there? She could always go back to the office. Maybe check out the supply closet. There had to be a supply closet. She remembered the closed door in the hallway. She bet there might be something in there she could use to pry open a window. Then she thought of the maids. Whoever cleaned the rooms would have to have access to all of the rooms. There must be a master key. Nevertheless, did she want to chance going back into the office to look for it? She stared warily in the direction of the office. Chills washed over her as she thought of the old man in the break room. Every few seconds she had been glancing back at the office and so far no one had come out. No one was following after her. Maybe she could go back inside. Maybe it was safe.

Ellie scooped up the key cards from the ground. She wasn't sure which one she'd already tried on the door. She grabbed one and slid it into the lock above the handle. The light lit up red. She put it on the bottom of the cards in her hand. Maybe the cards needed to be activated before they worked on the doors. She wasn't sure. She had no idea how the stupid things worked. She took the second card out of the stack when she heard something. It was the unmistakable sound of shoes crunching on gravel. Glancing over her shoulder, her heart began to race. Someone was walking across the vacant parking lot. Whoever it was had seen her. There was no mistaking that. She was standing beneath a security light. There was no hiding.

Heart racing, Ellie slid the second card into the slot. *Click!* The light flickered green. Unable to believe her eyes, Ellie slid the card a second time. *Green!* She pushed down the handle, and the door flung open.

"Hey!" the man crossing the lot picked up speed. Ellie could see him running toward her. Quickly she entered the room and slammed the door behind her, hearing it clicking locked. She slid the security latch and leaned her back against the door. She stood in the dark as her eyes adjusted. The window was to her left, the curtains open. Ellie grabbed the wand and pulled them shut just as the man began to bang on the door. She could hear him yelling at her to open up.

Finding her voice, she yelled back. "Go away! Leave me alone!"

"Let me in!" he yelled, still banging on the door.

"I'll call the police!" she yelled back. She prayed the man would leave. *What does he want with me? He wasn't infected. He seemed coherent.* The others she'd come in contact with seemed to lose cognateness when infected. *Unless, of course, he was newly infected.* All kinds of questions raced through her mind. *What if this guy was paranoid and looking for shelter for the night? Maybe he was just trying to find a place to hold up until this epidemic passed.* After the two men that'd tried to hijack her car, she wasn't about to take any chances with helping this guy. She was too afraid to take chances with trusting anyone.

"I need a place to stay!" the guy yelled. "Let me in!"

Ellie leaned her back against the door. She was afraid that the man would somehow get it open. She could hear him working at the handle.

"The office is open," she yelled back. "Get your own room!"

After a little while, the banging stopped. She hoped the man decided to give up and leave her alone. Her heartbeat began to stabilize, and her breathing slowed down. Exhausted, Ellie slid down the door, until her rear-end hit the floor. She stayed there, sitting on the floor, staring into the dark. She was too afraid to leave her spot by the door and didn't want to chance alerting anyone else to her presence by turning on a light. She closed her eyes and leaned her head against the corner of the wall where the door and wall met. Within minutes, exhaustion had taken over, and she'd drifted off to sleep. It wasn't long before the sound of something scraping interrupted her slumber. She kept hearing it.

The noise continued to grow louder until the unmistakable sound of a window sliding open in its tracks awoke her.

On all fours, Ellie scrambled across the room toward the bed. She got to her feet and snatched a lamp from the nightstand farthest from the window. Several times, she yanked hard at the cord until it finally snapped, releasing the plug from the wall. She thought of maneuvering herself next to the window and taking her assailant by surprise, whacking him upside the head when he entered. She could attack him before he attacked her. She was pretty sure he wouldn't be expecting her to attack first. Instead, she just stood there, on the far side of the Queen-sized bed, holding the bulky lamp in her hands. The heavy drapes moved, letting yellow light from the security lamp outside filter into the room, as the bulk of a large man climbed through the opening.

*Rush him!* she thought. *Take him out while he least expects it! Do it now!*

Ellie's feet didn't move.

*Now!* she told herself. *Do it now!*

Ellie still couldn't force herself to do anything. It was as if she'd lost all control of her body. In fact, she wasn't even sure she was breathing. She tried, but she couldn't even make herself scream. She just stood there like an idiot, clutching the stupid lamp, frozen in her tracks, while the voice in her head screamed at her to do something. Anything! Why the hell couldn't she move? She needed to do something. This man was going to hurt her. She couldn't just stand there and not do anything. What the hell was wrong with her? *Move, damn it! Move!* the voice in her head demanded. *Now!*

The drapes slid over to the side and Ellie could clearly see her assailant. He was now in the room with her. He stood just inside the open window, the light at his back. He was sizing her up.

"You should've let me in," he said, and then he charged at her.

Ellie's feet jumped into action without having to be told what to do. She hadn't even realized she was moving. Somehow, she and the oversized lamp, made it into the bathroom. Immediately, the ceramic lamp slipped from her grasp and hit the tiled floor, shattering everywhere. Leaning her full weight into the bathroom door, she locked the handle. Ellie patted the wall near the sink and found the light switch by the counter. The man aggressively shook the door handle and banged on the bathroom door.

"What do you want?" Ellie hollered. "I don't have anything!" She glanced around the bathroom. There was no window to escape through. Only a fan and vent in the ceiling which were way too small. She spied a minuscule bar of soap still in the wrapper, two miniature bottles; one with shampoo and the other conditioner, a tube of lotion, and a couple of individually wrapped plastic drinking cups. Nothing that'd help her. The rubber sole of her tennis shoes crunched on the pieces of the lamp as she spun around the room looking for a weapon. She yanked the white towels from the rack, tossing them onto the floor and grabbed hold of the bar. She tugged at it, hoping it'd come loose from the wall. She could use the bar in self-defense. She pulled again with all her weight, and the damn thing refused to budge. It must've been bolted into a stud.

*Bam!* The man rammed the door. *Bam! Bam!*

Ellie's foot crunched again as it slid a bit on the scattered pieces of ceramic. Reaching down, she grabbed a shard of the shattered lamp. It was the closest thing she had to a weapon. She grasped it in her hand and could feel the sharp edges threatening to slice into her skin. Eyeing the towels, she spotted a washcloth and wrapped it around the end she was holding. She took a few steps away from the door, flipped the light off, hoping it'd give her the advantage, and waited for the lock to give way.

\*\*\*

Pulling up in front of the motel, Mike drove through the small vacant parking lot. There was only one vehicle parked there. He thought of Ellie's car abandoned on the highway and the piece of shit, infected man, he'd stumbled across. He wondered if Ellie had ever made it to the little run down motel. Mike noticed the light on in the office and parked his car. He sat there for a moment, thinking about what he was going to say. He figured he'd start with whoever was working the nightshift and ask if Ellie had checked in. What was Ellie's last name? Had she told him? He wasn't sure. Guess he could inquire if an attractive woman in her twenties with long brown hair in short shorts with legs that... *No,* he told himself. *The world is falling apart around you, and you're thinking about this girl's sexy legs? What the hell is wrong with you? Pull yourself together!*

Swinging open the door, Mike slid out of his car. He stepped up onto the walkway, and was about to pull open the office door, when he heard some loud banging. For a second, he stood there listening. It was coming from the other side of the building. He was about to shrug it off and enter the office when he heard it again.

"What the hell?"

Curious, Mike headed in the direction of the sound. He kept his hand on the butt of his gun. He followed the sound until he reached an open window. The screen had been sliced open with a razor blade. He stopped in front of the window when he heard a loud cracking noise like wood splintering and then a woman's scream rang out from inside the room.

Mike grabbed hold of the curtain, yanking it and pushing it farther aside to see into the room. He'd left his flashlight in the car.

"Sheriff!" he yelled, as he climbed through the open window. "Stop what you're doing!"

The light drifting into the room from outside was just enough to see a bed and two-night stands. Across from the bed was a dresser with an older box television set resting on top. Mike heard a woman's sobs, coming from where he assumed was the bathroom. They were being muffled.

Mike switched on the light next to the door. A lamp closest to the window lit up, bathing the room in a soft incandescent light. He noticed the other nightstand on the other side of the bed was missing a lamp.

A man's gruff voice answered him. "What'd ya want?"

Mike took a few steps toward the bathroom. "I heard a commotion in here."

"Everything's fine," the man said. "The little woman and I are havin' a discussion. You'd better leave now."

Mike took another step toward the dark bathroom. "Sounded violent to me," he said. "I'd like to talk to your wife."

"It's none of your business," the man said. "Tell him you're fine."

Mike heard the woman's sobs.

"Tell him!"

Drawing his gun, Mike stepped closer to the bathroom. The door was open. The man suddenly wrestled a woman out of the bathroom. One arm was encompassing her waist. He was jabbing something sharp into the side of her neck.

Mike stopped dead in his tracks when he recognized the woman's face. The woman was Ellie. Tears streaked her rosy cheeks. He could see blood on her chin. Her bottom lip was swollen and had been split open.

"Stay back," the man warned. "Or I'll cut her. I ain't goin' back to jail. You 'ere me! I ain't!"

"I'm not here to take you to jail," Mike said, gun trained on the man. "Let her go."

The man chuckled. "I know how this works. I ain't no dummy. I let her go, and you take me to jail. I ain't doin' that!"

"You don't let her go…" Mike said, "I'll shoot you."

"You ain't gonna shoot me," the man laughed. "You can't. It's against the law. I have no weapon."

"Believe me, I'll shoot your ass," Mike warned. "If you haven't noticed, things *aren't* the same. There aren't any more laws."

The man's eyes shifted to the open window and then the bolted door. He pushed the ceramic shard against Ellie's throat causing her to wince. "I just want outta here," he said.

"Let the girl go," Mike coaxed, noticing the

man's bulging brown eyes shift again. "I don't care what the hell you do."

"She's goin' with me," the man said, taking slow, clumsy steps toward Mike. "For insurance…" He was now eyeing the door, the choice of his escape. Ellie shrieked as the shard punctured her skin.

Mike primed his gun. "Last chance."

Suddenly, the man pushed Ellie at Mike. She stumbled over her own two feet, slamming hard against him. Mike caught her in his arms. The burly man unlatched the door and ran. Mike didn't bother running after him. More than likely, the infected would take care of him.

"You okay?" He tilted Ellie's head to the side and checked her neck. Luckily, she only suffered a small puncture wound and a few surface scratches. As far as he could tell, she was okay. Nothing needed stitches or medical attention. No bones appeared to be broken.

Ellie, shaking uncontrollably, wrapped her arms around him and sobbed into his shoulder. Then the electricity went out.

# Chapter 16

The snarls coming from the backseat unnerved him. Bill kept glancing in the mirror at Benjamin. Seeing his baby boy strapped into the seat with blood caked on his puffed up face, wiggling against his restraints, broke his heart. He was having a hard time dealing with the reality of what was happening. *This really couldn't be happening, could it?* Bill swallowed, forcing down the large lump that was forming in his throat. Everything seemed so surreal, as if he was trapped in a crazy, messed up nightmare. Maybe he'd wake up. *Oh God, what he'd give to wake up.* To wake up with his wife snuggled up next to him in bed. His son eating Pop Tarts and watching cartoons on TV in the living room. That's what he wanted to wake up to. He wouldn't even complain about the television being up too loud. He'd welcome being awoken by the sound of cartoons blaring.

"Damn it!" Bill barked, slamming on the brakes. His car came to an abrupt halt, throwing him forward with a firm jerk. Benjamin groaned loudly. Bill glanced at him in the rearview mirror to make sure he was okay. He looked as okay as expected. This was the second time they'd come to a standstill. It was as if every freakin' person in the neighborhood had crashed into one another and abandoned their cars in the middle of the streets. "What the hell?" He couldn't even get out of their neighborhood. He wondered what was wrong with people. He looked around, studying the houses around him. Everything was eerily quiet and dark. The only lights on were either solar powered or running on a generator. The night was strangely still.

Throwing his car into reverse, he backed up, went forward and completed his three-point turn. He backtracked down the street and tore past their house, again. This time, when he reached the end of the street, his tires squealed as he made a sharp right. He'd already tried left. He drove two more blocks, when he came to a stop sign.

*So far, so good,* he thought. The street was open. Benjamin groaned. Bill glanced in his rearview mirror. Benjamin was no longer struggling to break free. His head was tilted to the side, his eyes squeezed shut. "It's okay, son. We'll be at the hospital shortly, okay? Hang in there."

Bill's sedan picked up speed. Benjamin's not struggling against his restraints, and his sudden quiet, worried him more than the growling and fighting to break free. Bill was going to try to bypass the emergency room downtown and bring him to the hospital in the suburbs. He figured the one in the suburbs would have less people, even though it was a few miles farther in distance. He was rethinking his initial plans. He hated driving into the city, but from where he lived, it was a straight shot down the freeway. Besides, he told himself that they probably offered better care and were better equipped for dealing with this sort of thing.

He remembered watching the news, earlier in the day, and the constant warning for people to stay indoors. He remembered seeing the hospitals filled to the brim with sick people. They were warning people not to go to the hospital unless you knew for a fact, you were already infected. They advised that uninfected loved ones not accompany the sick. Obviously, even though Bill himself wasn't infected, Benjamin certainly was. Accompanying his son to the hospital was a chance he'd have to take. It was a chance any parent would take. *Hell, Joanna, gave her life to try to save Benjamin.* He'd do the same.

"What the…!" Bill slammed on the brakes. A streak of white had darted out in front of him. Unfortunately, Bill hadn't been able to stop his car fast enough. Something thumped beneath his tires. His car swerved to the right, skidding. When the vehicle finally came to a halt, Bill glanced in his rearview mirror. Benjamin's eyes were still closed.

Bill flung open his door to take a look at what he'd hit, when a man came barreling around the corner of the house nearest him. "Shit!" Bill groaned, noticing the dog in the street. The man running toward him was probably the owner. "I, um, is this your dog? I didn't see him."

The little hairs on the back of Bill's neck stood on end as he watched the man, in the glow of his headlights leap over a white picket fence. Bill had seen enough footage on television of infected people being able to do crazy ass things, to know this man was infected. The poor dog had probably been running away from him. Without thinking twice, he lunged back into his car and slammed the door shut, locking it. The man flung himself against the door, wildly pawing at it. His frenzied growls and pounding seemed to arouse Benjamin who began to growl in the backseat. Bill glanced at his son's reflection. As creeped out as he was by the guttural sounds his son was making, he was happy to see him awake and moving. That meant there was still hope. He was alive.

Flustered, Bill turned the key in the ignition, and then realized the car was still on. He'd put it in park after hitting the dog and had not switched it off. He was having a hard time thinking straight.

The man continued to pound on the window. Bill flung the car into reverse, feeling the tires roll over the dog. He cringed at the thought, but knew the poor animal was dead, he then turned the wheel, shifted the car into drive, and raced forward as the man leaped at the car, bouncing off the side and landing on the pavement. The sickening thud had caused Bill's stomach to leap up into his chest. In his side mirror, he could see the man lying in the road, trying to get up and falling back down.

*Should he stop? Should he check on the man? What the hell should he do? Call an ambulance?* Then he remembered that the phone lines were down. There was no one to call. He couldn't even call for help for his own son, let alone a stranger. His conscience was telling him to go back. He needed to help that man. And the poor dog… the dog, thank God, was dead and not suffering. He'd died instantly on impact.

Benjamin uttered a sickening groan that made Bill's mind up for him. He watched as his son's head slumped again to the side and his eyes closed. He needed to get Benjamin to a hospital, fast! He hated the decision he was about to make, but he couldn't stop to help that man. He'd have to leave him.

Racing down the street, Bill was happy to finally make it to the freeway. As much as he detested the thought of going into the city that was the route he'd decided to take. With as much trouble as he had getting out of his own neighborhood, he couldn't imagine trying to get to the hospital in the suburbs. He raced down Interstate 5 when he noticed a fire to his right, just off the freeway. There was a large shopping center off the road running parallel to the Interstate. People were running amuck, and smoke was filling the freeway. Bill couldn't believe what he was seeing. It looked as if a Walmart was being looted. He shook his head and then coughed, gagging on the thick smoke. Even though he'd only taken his eyes off the road for a second, the smoke had masked a huge pile up directly in front of him. Bill slammed on his brakes. The car skidded out of control, brakes squealing. The last thing Bill saw before hearing the sickening sound of metal crunching loudly around him was Benjamin's favorite teddy bear hitting the windshield.

\*\*\*

With an arm around her shoulders, Mike guided Ellie from the motel room. They stepped outside into the dark. Ellie shivered. The only light was coming from the moon. Even the security lights were off.

"Must be a power failure," Mike said, thinking

out loud. He looked in the direction of his car. Or where he'd parked his car anyway. "You've gotta be kidding me!" His arm dropped from Ellie's shoulder. He patted his pockets for his keys as he marched toward the office.

"What the hell!" He couldn't believe his friggin' car was gone. He'd been in such a hurry, and with the crazy turn of events, he hadn't been thinking straight and must've left the keys in the ignition. "God damn it! Fuck!" he swore. "That asshole! I knew I shouldn't have let him go! I should've shot his ass!"

"What is it?" Ellie ran up behind him, not wanting to be standing there alone. "What's wrong?"

"I can't believe this!" He threw his hands up in the air as if to ask, *What more are you going to do to me?* "My *car*! It's gone! How the *fuck* am I gonna explain this?"

"Oh," Ellie said. She crossed her arms over her chest, not because she was feeling cold, but because she was feeling insecure.

"Shit, shit, shit!" he cussed. "I can't freaking believe this!" Mike glared at the front office. A soft glow of emergency lighting, probably being run by a generator, spilled out onto the pavement through the front glass door. Mike stormed up to the door and yanked it open.

"Wait!" Ellie warned. "The manager! He's infected!"

Mike stopped and stared at her for a moment before stepping inside.

Not wanting to go inside, yet not wanting to stand outside alone, Ellie followed him. She stood by the counter as Mike went around the back. He grabbed the phone on the desk, listened for a moment and then frowned. Ellie gnawed nervously on her swollen lower lip which was stinging like hell, as he slammed the phone down.

"Lines are down," he muttered.

Not surprised, Ellie nodded. She glanced over her shoulder at the empty parking lot. She kept expecting to see someone or something jump out of the shadows. "He's in the backroom," she said, not taking her eyes off the lot.

"The manager?"

"Yeah…"

Mike stared in the direction of the dark hallway. "You sure he's infected?"

Ellie turned and nodded. "Um, yeah."

"Down there?" he asked, not waiting for an answer. Gun drawn, Mike carefully stepped into the hall. This time Ellie didn't follow. She stood there, arms still protectively crossed over her chest and shivered. She could hear his footsteps. Her teeth clenched in anticipation. She looked again over her shoulder in the direction of the parking lot. She couldn't shake the feeling that someone or something would sneak up behind her.

The sound of a door creaked open from somewhere down the hall. Ellie felt her muscles tighten. The first thought she had was that Mike must've opened the door to the breakroom, but after waiting a moment, and not hearing any commotion, Ellie remembered the other door. The one she thought belonged to maybe a storage closet or a maintenance room.

Something made a loud crashing sound. Ellie's heart raced. She glanced again behind her. Then

132

there was a horrible clanging sound followed by a crash. "Mike?" she called softly. Gathering her courage, she crept to the opening of the hallway and stood there, waiting for a reply. She worried for Mike's safety. "Mike…?"

"Yeah, I'm okay…" he said.

Ellie forced herself to saunter down the dark hallway and came up beside him. It was hard to see him. The door to the other room, obviously a maintenance closet, was open. She could just make out a bunch of stuff on the floor. She figured, Mike must've knocked over a shelf of what looked like cleaning supplies. An aerosol can was next to her foot. She bumped it with her shoe and it noisily rolled across the tiled hall.

She then turned and eyed the other door. The door to the room the infected man was in. "The manager was in there," she whispered. There was still light seeping out from beneath the door. It just wasn't as bright as it had been before the electricity went out. She wondered how long the generator would last. She worried about being plunged into darkness.

Mike didn't say anything. He walked over to the door. Ellie didn't follow. She stayed where she was, too frightened to move. She listened as Mike turned the doorknob and opened it a crack. Sucking in a sharp breath, Ellie cringed, waiting for the infected man to crash into the door, but nothing happened. Light spilled out into the hall as Mike opened the door all the way and then stepped into the room. Ellie waited a moment, still too freaked out to move.

"He's dead," she heard Mike say.

Ellie let out her breath with a sigh and stepped

into the room. A silver-haired man lay on the floor next to a small round table. The fluorescent bulbs of the overhead lighting flickered. Mike was kneeling next to the body, with his fingers pushed to the side of the man's neck, feeling for a pulse. Ellie walked over toward the body. She stared at the man's distorted face. She shook her head. "It's like they're having some sort of allergic reaction," she said. "Reminds me of when I had hives from penicillin… well, except, of course, my eyes didn't change color and I didn't go around attacking people… It's as if the fever drives them insane."

Mike stared up at her. "He's still warm."

Ellie frowned. She felt bad for the man. Dying all alone. Suffering. "You're sure he's dead?"

Mike nodded. "No pulse," he said, getting to his feet.

Ellie gnawed on her bottom lip and glanced around the room. She noticed the fridge and suddenly realized how thirsty she was. She walked over to it and was relieved to see bottles of spring water. Mike joined her. She pulled out one for each of them. "Now what do we do?" She twisted off the cap and took a sip.

Mike set the bottle down on the table and pulled out his cell phone. Still no service. "Well, we have a choice," he said. "We can stay the night here and wait 'til morning or we can hightail it outta here."

"How?" Ellie asked. "We have no car, and the phone lines are down."

Mike eyed the body on the ground. "We look for the manager's keys and borrow his car."

"And go where?"

"To the station," he said.

Ellie thought this over. No matter how exhausted she was, she didn't want to stay there overnight. She wanted to go home in the worst way. The sheriff station was probably their best bet. She'd at least feel safe there until she could figure out how to get home. "Okay," she said. "Where do we begin looking?"

Mike looked again at the body. Ellie watched as he nudged it with his boot, waited for a second, and then frisked the man's body. He extracted a wallet and tossed it onto the table. He reached back into the man's pocket and pulled out a set of keys. "Bingo," he said.

Ellie picked up the man's wallet and stared at his driver's license. He looked so different. So normal. She would've never recognized him. She thumbed through the few family photos he carried with him. They were photos of whom she believed were his children and grandchildren. "Thank you, Peter MacArthur, for letting us borrow your car. Rest in peace." She set the wallet back down on the table feeling sympathy for the man and his family. "Do we just leave him here?"

Mike nodded. "We'll make sure to report it. Hold on. I'll be right back."

Ellie took another sip of water. Mike left the room. She heard him doing something in the hall. She recognized the sound of the aerosol cans rolling on the floor. He returned with a white sheet. "This was in the storage room." He shook open the folded sheet and gently laid it over the body. "Come on, let's look for his car."

***

Searing pain shot through his neck into his head

like a bolt of electricity. Bill forced his eyes open. He blinked hard. He tried his hardest to remember what'd happened. Within seconds, his memory returned. Blinking, trying to focus, his eyes spied Benjamin's stuffed bear on the dash. The windshield was a spider web of cracks. *An accident. Benjamin.*

"Benjamin," his voice cracked. "Benji." Bill felt around for the clasp on his seatbelt. Finally, his fingers came in contact with the release. He fumbled with it until the seatbelt sprung loose. He turned in his seat trying to get a look at Benjamin. He screamed as another hot bolt of pain shot through his head. *Whiplash?* he wondered. *How long had he been unconscious?*

He could barely make out Benjamin's form in the back seat. It was so dark. The only light filtering in the windows was from the moon and the flickering of fire from the buildings alongside the freeway. "Benji? You okay son?"

There was no sound or movement coming from the backseat. Bill reached for him. He wanted to touch him. He stretched his arm, pushing past his pain, in the direction of the small boy. His fingertips brushed Benjamin's cheek. He was hot to the touch. "I'm going to get you to the hospital, son. Everything's gonna be okay. I promise." Even as he said the words, he didn't believe them. He just didn't know what else to say.

Bill grimaced as he settled back down into his seat. He pulled at the door handle and tried to open his door. It wouldn't budge. He tried again and leaned into it with all of his weight. Still no movement. Something was blocking the door. Either that or the impact of the crash bent the frame.

He reached for the passenger side door, grunting with the effort. After a couple of tries, his fingers grasped the handle, but he didn't have enough strength to push the door open. Clenching his teeth against the hurt radiating down his right arm from his neck, he crawled over the center console into the passenger seat. Bill tugged on the door handle and pushed. To his surprise, the door opened easily.

"We're gonna be okay, son," he said. "I got the door open." Bill grabbed Benjamin's stuffed bear and then reached over the seat to manually unlock Benji's door before sliding out of the car. He grasped the side of the car to steady himself. His legs felt weak, and his head was spinning. Bill closed his eyes against the combination of pain, weakness, and dizziness. The coolness of the metal felt good pressed against his cheek. *Benjamin,* he thought, gathering his strength. *Benjamin needs me.* Bill tugged on the handle of the back door, opening it. Benjamin didn't move. His little body was motionless, head leaning to the side, still strapped in with his seatbelt.

"Benji, buddy," Bill said, softly, unlatching the seatbelt. He set Benji's favorite bear next to him on the seat. He put his hand on his son's forehead. He was still hot to the touch. His skin also felt clammy. Benjamin didn't move. Bill gently shook the small boy's shoulder, trying to wake him. "Sport?"

Not knowing what he should do next, Bill stood next to his car and looked around, taking in his surroundings for the first time. The freeway was abnormally dark. The streetlamps were out. There was a pile-up of cars in front of him. He couldn't tell how many. The freeway heading the opposite direction was eerily empty. He looked toward the buildings on fire.

Before the accident, it was just the Walmart he remembered seeing on fire. The fire had been spreading to other nearby shopping centers along the side of the freeway. There were no firetrucks or sirens. Bill frowned. He looked again at the pile-up of cars he'd crashed into. There was no highway patrol. No firemen. No ambulances. *Where were all the people? Who was going to help them?*

On unsteady legs, Bill walked up to the car that he'd rear-ended. The front of that car was pushed up into the car in front of it. He gazed into the passenger window. No one was inside. The driver's side door was open. There was another car to the right of it, that'd been facing oncoming traffic. Bill forgot about his pain and jaunted toward it. He thought he could make out a figure inside.

"Oh my God," he gasped. There was blood on the windshield. "Hey! You okay?" He knocked on the glass. The person in the driver's seat didn't move. The headlights of the car facing it, gave off just enough light for Bill to be able to see blood and someone with dark hair in the driver's seat. He couldn't tell if it was a man or a woman. He tugged at the door handle. It was locked. He pounded on the window. Still no movement. He looked around, still unable to believe with the number of cars that were piled up, that no one was around. *Where the hell was everyone?*

"I'll get you help!" he yelled to the person through the glass, unsure of whether he or she was dead or alive. He couldn't just leave them there without knowing. He walked around the mass of cars in a daze, looking for something or someone.

Bill cringed when he saw it. He covered his mouth, as bile rose in his throat. The carnage was unlike anything he'd ever seen. Dead bodies were strewn on the freeway amongst the cars, and pools of dark blood were highlighted in the headlights of a deserted tow truck on the side of the road. A strong scent of iron, wafting on the cool, damp air, penetrated his senses and turned his stomach. Bill limped toward the tow truck as he looked around for the driver. He was nowhere to be seen. Glancing back over his shoulder, he wondered if the tow truck driver was one of the many bodies scattered across the freeway. Bill was curious to get a closer look at them, but not curious enough. He couldn't get up the nerve to get any closer. Were they attacked by the infected? He worried that whatever got these poor souls, was still lurking about.

Cautiously, Bill approached the tow truck. The door had been left open a crack; lights were on in the cab and the keys in the ignition. Bill looked around the cab and climbed up inside. This truck was his best bet to get Benjamin to the hospital. He could drive it along the side of the freeway to avoid most of the cars. Sitting up in the cab, he looked at the cars in front of them. They were all abandoned. Most were just left there. Since it was so dark, he couldn't see very far. He could only see what was in the headlights or the light of the moon when it peaked in and out of the clouds. Still feeling a bit woozy after the accident, Bill tried to focus his energy. He remembered the person trapped in their car that might or might not be alive. Searching around, he found a crowbar on the floorboards of the backseat. He grabbed the cold metal and rushed as fast as his injuries would allow, in the direction of the car.

For some reason, getting back to that car felt like it was taking an eternity. His darn leg was beginning to stiffen, and his head was throbbing. When he finally reached the car, he smacked the window a couple of times with the palm of his hand trying to alert the driver. "Hey! I'm back!" The person inside, didn't move. Bill edged his way around the car to the passenger side. He took a step back and swung the metal bar at the window shattering it. He swung again and glass crumbled. "Hey!" he yelled into the window. "I'm gonna get you out of there."

Reaching into the car, Bill unlocked and opened the door. Still no movement. Cautious, he poked at his or her shoulder with the end of the crowbar. He didn't want to take any chances on the person being infected. There was still no movement. Gaining courage, Bill leaned in and got a better look. It was a woman. She was leaning forward. Her hair covering her face. He clutched her cold arm and then her wrist. As far as he could tell, no pulse.

Sighing, Bill got out of the car and stared in the direction of his own car. A sudden memory flashed before his eyes causing great concern. He'd left the door open. His heart began to race. Hadn't he unlatched Benjamin's seatbelt? Pushing past his pain, he imagined the worst, and dragged his leg that no longer wanted to move, as he headed for his car. His mind played tricks on him as he imagined Benjamin wandering along the freeway, disoriented and alone, carrying his stuffed bear. Then he remembered that Benjamin was still handcuffed and gagged to keep from hurting anyone else. More than likely, he wouldn't be able to get too far. To Bill's relief and horror, Benjamin was right where he'd left him. He hadn't moved, and panic hit him hard like a ton of bricks. *Was he breathing?* Bill frantically touched the boy's forehead and cheeks. He was still burning up with a fever. He felt for the pulse in his neck and was relieved when he found it. Benjamin was still alive.

"Come on, son," Bill said, softly. He set the crowbar on the roof of the car and then leaned down. He slipped his arms around the little boy and grunted as he hoisted him out of the backseat. Benjamin didn't make a sound. Bill was having a hard time distributing his weight since his left leg was somewhat useless. He leaned against the car for support and slung Benjamin over his shoulder. The boy's body was limp, as if it were nothing more than a mere ragdoll. Once Bill felt he had a good enough grip on Benji, he grabbed the stuffed bear. The bear had always been like a security blanket to his son, so he didn't want to leave it behind, and the crowbar was for his own security. He then began to make his slow, somewhat unbalanced descent, to the tow truck.

Fire was still blazing out of control to his right. Bill glanced in the direction of the flames. The buildings were far enough away, that he wasn't too worried about it reaching them. It just seemed eerie not to see any firemen trying to put out the flames. Hell, he wasn't even seeing any people running about anymore. Again, he wondered how long he'd been unconscious since the accident. He remembered, right before the crash, having seen the Walmart on fire and people running about looting the place. At the time, Walmart was the only store on fire. Now, from what he could see, every building in that shopping center was on fire and spreading along the freeway. They'd had a very dry summer, more so than the usual, and all of Southern California had been in a drought. The dry grass and weeds were all ablaze, and the light ocean breeze wasn't helping to contain it.

Again, Bill wondered what had happened to all the people. He couldn't get over it. They were all gone. He tried not to dwell on it and focused his energy on carrying Benjamin. The tow truck was just up ahead. He could see the headlights. He probably should've shut them off to prevent draining the battery. He had no idea of how long the tow truck had been sitting there with the lights on before he'd discovered it.

"We're almost there, Sport," he said, picking up speed. Seeing the truck growing closer, gave him hope. Soon, he'd get his son to the hospital. And while he was there, he'd get his own injuries taken care of. He only wished that his wife had been so lucky. He still felt numb. Like she wasn't really gone. And none of it had really happened. But it *did* happen. What was he going to tell Benjamin? How would he break the news to him? Would he remember what had happened? Bill shook his head. He could never tell him. Not how she died. He'd take that knowledge with him to the grave. No one needed to know. Not ever!

Bill set the crowbar on top of the cab freeing his hand so he could yank open the driver's side door. He set Benjamin down, propping him up in the seat. He then limped around to the passenger side and pulled at the door handle. It was locked. Frustrated, because he felt that he'd been wasting valuable time, he slugged the door, and then made his way back to the driver's side. He quickly decided it might be easier to just lift Benjamin over the center console and into the passenger seat. He struggled a bit, but eventually managed to get the little boy settled into the other seat. Bill was leaning across the console, pulling the seatbelt over his son's chest, when he felt something grip his leg. Almost simultaneously, he heard a guttural growl. Chills encompassed his body and goose bumps covered his flesh.

"What the...!" Bill turned to look over his shoulder while instinctively kicking his leg. Forgetting his pain, he flipped himself over and kicked again. A woman with a mass of tangled red hair was clawing at his legs. Her fingernails were raking his jeans. Bill kicked her hard in the stomach with his good leg, knocking her back. But within seconds the woman was up on her feet, pouncing on him, grabbing hold of his injured leg. Bill screamed out in pain. He looked for the crowbar and remembered having set it on top of the cab. The woman's teeth chomped down on his calf. Bill could feel the strength of her bite through the denim. He prayed that the material was thick enough to keep her from puncturing his skin. The last thing he needed was to become infected himself. With his good foot, he kicked her hard in the head. The woman lost her balance and stumbled backward in her high heels, twisting her ankle in an unreal way. Bill cringed, hearing the snap of her bones. Reaching for the door handle, he slammed the door shut. The woman quickly regained her balance and rushed at the truck. She pressed her distorted face to the glass and began to chomp, drooling all over the surface.

Turning the keys in the ignition, Bill was both

thankful and surprised, when the truck engine easily roared to life. *At least something is going in my favor,* he thought. He took off, driving along the side of the highway, trying to get around the pile-up of cars. The crazed woman chased after them, dragging her broken ankle. He figured, by the time they'd reach the hospital, even though he wasn't that far away, it'd be morning. Bill was hopeful that tomorrow would be a better day.

# Day Two

# Chapter 17

Amanda groaned. She reached back and rubbed at her sore neck. She'd slept in an odd position, curled up in a ball on the floor on the passenger side of the car. It took her a second to remember where she was. Her knees were pulled up to her chest and her face buried in her arms. She'd been too petrified to even breathe let alone move. The infected stopped pounding on the car long ago, yet she couldn't get up the nerve to move. She was too afraid that they'd hear her and come back. At some point, in the wee hours of the morning, exhaustion had taken over, and she'd passed out.

Morning sunlight drifted through the thick haze of fog coming in from the ocean. In San Diego, they called it June Gloom, even though it was now early August. The sky reminded her of a typical June Gloom sort of morning. The haze would burn off by midday. Amanda was staring up out of the window from the floor. She couldn't see much, except for the sky and some buildings. She was still too afraid to get up, but she needed to. Now she felt extreme pain in her back and legs, and her left buttock was numb. She needed to get up and stretch. And she also needed to find a restroom. *Stupid bodily functions!* she thought, frowning. The last thing she wanted to do was find a place to go to the bathroom.

Amanda stayed still and listened. She felt like her hearing was hypersensitive. Her ears tingled in response. If a pin dropped a block from there, she'd bet her bottom dollar that she'd hear it. The strange thing was, no matter how hard she listened, she wasn't hearing anything. Just silence. She wasn't hearing voices, vehicles, nothing. It was so bizarre. *Wait... a bird.* She suddenly heard chirping. At least she could hear something familiar. It was a little consoling, but not much. *Where were all the people?* She was downtown, close to the freeway. She should be hearing the everyday noise of traffic. There was nothing. Absolutely nothing.

Lifting herself up, Amanda slid as quietly as she could into the passenger seat of the cop car. Her body hurt like hell, and she desperately wanted to scream out. Instead, she bit her tongue and rubbed again at the painful knots in her neck and shoulders while examining the damage done to the car.

Dried blood and saliva was smeared all over the driver's side window. Amanda cringed. She then looked at the back window and sucked in a deep breath. She quickly turned around and scooted back as far away as she could until the middle of her back was pressed against the glove box. The rear window had been shattered and there was a man lying across the opening into the backseat. His legs were still sticking out the rear window. She watched him for a moment. He wasn't moving.

Amanda tried to calm her heart. Whenever she felt overly anxious, her heart began to palpitate. She began experiencing these palpitations a couple of years ago when she'd gone through her divorce from a scum bucket of a husband. Stress seemed to be the number one trigger. Her ex had made her life a living hell during their numerous years of marriage, the mental and emotional abuse scarring her indefinitely. And then he'd made sure to make their divorce just as painful and miserable. She was forever grateful that they'd never had children together and once the divorce had been finalized, she never had to see him again.

Pressing her hand to her heart, Amanda concentrated on breathing steadily while keeping her eyes trained on the man in the plaid shirt. He still wasn't moving. From what she could tell, he wasn't even breathing. She zeroed in on his back, watching carefully, to see if his ribcage moved. It didn't. She then noticed the blood and glass. At first glance, the glass had blended in, coated with dried blood. A shared of it was protruding from the man's side. He must've impaled himself when climbing through the rear windshield.

"Serves you right, bastard," she whispered, getting up the courage to move closer to the barrier that was separating the backseat of the cop car from the front. The man's lifeless head was turned, facing her direction. His unseeing eyes were wide open, a yellowish white in color. Dark, thick blood had oozed from his mouth, staining his puffed up lips.

Amanda wrapped her arms over her chest and shivered. She glanced out all of the windows and didn't see anyone else about. She wondered where she should go now. Should she try the hospital again? *No,* she thought. *Best to stay clear of the hospital.* She'd try walking back home. Maybe, on the way, she'd come across someone that could help her.

Not wanting to leave the safety of the cop car, but knowing she had to. Amanda got up the courage and unlocked the passenger door. She closed her eyes, took a deep, calming breath, and pushed open the door. To her surprise, it only opened a crack, and then it wouldn't budge.

"What the… ?" Amanda pushed the door again. *Thump!* The door was hitting something. She pulled it back and then pushed it open again. *Thud!* Amanda looked down at the ground and could see an arm, a man's arm with lots of hair, and then a shoulder, and long straggly black hair. She'd been banging the door against someone's head. Startled, she squealed, and let go of the door. The body didn't move. She quickly realized she'd left the car door open, and then slammed the door closed.

She climbed over the console into the driver's seat and pressed her forehead against the glass as she peered out the window through the smeared blood. Her stomach lurched. *Dead bodies.* They were everywhere.

Panicked, Amanda began to hyperventilate. The mob of infected people, the ones that'd been trying to get into the car last night, were all dead. All of them. Her heart pounded in her ears, and her breathing was fast and erratic. She sat down in the seat and leaned forward to put her head between her knees, but the darn steering wheel was in the way. She slammed her fist against the steering wheel and began to cry.

"Get ahold of yourself," she whispered, trying to catch her breath. "Calm down." Her body wouldn't listen, and her stomach lurched again. She tried to force herself to think of something positive about her situation. *If all of the infected are dead, then no one can hurt me. That's positive, right?* she asked herself. *Wrong!*

Her mind then drifted to Jasper and tears streamed down her cheeks. Did that mean that Jasper was dead, too? He was infected. Poor Jasper. Was it a painful death? Maybe, just maybe, he'd made it into the hospital and was okay. Maybe there were only *some* infected people in the hospital, and the upper floors were safe. Again, she thought of trying to enter the hospital. If the infected people trying to get into the cop car last night were dead, then more than likely, the infected people within the hospital would be dead, too.

Amanda took in a few more deep breaths and lifted her head. With the back of her hand, she swiped at her tears. She was still feeling a little light-headed, but at least she knew what she had to do. She'd try the hospital one more time before walking home. Maybe some doctors and nurses had been holed up all night, along with those that'd been cured, like Jasper. *Yes,* she thought. *Just like Jasper.* Besides, she needed to find a restroom. And she knew she could find one in the hospital. She'd be fine. Jasper would be fine. The infected were dead, and the living would be around to help her. Everything would be okay, and life would soon go back to normal.

Taking in another deep breath, she forced herself to believe going to the hospital was what she needed to do. She opened the driver's side door until it hit a woman's body lying nearby. Amanda sat there for a moment making sure the woman in the blue dress with the paisley flowers didn't move. She nudged the body again with the door. No movement. On stiff, yet wobbly legs, Amanda's bare feet stepped onto the cold asphalt. Her eyes widened in disbelief, as she took in the amount of dead bodies scattered around her; old, young, men, women, and children. Too many children. *Oh God,* Amanda whispered. She closed her eyes and forced herself to gain courage against the horror. Upon reopening her eyes, she cringed, and her stomach lurched. Flies were already beginning to collect, and an acrid odor was developing. Amanda covered her mouth and nose with her hand, using it as a makeshift filter against the pungent smell. She forced herself to hold back the bile rising in her throat and began to carefully hop over the distorted, puffed up bodies. With each step, she worried that one of the infected may not be dead yet and would attack her.

***

Ellie awoke lying down in the reclined passenger seat. She turned to see Mike Wilson sound asleep in the driver's seat. It ended up that the manager of the motel owned a lemon of a car that was not only on its last legs, but had less than an eighth of a tank of gas. They'd only gotten maybe ten miles away from the motel when the entire car began to shake and shudder. Mike had been cussing up a storm when the car died, and Ellie had been rethinking their decision to head for the sheriff station. She wished they had decided to have stayed the night in the motel. It would've been safer.

After the car died, Mike had noticed how tired Ellie was and suggested that they catch a couple of hours of shut-eye. At first, Ellie had argued against it. She didn't like the idea of sleeping on the side of the road after the experience she'd had with the carjackers. However, Mike insisted. Ellie gave into her exhaustion as soon as he said he'd take the first watch and showed her his gun.

Still in a daze, Ellie laid there, facing Mike. She couldn't help but notice how handsome he was. She normally noticed good looking guys, but then quickly dismissed them. She hadn't had the best of luck when it came to men and relationships. Not that she was even contemplating a relationship with Mike. She couldn't believe she'd even entertain the idea, especially when the world around her seemed to be falling apart. But regardless, it'd been a very long time since she'd been this close to a man, one that she was attracted to. She studied his square jaw and his thick 5 o'clock shadow. His lips were plump and kissable. She imagined what it'd feel like to press her lips against his. She wanted to feel his warm skin against hers.

What felt like butterflies, came to life in her tummy. Her eyes raked over his wide shoulders, thick chest, and worked their way downward. Her gaze lingered there for a moment. When she looked up, Mike was watching her. He grinned. That's when she realized he'd just caught her admiring him. And even worse than that, she'd been licking her lips.

Quickly averting her eyes, Ellie could feel herself blushing. She hoped that Mike hadn't noticed her staring down there. Not that that was what she was thinking of. Her gaze had just happened to be in that general direction. Ellie prayed that he'd just opened his eyes and hadn't noticed.

"How'd you sleep?" he asked, sitting up in the driver's seat, stretching.

"Um, okay," Ellie said. She sat up and stretched too. She suddenly felt very aware of her appearance and tried to smooth down her thick hair with the palms of her hands. Her bottom lip that'd been busted open, burned when she spoke.

"Good," he said, looking around. "Looks like we're gonna have to hoof it."

Ellie frowned and looked out the window. She knew he was right. Last night, Mike had spent quite a bit of time trying to get the car to run before giving up. It was doubtful that the car would magically start working this morning.

"We should get a move on before the day gets too hot. We need to find more water." He grabbed the four bottles of water they'd confiscated from the fridge in the motel breakroom. Two of the bottles were half empty. They sipped sparingly from them last night after the car broke down.

"Okay," Ellie agreed, while looking out at the early morning sun. It was already feeling uncomfortably warm out. She guessed that it was already in the 80s and in a few hours, if not less, it'd be in the low 100s.

Mike twisted the key in the ignition. The car sputtered and then died. "I'm an optimist," he said. "Thought I'd give this bucket of junk one last try." He then pulled out his cell phone and frowned before slipping it back into his pocket.

"Still no service?"

"No," he said, handing her a bottle and a half of water to carry.

"Hmm." Ellie's heart sunk. "Not a good sign."

Mike didn't answer. He slid out of the car, adjusted his hat, and closed the door. Ellie followed suit and joined him. "Ladies first," he said, pointing the way.

Ellie shook her head and smiled. She began to walk alongside of the vacant highway. Even though she was worried about what was to come, she was thankful that she wasn't alone. "How far to the sheriff's station?"

Mike looked ahead and walked alongside of her. "Do you really want to know?"

Ellie looked down at the ground, studying the sand covered asphalt. "That far, huh?"

"We'll keep an eye out for a vehicle," he said. "And a place to get a bite to eat."

Ellie's stomach growled at the mention of food. She'd been such a nervous wreck, that she hadn't realized just how hungry she was. "Yeah... sounds like a plan."

They walked for a while in silence. The only sound was their feet crunching down on the sand covered pavement. Ellie's mind was running a mile a minute, but she conserved her energy. She was already feeling overly hot, and fatigue was setting in. Sweat was beginning to run down her back. She grabbed her tangled hair which was wet underneath with perspiration, and pulled it to the side over her shoulder, to try to cool herself down. She wished she had a scrunchie or something to use to pull it up.

Mike continued to walk alongside of her, in the street. Ellie stayed on the edge of the asphalt, next to the sand. She didn't trust that a car might appear out of nowhere and zoom down the road and run them over. After an hour of walking, and no vehicles in sight, she gravitated into the middle of the road.

"Hey," she said, her voice cracking, and then cleared her throat. Her mouth was parched since she'd been sipping her water cautiously, trying to make it last. "Is the highway always like this?"

"Like what?" Mike asked.

"Desolate," she said, shrugging her shoulders. Ellie could feel the stinging of her skin burning as she shrugged. "It's been over an hour, and we haven't seen one car."

Mike looked straight ahead. He didn't answer. Ellie took that as a really bad sign.

"Look," he said, with a curt nod. "I see a house out there."

Ellie shielded her eyes and looked in the direction of his stare. There was a small white shack off in the distance. It blended in with the sand. If Mike hadn't pointed it out, she probably would've missed it. "Kinda out in the middle of nowhere. You think it's safe?"

"We're getting closer to town," Mike said. "Some desert folk like their homes to be away from the rest of the population. They like the privacy. Yet, they aren't too far away from the conveniences of town. Should be fine."

"It looks like it's still a long walk." Ellie stared in the direction of the dingy little shack. "If we're close to town, shouldn't we just keep going? I mean… isn't it kinda out of the way?"

"We're not *that* close." Mike took off his hat and ran a hand through his sweat-soaked hair. "And we need water."

Ellie had less than a quarter of her 2nd water bottle left. She'd been sweating out more fluid than she'd consumed over the last hour. She knew he was right. They'd die of heat exhaustion and dehydration before they'd make it to town. It was still early, yet the heat was already beyond bearable.

"Besides, they might have a vehicle we can borrow."

Ellie nodded. What Mike was proposing sounded logical to her. And being a sheriff officer, she had him to protect her. "Okay."

"Let's cut through the desert," he said, making his way toward the sand.

"Oh! Um…" The last thing Ellie wanted to do was walk through the desert, but she didn't have much of a choice. Unwillingly, but not wanting to protest, she followed Mike into the scratchy tumbleweeds. Hot, gritty sand immediately worked its way into her canvas shoes.

*** 

When Bill awoke, he rubbed at his eyes with his fists. He'd driven as far as he could until he came to a halt on the freeway. All of the lanes were blocked with hundreds of abandoned cars. And unfortunately, he'd come to a point where he couldn't get around them. Even the shoulder was blocked. He'd gone back and forth with the idea of walking, carrying Benjamin the rest of the way to the hospital. He knew it was only a few more miles down the highway. However, with the infected wandering about in the dark and his own injuries, he knew his chances of them making it to the hospital unscathed were slim. He'd made the decision to try to get a few hours of sleep until the sun came out. He felt he'd have a better chance at getting Ben to the hospital, if he could see what he was up against.

Groaning, Bill winced against his pain. Whiplash had set in. His neck and back didn't want to move. He truly felt like he'd been run over by a Mac Truck. *How the hell was he going to cope with the pain?* Whiplash wasn't new to Bill. He'd unfortunately been in a bad wreck once before. At that time, he had some heavy duty painkillers that they'd put him on once admitted to the ER. Painkillers had been his best buddy for a while. He then remembered the withdrawals he'd gone through when the doctors weaned him off the meds. Eventually, he'd rehabilitated after a long hard row. Bill pushed the memory from his mind and forced himself back to the here and now. Benjamin needed him. He needed to think.

In an awkward, stiff movement, Bill turned in his seat to get a better look at his son. A hot bolt of pain seared through his head from his neck. Another bolt shot down his bad leg. Bill grimaced, as his eyes fell on his little boy, and he took in the state of his condition. Benjamin's body looked so tiny, slumped in the seat. The only thing keeping him from sliding off the seat and onto the floor was the seatbelt restraining him. Bill was beyond worried. He was afraid to touch Benjamin's cheek. What if he were to find it stone cold? That was his worst fear. He couldn't outlive his boy. *Not* his boy!

Sucking in a sharp breath and closing his eyes, Bill lightly brushed Ben's right cheek with the back of his fingers. To his relief, his skin wasn't cold. To his horror, he wasn't hot either. He was just warm. What did that mean? Was he dying? Or was Ben okay? Maybe he beat the fever. Maybe he was getting better. A spark of hope grew in Bill's mind.

Lifting the boy's limp arm, Bill fumbled around

trying to find his pulse. It took him awhile since he wasn't moving too well. Eventually, he found Ben's pulse and the tiny spark of hope lost some of its luster. His pulse was faint. Frowning, Bill knew that he needed to get Ben to the hospital, immediately. Even if Ben had managed to beat the fever, he was severely dehydrated. Bill glanced at the rows and rows of abandoned cars on the freeway. Grunting against the pain, he forced himself out of the truck. Bill looked around for any signs of life before getting Benjamin out. Again, he wondered where all the people were? His guess was that once they realized traffic was never going to let up, they all decided to walk.

Bill lifted Benji out of the truck and slung him over his shoulder. He then grabbed Ben's bear, even though he knew it was silly to be carting it around with them. He just wanted Ben to have some sort of comfort from home when he awoke. In severe pain, and his knee not wanting to cooperate, Bill stiffly wandered along the edge of the freeway in the direction of downtown. All cars were deserted. Some had doors left open. Some were closed. Actually most were closed. It was as if the owners had locked them up for safekeeping so that they could come back for them later. Other cars weren't so lucky. There were a few that'd crashed into others. But still, they were empty.

Trying to keep his mind off his pain, Bill continued to walk, slowly dragging his leg. It was still early in the morning and a bit hazy. The damp air was already beginning to feel warm, but not uncomfortable. The haze would burn off soon. Bill noticed another good-sized pile-up, ahead. He still had a ways to go before he reached the wreck. It was a big one. He squinted his eyes, trying to scope out the wreckage. Flashing lights. An ambulance? Maybe. He wondered if this was the initial accident that had caused the traffic to back up and the other accidents to have happened in its wake. Almost like a domino effect.

"What a mess!" he whispered, his eyes still scanning the cars around him, while trying to shift Benji's weight. Even though his son was of a slight build, he was becoming increasingly heavier to carry with each step.

Bill looked toward the center of the freeway and noticed a few scattered bodies on the asphalt, and grimaced. Up ahead, the flashing lights grew brighter. Bill kept on going.

*It's an ambulance!* he thought. Then he noticed even more lights farther down the freeway. *Cop cars!* He prayed that he'd find some help for him and Benji. He picked up the pace, dragging his leg behind him.

The closer he got to the huge accident, the more bodies he'd found. Some were on the asphalt, others in cars. He didn't stop to make sure the people in the cars were dead. He just kept walking. At the moment, all he could do was to keep pressing forward. As guilty as he felt, not checking to make sure these people didn't need help, he felt he didn't have much of a choice. He didn't have the strength. He worried that at any moment, his body would give out, and both he and Benjamin would join the rest of the bodies.

The lights were growing brighter. He was almost there. Seeing the ambulance was the only thing keeping him slowly propelling forward. It kept him optimistic that he'd find help.

"We're almost there, sport," he said to Benjamin while trying to shift the boy's body farther up onto his shoulder. His arm was growing weak. As he shrugged his shoulder, his other hand had lost grip on the teddy bear. He felt the fur slip from his hand. He took a few more awkward steps and almost lost his grip on Benjamin also. Getting to the ambulance was more important than a teddy bear. Then he thought of how much it'd mean to Benjamin to have his bear. For a second, he stopped walking. He turned and glanced back at the bear. He couldn't physically pick it up without setting Benji down. He told himself that he'd come back for it later. He had no other choice. After what seemed an eternity, Bill walked up to the driver's side of the ambulance. Immediately, his heart stopped. The driver was slumped over the steering wheel.

"Hey!" Bill called. The driver didn't move. He shifted Benjamin and then knocked on the window. "Hey! Hello!" Still, no movement. "We need help!" He knocked again. Nothing. Bill tugged at the door handle. Locked. "Damn it!" He looked around and then decided to try the back of the ambulance. The doors were shut. To Bill's surprise, he was able to open them. "Hello?" He peeked inside. No one was there. The gurney was gone. That meant the paramedics were out there somewhere. Probably in that pileup. Maybe he could leave Benjamin here and go look for help. The paramedics couldn't have gone far. Surely, they were still around. He doubted they'd have left the scene of the accident without the ambulance. He had seen the flashing lights of police cars up ahead, too. Someone would be able to help them. They couldn't all be dead. Then he frowned as he pictured the ambulance driver slumped over the wheel. It just didn't make sense. Why would the paramedics leave one of their own behind? Maybe he fell ill while they were out helping others. Maybe. There was no time for contemplation. He needed to find help.

Bill hoisted Benjamin into the back of the ambulance. He then climbed in behind him. He scooted the boy to the back, laid the limp little body on a built-in bench, and then knelt down beside him. "I'll be back with help," he said, gently stroking his son's white, puffy cheek. He was still warm, but not hot. He still didn't know whether or not that was a good sign.

Climbing out of the ambulance, Bill noticed a man, adjacent to him, walking between the cars, two lanes over. He then spotted several more figures, farther down the highway. His gaze then fell on Benjamin's bear where he'd dropped it. He wandered in the direction of the bear. It wasn't too far away. If Benjamin awoke in the ambulance while he was gone, he'd at least have his bear with him for comfort.

"Hey!" he called to the man who was stumbling about, moving in the direction of the massive pile up, up ahead. The man's head snapped to the side. Bill wasn't sure of what to make of the man's movements. Was he injured? Was he infected? Bill wearily eyed the teddy bear and then yelled again, "Hey! Have you seen a paramedic? My son needs help." The man didn't move. He just stood there, watching him.

Bill walked toward the bear, keeping his eye on the man, just in case. He wished he could see his face more clearly. Then he'd be able to tell if he were infected or not. He'd seen enough to know the signs.

"No!" the man finally yelled back, surprising Bill. "My family… I'm trying to find my family…" Then the man let out a blood-curdling scream. A figure had pounced on him from behind, taking him down. Bill hadn't even seen where the figure had come from. It seemed to have appeared out of nowhere. The man screamed out from somewhere between the cars. Bill eyed the spot where the man had been standing. He wanted to help him. The horrific screams echoed in his ears. The figures he noticed wandering the freeway, quite a ways back, began to pick up speed. At first Bill wondered if they were running to help the man, but then noticed one of them leap onto a car, run across the roof, and fly off the hood with animal-like reflexes. The figures were gaining speed, drawn to them by the sound of the man's screams. Bill's heart thudded in his chest, watching the infected coming toward him, as if in slow motion.

Bill eyed the bear, again. He was so close to it. It was only a few feet away. He limped as fast as he could, reached down and swooped up the teddy bear. He could hear the pounding of feet on asphalt, and then them climbing over tops of automobiles, growing closer. A car alarm went off; there was crunching of glass. Bill tried not to think about how close the infected were getting. He knew that they were right behind him. He'd seen four people when he'd snatched up the teddy bear; three men and a young girl. Being of an athletic build, the young girl was gaining on him the fastest.

Thinking of Benjamin, Bill pushed himself to the extreme. Benji needed him. If he died, what would happen to him? Joanna was gone. Who would take care of him? He'd be all alone in this chaotic world.

Bill was so close to the ambulance. So close! He'd left the door wide open. He sprinted, the best he could in his condition, to the vehicle. Forcing himself, with strength he didn't have, he jumped up inside. He grabbed hold of the door and began to pull it closed, when it hit something. It wouldn't shut! Bill's eyes widened. The girl's arm was in the door. She was growling, snarling and clawing at him. He held tightly onto the door handle and pulled with all his might. He had to do something before the others arrived. He couldn't hold onto the handle forever. Already he was feeling the handle slipping from his sweating hands. *Think!* He had to think! He heard other growls getting closer. My God, it was like the infected had become wild animals. His mind flashed to Joanna and the way Benjamin had brutally attacked her. Benjamin had become something else. He hadn't been in his right mind.

Bill eyed a metal box containing a First Aid kit and some other medical instruments, but they were all out of reach. He would need to let go of the door, and that wasn't an option. The arm twisted and grabbed hold of his sleeve. The door opened a bit more as she used her shoulder, trying to force her way in. Bill pulled on the handle with all of his weight, trying to crush her arm. He could hear the other growls grow louder. There was a sudden banging on the side of the ambulance. His heart leaped in his chest.

Not able to come up with another solution, Bill removed his right hand from the handle and began to punch the clawing arm, trying to dislodge it from the door. The girl began to twist her arm more furiously, and blood dripped down the inside of the door, her flesh was ripping, as she continued to work her way inside. The banging on the outside of the ambulance grew louder and the growls more intense. Then, a set of thick, sausage fingers with hairy knuckles, not belonging to the girl, curled around the opening of the door, right above the arm.

Bill winced. Something sharp was jabbing his upper thigh. It took him a second to realize what it was. *Keys!* he thought. *My keys!*

He eyed the lump from the key ring in his pocket, and then his fingers that were slipping from the door handle. He returned both of his hands to the handle until he felt he had a better grip, and then, with his right hand, he quickly let go. Reaching into his pocket, he fumbled with the key ring for what felt like an eternity, but in reality, it was only seconds, and then yanked them from his jean pocket. With the car key, he jammed it into the girl's arm, stabbing her several times. Finally, the girl yanked backward, her arm pulling free of the door. The door slammed hard on the sausage fingers. He then opened and slammed the door again. The fingers released.

Heart throbbing wildly, breathing erratic, Bill latched the door. He knew it'd only been a matter of minutes, but he'd felt like he'd been struggling with closing that door for hours. Bill scooted backward until his back was against the wall. The infected continued to pound away on the ambulance. Bill leaned over the bench built into the side of the wall and scooped Benjamin up into his arms. He hugged the little boy close to him. He remembered how his son couldn't open the bedroom door to get to him.

It was as of the fever had destroyed his ability to think. He doubted the infected would figure out a way inside the ambulance now that the door was closed. It was as if the fever drove people to the brink of insanity and then they keeled over and died, but not after taking more people down with them.

At the thought of the dying, Bill hugged the little boy harder. "Please, don't die," he begged, tears escaping his eyes. He kissed his son's forehead. "I'll get you help, Sport. I promise. Just don't die on me."

# Chapter 18

Surprised that no one had attacked her, Amanda gathered her courage and peered through the glass doors of the hospital. There were bodies scattered on the tile floor inside. She glanced over her shoulder to make sure no infected were closing in on her while she checked out the hospital. Nothing moved. And there were still no sounds of people or traffic. The eerie silence seemed to be affecting her more than the dead bodies surrounding her.

Amanda cupped her hands and pressed her face as close to the glass as possible to get a better look inside. Still, there was no movement. The infected police officer that'd freaked her out last night, was slumped down on the floor, his back against the glass, skin white and puffy, head tilted to the side. Amanda wondered if the patrol car she'd taken refuge in had belonged to him. She pulled on the locked door and shook it. She bent down and tapped on the glass next to the police officer's head. He didn't move.

Again, she nervously glanced over her shoulder. Still no movement. She wondered if she should even bother with trying to find another way into the hospital, or just go somewhere else. If she could just make it inside, she could phone for help. She'd also be able to look for Jasper and find a nurse or doctor to consult with about his condition. Surely, they were holed up somewhere safe inside. She doubted that everyone inside was dead. At the thought, Amanda suddenly felt all alone and wanted to hyperventilate. What if everyone *was* dead? What if she was the last person alive? She quickly pushed the absurd notion from her mind. It was silly to think like that. There was no possible way that everyone was dead, but her. She was freaking herself out. The hospital had been filled with infected people. That's where they gravitated to for help. Those that didn't receive help had died. She should forget the hospital and go somewhere safe. Somewhere away from the infected.

Taking small shallow breaths, she tried to force herself to calm down. She needed to concentrate on finding help. A panic attack would only make matters worse for her. She concentrated on slowing her breathing. She looked up and down the street.

*What about Jasper?* she thought. *He might be locked inside.* She wearily looked again at the locked doors. The hospital had probably been locked down to try to contain whatever this thing was from spreading. She eyed the dead bodies on the pavement. Obviously, it didn't work.

Amanda carefully walked down the cement steps. She stood at the bottom and decided she'd walk toward the city, away from home. A part of her wanted to head in the direction of home, but she remembered the traffic last night. Everything on the freeway had been at a standstill. Right now, she needed to find a phone… to find a populated place, with people to help her. Stepping over the bodies, one at a time, careful not to step on one, she kept one hand over her mouth and nose. The smell was growing, and so was her nausea. Stepping in something wet and squishy with her bare feet, Amanda cringed. Her stomach lurched while feeling the gooey substance between her toes, and bile rose into her throat. She didn't want to know what it was or where the substance had been expelled from, or from which body. She didn't look down to examine it. The last thing she wanted to do was to start throwing up. She eyed a fountain up ahead in front of the hospital and forced herself to move on, carefully watching where she was stepping. There were bodies near the fountain as well. She tried to concentrate on getting to the water. Seeing the water jetting up in the middle of the fountain made her realize not only how bad she needed to find a restroom, but just how thirsty she was.

When Amanda reached the edge of the fountain, she sat down on the cement wall and dipped her hands into the water, splashing it on her face. The water was cold and rejuvenating. She was wondering if she'd get sick if she drank some of it. Maybe just a sip. Was the water chlorinated like pool water? She wasn't sure. *They must add something to the water to keep it from being riddled with algae and bacteria*, she thought. Deciding against drinking it, Amanda swung herself around and plunged her feet into the water. She wanted to wash off whatever that gooey excrement was that she'd stepped in. She walked around the inside of the fountain, feeling the smoothness of the navy blue tiles beneath her feet. She froze when she noticed a woman's body floating on the other side. Quickly, she scrambled to the cement ledge and climbed out. She thanked her lucky stars that she didn't chance drinking the water. It was bad enough that she'd splashed it on her face.

Looking around, Amanda tried to figure out where to go from here. All she knew was that she needed to get out of here. Get away from the bodies. The amount of infected people that'd been trying to obtain help for themselves, and their loved ones last night, was unbelievable. It broke her heart. All these people were so desperate for help. Just as she had been to find help for Jasper. Now they were all dead. No one could help them. Tears pricked at her eyes as she continued to work her way over, around, and through the maze of bodies. She wondered if all hospitals were like this one. Had they all been swarmed? Were they now filled inside and out with corpses?

To her relief, Amanda eventually made it to a side parking lot near the hospital. She let out a deep breath, unaware of the fact that she'd been holding it for so long. She noticed that the number of bodies had lessened the farther she moved away from the hospital. That was a good sign. It meant she was moving in the right direction, away from the infected. She wondered if she'd soon be stricken with whatever the hell this virus was, and lose her mind. Chances were pretty good that she'd get sick too. She pressed her wrist to her forehead as a precaution. As far as she could tell, no fever. Her skin was still cool and clammy from the fountain. Amanda generally caught every little thing going around. If someone even sneezed in her general direction, within a day or two,

169

she'd begin sneezing, too. She'd always tease that she'd live forever because her body would eventually become immune to everything, since she'd already caught everything.

Again, Amanda's mind drifted to Jasper. She'd been in close proximity to him while he was ill. In fact, she was quite surprised she hadn't become sick already since she'd been cooped up with him in her apartment when he first came down with a fever, and then later in the car on the way here, she'd been breathing in his germs. Maybe she'd get lucky. Amanda glanced back at the hospital. Why would she believe that God spared her life and not these other people? She was no one special. There was no reason for her not to become one of the unfortunates.

Amanda stopped by a young Birch tree in the lot, tied to a stake, anchoring it to the ground. Feeling a bit lightheaded, she grabbed hold of the trunk and steadied herself. She stood there for a moment, catching her breath while studying the cars parked in the lot. From what she could tell, they were all empty. She then peered into a silver sedan parked closest to her and tried the handle. It was locked, and there were no keys in the ignition. Not that she really expected people to be dumb enough to leave their keys in the ignition. She just kind of hoped that with all of the commotion last night, people would have become scatterbrained.

Maybe she should try each of the cars in the lot. See if anyone left their keys behind. She might get lucky. But then again, she might just be wasting her time. At this moment, she really wished she knew how to hot-wire cars like her cousin Mike, but she never paid attention to how he did it. She had been what most people would refer to as a wild teenager. One of her favorite past times had been going for joy rides with Mike, in cars that he stole, on the weekends. She, herself, never had stolen one, but she had loved the thrill of the ride all the way until they got caught. That'd been enough to scare her straight. Well, almost.

Being that her cousin had been eighteen at the time, he hadn't fared too well. She had only been fifteen, and was lucky. She'd gotten off with a slap on the wrist and some menial time doing community service. However, seeing what her cousin had gone through had been the wakeup call she'd needed to put life on track.

Amanda thought back to her troubled youth and how stupid she'd been. Even when she'd straightened herself out, she still managed to muddle everything up. She was always doing stupid things, or hooking up with people that were doing stupid things. Her mind drifted to Jasper. Her relationship with him was a prime example of stupid. Not that she wanted anything bad to happen to him. She prayed that he was all right. But she knew he wasn't good for her. She knew he was a cheat and a liar. Why she continued to see him was beyond her knowledge. Right before all this craziness happened, she'd planned on breaking it off with him. She was going to tell him good-bye for good. They were in the middle of an argument about his ex when he'd gotten sick. She couldn't leave him when he was sick.

Amanda worked her way through the parking lot, peering into the windows of cars until she reached a sidewalk. The plan was that she'd follow the sidewalk until she found someone to help her. *That and shoes would be nice,* she thought. She'd seen a lot of available shoes on the dead people, but couldn't get herself to take a pair. Even though they obviously wouldn't be needing them, it didn't seem right to take them. That, and the thought of wearing shoes that were on a corpse, creeped her out.

The ground was cold and hard under her feet. Amanda crossed her arms over her chest and shivered. She wasn't shivering due to the cold. The morning sunlight was burning through the fog, and she could feel the warmness beginning to caress her skin. She was shivering against the horrors surrounding her. Nothing felt real. It was as if she was trapped in a bad dream and couldn't wake up. *This isn't real,* she told herself. *It can't be. It just can't.* Knowing full well that this *was* real, tears trickled down her cheeks. She was lost, alone, and feeling helpless.

***

From behind, Ellie watched as Mike easily cut through the desert foliage. The distance between them grew as Ellie's pace slowed down. She didn't say a word. She was too tired to speak. She kept quiet and followed. Her stomach grumbled, and Ellie pressed her hands to the dull aching pain in her gut. Not only was she tired, hungry, and thirsty, but she was feeling faint. Probably from dehydration. Ellie's body wanted to stop, to sit down and rest. But her brain told her to press on. Not that there was anywhere to sit down anyway. Not comfortably. Besides, her legs were being scratched up enough walking through the desert. The last thing she needed was to sit amongst the prickly mass of plants.

Mike looked over his shoulder at her. "You okay?"

Ellie forced a smile. "Yup."

"Just making sure," he said, slowing his pace, waiting for her to catch up. "Don't want you to pass out on me."

Ellie didn't answer. She wasn't about to admit to him that she just might pass out. She didn't like feeling weak.

"Then I'd have to carry you," Mike continued, searching her face.

Ellie forced herself to grin again. "Yeah, we wouldn't want that."

"We're almost there," he encouraged.

Ellie nodded.

They came up along the side of the property. A chicken wire fence encompassed the sand and tumbleweed backyard. Ellie followed Mike around the fence toward the front of the house. They walked across a makeshift gravel front yard, infested with weeds. The gravel crunched underfoot as they approached a cement front porch. When they reached the front door, Mike knocked. There was no answer. Mike knocked again and waited. Still no answer. He also rang the doorbell.

"Looks like no one's home," Ellie stated the obvious.

Mike raised an eyebrow at her. "Looks like it." He walked over to a window to the left of the door. He knocked on the window. "Hello! Sheriff! Anyone home?" He waited for a moment and then placed his hands on the window, trying to move it. It didn't budge.

"Well, now what?" Ellie asked, staring in the

173

direction of the highway.

"We find a way in," Mike said, walking past her. She followed after him.

"Isn't that illegal?"

Mike turned and looked at her over the rims of his aviator sunglasses. "What do you suggest we do?"

Ellie pursed her lips before answering, "You have a point."

Mike walked around the small stucco house to a gate. He unlatched it and entered the chicken wire fenced in backyard. He tried another window. Locked. He then found a faucet with a hose attached near a sliding glass door and nodded at it. Taking his cue, Ellie grabbed the hose and turned on the faucet. To her relief water sputtered and then flowed from the hose transforming the sand beneath her feet into a thick paste. She kept her hand on the end of the nozzle, feeling the water temperature; at first, hot, and then cool. She put her lips near the nozzle and drank until her stomach hurt, not even noticing Mike prying open the sliding glass door and entering the house.

Ellie was switching off the faucet when Mike stuck his head out the door. "It's empty," he said.

"Oh," Ellie waved the hose at him, "did you want some?"

"Got a drink from the sink," he said and disappeared back into the house.

Ellie dropped the hose into the sludge that'd formed in the sand and followed Mike into the house. It was dark inside, and significantly cooler, even though it was warm and stuffy. She stepped into a small living room with an old sofa that was littered with newspapers, a coffee table piled high with a jumbled mass of magazines, and a small box television set, propped up on a beat up oak table, across from it. An acrid scent lingered in the house. Ellie waved her hand in front of her nose. "God, what's that smell?"

"Don't go into the bedroom," Mike warned, opening the fridge in the small kitchen. Ellie eyed the closed door to her right.

"And what's left of the food in the fridge isn't looking too great neither," Mike said. "No electricity, plus already rotten food, doesn't make for a pleasing experience."

"Is someone… is someone in there?' she asked, still staring at the closed bedroom door.

"Someone *was* in there." Mike closed the door to the fridge and began searching the cupboards. "Don't open the fridge. Not good."

"*Was…*" Ellie repeated.

"*Was,*" Mike said.

"Man or woman?"

"Does it matter?"

"Yes."

"Man."

"Was he old?"

"Older," Mike answered. "Why?"

"I don't know." Ellie shrugged. "Seems easier to accept, I guess."

Mike didn't say anything to that.

Knowing the source of the smell made Ellie's stomach lurch. She pressed her hand to her mouth and closed her eyes. When she re-opened them, Mike had his arm around her, guiding her to the sofa. He cleared the newspapers from one of the cushions and motioned for her to sit down. "Here. They're a bit stale, but edible." He handed her a box of saltine

175

crackers and then set a red plastic cup filled with water on the coffee table. "Eat."

Ellie wrinkled her nose and frowned at him. How was she supposed to eat while breathing in the disgusting odor of a rotting corpse?

"You need your strength," he said, reading her expression. "Just be happy that decomp has just begun. Trust me. The smell will be much worse by tomorrow. Try to eat and refuel. Okay?"

Ellie nodded, taking a stale cracker from the box. Her stomach clenched.

"I'm going to pack up what food I can find." He turned and left her on the couch. Ellie forced herself to chew. She was having a hard time getting herself to swallow the sawdust like substance. Maybe she needed more water. Reaching for the cup, Ellie noticed the handset to a cordless phone sticking out from beneath an old clothing catalog. She picked it up and pressed "talk". To her dismay, the phone was dead. Not that she really expected otherwise. But she figured that she'd give it a shot anyhow. Again, she thought of her parents and her sister. She wondered if they were okay. She prayed that they were. If only there were a way she could get a hold of them to make sure. Maybe once they reached the Sheriff's station, she'd be able to. She hoped that they'd have a more secure phone line she could use. She prayed the virus hadn't spread to Florida. With the speed that it'd been spreading on the West Coast, she doubted they were untouched. The last she'd heard it'd been reported globally, but she tried to remain positive. Maybe things weren't as bad as they appeared. It was the only thing she could do to remain somewhat sane.

Looking around, Ellie wondered where the bathroom was. The only door, besides the front door, and the sliding glass door, was to the bedroom. "Is there a bathroom?" she asked.

Mike had every cupboard open in the kitchen and was now rummaging through the drawers. "In the bedroom."

"Oh," she said, eying the closed door again.

"You can always go outside. No one's around."

Ellie frowned. The last thing she wanted to do was go to the bathroom outdoors. She'd only do that as a last resort. It was the one thing she liked the least about camping. Not that there was much she liked about camping to begin with.

Covering her nose with her hand, Ellie got up from the couch and headed for the bedroom. Putting her hand on the knob, she grasped the hard metal and felt the coolness pressed against her palm. Closing her eyes, she tried to calm her nerves before entering. *I can do this.*

She twisted the knob and carefully opened the door. *Just head for the bathroom,* she told herself. *Don't look at the body. Don't look at the bed. Head straight for the bathroom.*

Not taking her own advice, her eyes raked the room for the dead man. The bitter scent of death hit her hard, penetrating the hand she was using to cover her nose. Ellie coughed at the sour smell. It burned the back of her throat. The blinds were drawn and the room was darker and cooler than the living room and kitchen. Ellie stared at the empty bed with the rumpled beige sheets. No body. She didn't know why she expected to see the man lying in bed as if he'd died in his sleep. She scanned the room. A photo in a silver frame on a bedside table caught her attention. Ellie wandered over to the bed and picked up the frame. A silver-haired man and a white-haired woman were smiling back at her. He had his arm around her. They both looked happy. There was a brilliant orange sunset lighting up beautiful rock formations in the distance. Ellie recognized the location. The photo had been taken in Red Rock Canyon. She'd been there once before. She and her boyfriend, *ex-boyfriend*, had done some hiking there a few years back. Not long after that trip, they'd broken up.

Setting the photo down, Ellie frowned. Seeing the picture had personalized the dead man. There was another photo on the other side of the bed in a matching silver frame. It looked like a wedding photo. Ellie walked around the bed to get a better look, and then stopped. The man from the photo was lying on the floor, face down, in a white T-shirt and blue checkered boxers. Her eyes clouded with tears.

"You okay?"

Ellie's heart skipped a beat, not expecting Mike to enter the room.

She nodded. "Yeah."

"I think I've scavenged as much as I can. Ready to go?"

It took Ellie a moment to find her voice. "Um, yeah. I just need to use the restroom." She crossed the bedroom, walking past Mike without making eye contact, and entered the bathroom wondering what had happened to the man's wife.

\*\*\*

Once the commotion settled and all was quiet,

Bill laid his son back down on the bench. He buckled the boy in to keep him from accidentally rolling off. While waiting for the infected to leave, Bill had explored all of the nooks and crannies of the ambulance. To his relief, he'd come across a stash of bottled water. He tried to rehydrate Benjamin by dripping a little bit of water into his mouth. He'd worried about him choking, but to his relief, he didn't. He didn't do anything. Bill hoped that the water would make a difference in Benjamin's condition. The ambulance was equipped with emergency supplies, including IVs, but Bill was afraid to try to administer one. He didn't have a clue as to where to begin. The only medical knowledge he had was from watching "Scrubs" on TV.

Climbing into the passenger seat of the ambulance, Bill looked out the windshield and the side windows to see if the infected were still around. There was no sign of them. He sat there for a few minutes studying the dash, the keys were still in the ignition, and then the pile-up of cars, scattered around them on the freeway. If he stayed as far to the right lane as possible, he might be able to pass the mess blocking the road. The trick would be getting this ambulance running. Bill had once been told that ambulance drivers kept the engine running because they were diesel and it was more fuel economical. He also knew that diesel engines took longer to warm up. He was concerned because the engine was off, but the lights were on. Why wasn't the ambulance running? Did it run out of gas? Did the battery die? No, the lights wouldn't be working if the battery died. Or at least, he didn't think so.

Feeling that he'd waited long enough, and if the

infected were still there, he'd have noticed them by now, Bill reached over the driver that was hunkered down over the steering wheel. He pulled the handle on the driver's side door and then pushed it open. Sitting back down in the passenger seat, Bill turned, facing the dead ambulance driver, and lifted his good leg. He placed the leather sole of his boot to the corpse's shoulder and gave it a hard shove, knocking the body over. He pushed again, this time placing his foot a little lower, until the body completely dislodged itself and tumbled onto the asphalt.

"I'm sorry," Bill said, trying to move the body just enough to close the door. He felt remorse for the guy, but he knew there wasn't anything he could do. The man was already gone. "I'm sure you were a good man."

Bill turned the key in the ignition. It took a few tries before the engine roared to life.

# Chapter 19

Wandering down the street, Amanda felt lost. Everything was silent. No familiar sounds of traffic or people. Every once in a while she'd hear a bird or two, but even they were abnormally quiet. No matter which way she walked, cars were left abandoned in the streets. From time to time, she'd come across another dead body. Some were in the street, some were on the sidewalks, or trapped within the vehicles. She tried not to look too closely at them. She stared just long enough to make sure they weren't alive. She still worried about being attacked by an infected person, and tried her best to keep a safe distance from any and all bodies. So far nothing notable had happened.

*If there is anyone else alive…* Again, Amanda wondered if she was the last person on Earth. *What if all of the buildings were filled with dead people? All of the stores… the restaurants…. the apartments… what if?*

Deep in thought, pondering the possibility of

being the last person on Earth, from the corner of her eye, Amanda she saw something move in a window above a café. She stopped walking and stared at the window on the second floor. It was open. And there were beige chiffon curtains covering it. A breeze kicked up, ruffling the light material.

Amanda sighed. The movement had been caused by the wind. She decided to walk up to the door of the café located below the window, and give it a try. She yanked on the handle. The door didn't budge. She peered through the dark windows. The café was empty and locked up, just as all of the other shops and buildings had been. There were no lights on. She shook the handle harder, jiggling it. Still nothing. Not that she really expected something to happen, but she tried anyhow.

Backing up from the building, she took one last upwards glance at the open window. A face was staring back at her. Amanda blinked hard. *Was she seeing things? No. She wasn't.* The face was still there. A girl, she guessed to be no older than fourteen, with long dark hair, large brown eyes, set in a round face, stared back at her.

Amanda waved. The girl, slow to respond, shyly waved back.

"My name is Amanda."

The girl didn't respond. She just continued to stare. Amanda wondered if she couldn't hear her. Or maybe the girl didn't speak English. Being so close to the border of Mexico, many people spoke Spanish. "Me llamo, Amanda."

Still no response.

"I need to find a phone," Amanda explained, hoping the girl wasn't deaf. She didn't know sign language. "Do you have a phone?"

The girl didn't answer, but looked over her shoulder. Amanda thought she looked worried.

"I'm Amanda," she repeated, in case the girl hadn't heard her the first time. "What's your name?"

The girl nervously bit her bottom lip.

"It's okay," Amanda said. "I'm nice. I just need to find a phone, so I can call a friend for a ride home."

"Jennifer," the girl said. "Jenny."

"Hi Jenny. Do you have a phone I can use?"

Jenny shook her head.

"Do your parents?"

Jenny looked over her shoulder again and then returned her attention back to Amanda. "The phone doesn't work. No electricity."

"Oh," Amanda said. "Do your parents have a car? Do you think they could drive me home?"

"Don't you know?" Jenny shook her head while looking appalled by Amanda's lack of knowledge. "The roads are blocked. Accidents."

"All roads?"

"That's what the news said last night before the electricity went out. They said *not* to drive because of all the accidents. *And* they put up roadblocks everywhere too. There's nowhere to go."

"Oh, um…" Amanda didn't know how to respond. It made perfect sense though. Cars were left abandoned everywhere. Heck, she'd abandoned her own car on the freeway yesterday evening when trying to get Jasper to the hospital. Even if the phone lines were up, and she could get ahold of someone, would they be able to come get her? It was doubtful.

"I should probably go now," the girl said. "I

don't want to get in trouble."

"Wait!" Amanda was desperate. The girl was the only person she'd seen alive since last night. She didn't want her to go. "Please, um, do you have any shoes I can borrow?" She looked down at her feet. "I've had a really rough night. And it looks like I may have to walk home."

The girl shook her head. "My shoes won't fit you. And my Mom would be mad if I took hers."

"Please," Amanda said. "Don't go. Um, ask your Mom for me…"

"No. I'll get in trouble."

"Please, I beg of you. Or see if I can come in and rest for a little bit."

"I can't. You might be sick."

"But I'm not." Amanda could feel her eyes begin to cloud up with tears. She didn't know where to go next. She'd just have to continue walking. "Let me talk to your mom. Please."

Just then, she heard a crash coming from across the street and down a little way. It sounded like someone knocking over metal trashcans. Amanda could feel the hairs on the back of her neck stand on end. She then heard men's voices laughing and cat calling. There was another loud crash. This time it sounded like glass shattering.

"Please," Amanda said, feeling frightened. She now wished she could go back to believing she was the last person left alive. "Let me in."

The girl shook her head. "You might be contagious."

"You can't just leave me out here!"

The sound of a car alarm went off causing Amanda's heart to skip a beat. Then there was whooping and laughter. It was growing louder. Whoever they were, they were getting closer. And it sounded like they were up to no good. Unfortunately, Amanda had had run-ins with men like that in the past. Not a good situation.

Amanda looked back up at the window. It slammed closed and the girl was gone.

There was another loud crashing sound and another car alarm going off. Amanda ducked down on the sidewalk behind the car nearest her, a newer model, fire-red mustang. She pressed her cheek to the door and stayed put. She could hear the men's jeering getting louder. Their feet pounded on the pavement. They were running in her direction. She hoped they hadn't seen her.

Getting down on all fours, she peeked under the car. She could see the men's feet in the street. They had stopped running and were on the other side of the car. Amanda held still. She worried that she'd somehow do something to draw their attention to her.

"Hey! Look at this place!" a man's voice called out from somewhere farther away.

"What is it?" asked one of the men near her.

Amanda cringed. One of the three sets of feet, wandered closer to the front end of the car. Amanda quickly moved to the rear of the car and stayed in a crouching position.

"Hey homey, let's go see what he's got."

"Wait!" the man closest to her said. "Gotta do somethin' first." His feet turned and took a few steps in her direction. He was now nearing the rear of the car where Amanda was hiding. Amanda kept watching his feet, and then, on all fours, she crawled from the rear of the car, back up onto the sidewalk, and to the side of it. Little pebbles from the asphalt had dug into the palms of her hands, stinging her flesh. She kept her eyes on the set of feet closest to her. When the feet stopped moving, she stopped crawling, and held her breath.

*Crash!* The splintering sound of glass penetrated her ears as the man bashed in the rear windshield with a baseball bat. *Crash! Crash!* The alarm went off, joining the other car alarms in an array of honking. The man took another swing. *Crash!*

Amanda worried that the man would round the car at any moment to bash in the side windows and would find her. She didn't want her head to be next on the gangster's list of things to bash. She thought about sliding under the car to hide, but since she was on the sidewalk now, the curb blocked her from being able to get underneath. And if she crawled around to the front of the car, the other men would see her. There was nowhere for her to go. She could make a run for it. But would they chase after her? They'd surely catch her since she was at a disadvantage being barefoot.

*Crash!* The man was bashing in the tail lights when he unexpectedly bellowed out in pain. Then another sound accompanied his cries. Amanda recognized the snarls of an infected person. The hoodlum landed on the ground, kicking, and screaming. His head turned to the side, facing her. The infected was a bald, slender man wearing a grey T-shirt, and a tattered pair of Levis. He was on top of the hoodlum, too busy ravaging his prey to notice her. Amanda froze, watching the gangster being mauled. Blood pooled on the pavement. The gangster's so called friends took off running in the opposite direction.

"Hey!" Amanda heard a girl call out. She looked for the source of the voice. It was Jenny. She was outside, standing at the street corner, near the edge of the building, beckoning for her to follow. Amanda eyed the infected man still brutally ripping the gangster to shreds. In order for her to do what Jenny wanted, she'd need to run past him.

Jenny furiously waved her arms in a desperate attempt to get Amanda's attention. The gangster finally stopped struggling, and his screams died out. Amanda worried that she'd waited too long. She wasted her opportunity to run past the infected, unseen. What would stop him from attacking her next?

Without thinking twice, Amanda made a snap decision, and sprang to her feet. She kept her eyes on Jenny. Jenny rounded the building and disappeared from sight. The infected man lifted his head as Amanda ran past and snarled. She kept her eyes on where she'd last seen Jenny and hoped that she'd be led to safety.

Making a sharp left, Amanda headed down a narrow alley. Jenny was on the other side of a tall, chain link fence with barbed wire looped around the top.

"Hurry!" Jenny shrieked.

Amanda stepped on something sharp and screamed. Hot, searing pain bolted up her leg from the wound. She reached down and yanked out a shard of glass. Snarls came from behind her as she stumbled through the gate. Jenny grabbed her arm, propelling her out of the way, slammed the gate shut, and latched it.

The infected smashed his body into the chain-link. His puffy distorted face, covered in fresh blood, pushed into the wire mesh. Blood stained teeth bit at them with fierce determination. His golden eyes narrowed, focusing on the two girls.

"Come on," Jenny said, taking Amanda's hand. "I don't know how long that'll hold him."

Amanda let Jenny guide her around the back of the building, while constantly looking over her shoulder, expecting the gate to give way. Jenny opened a door and ushered Amanda into the dark building. She quickly turned the deadbolt, locking the heavy door behind them. The room was dark, and Amanda couldn't see anything. She was afraid to move.

"This way," she heard Jenny say, then felt a tug on her sleeve. She moved through the dark, letting Jenny guide her. When the door opened, on the other side of the room, light trickled in from down a hall. Amanda looked back behind her. She could make out boxes and shelves. She'd been in a storage room behind the café. "Stay away from the windows. No need to draw attention."

Amanda did as Jenny instructed. They quickly walked past a kitchen, bypassed the café, and headed to the right side of the building. She followed Jenny up a narrow staircase that led to the apartments above the café.

"My parents own the restaurant," Jenny said, opening the second door on the right. "They rent out the other apartment units to family and close friends from Mexico." Jenny stopped not yet entering the room. She looked Amanda up and down. "My parents are going to kill me for bringing in a Gringo."

Amanda threw Jenny a bold look. "I'm thankful for your kindness, but I'm no *Gringo*," she stated in perfect Spanish. "My *abuela* is from Mexico."

Jenny looked surprised. "Good. That might help you."

"Where have you been?" A short, round, woman with wavy black hair grabbed hold of Jenny in a bear hug. "I couldn't find you! I thought you were attending to your grandmother..." The woman stopped talking when she noticed Amanda for the first time and raked her with her eyes. "Who's this?"

"She needed help."

"I'm Amanda," Amanda introduced. "I'm so very thankful..."

"Get her out of here!" the woman spat in Spanish. She was unaware of the fact that Amanda could understand her.

"But Mama," Jenny said. "She needs..."

"I don't care what she needs. She's a stranger. She might be ill. Make her leave!"

"No, I can't do that. There are bad people out there. They were going to..."

"We only have enough food for the family. Make her leave!"

"Mama, please. She needs our help."

The woman made the sign of the cross over her chest. "Heaven forbid your father sees her. Get rid of her quickly."

Amanda quickly stepped in and addressed Jenny's mother in Spanish. "I'll only stay for a little while. Just long enough to refresh. I'm very thankful for your gratitude."

"Take her to get cleaned up," the woman said to

Jenny, refusing to address Amanda. "Your grandmother needs me." She pushed past them and left the apartment.

"Come," Jenny said, leading Amanda to a dark little bathroom with no windows. "We still have running water, but it's cold."

"Is your grandmother okay?" Amanda asked.

"She's got the sickness." Jenny grabbed a small towel from a rack and set it down on the counter. She then lit a candle. "Clean yourself up. Bandages are under the sink."

"Oh." Amanda looked down at the bloody footprints she'd left on the floor. Her mind had been so preoccupied that she hadn't noticed the stinging pain of her wound until now. "I'll clean those up. Sorry. I'll try to be quick. I don't want to get you in trouble with your father."

"Don't worry about that."

"You don't think he'll mind?"

"He went to find my brother. He's not coming back."

Amanda didn't know what to say. She didn't have the heart to say anything. Jenny continued, "If he was okay, he'd have returned last night. He didn't. Mama is in denial." She turned and left Amanda in the bathroom to tend to her wound.

\*\*\*

Looking out the window, Ellie realized just how desolate the desert was. Most definitely not the best place to be stranded. But then again, she thought about San Diego County, and how many people lived there. With this so called virus, or whatever the hell it was, Ellie still thought it looked as if people were having some kind of strange allergic reaction, except for the yellow eyes and attacking people thing, she bet southern California would be an utter mess. The virus must've been spreading like wildfire. It was probably safer to be in a less populated area. However, on the flip side, being less populated meant fewer supplies. Not to mention it was frickin' hot in the desert. For the second time, Ellie reached for the old stereo and scanned for stations. Still nothing but static. There was absolutely nothing coming in on AM or FM. Either all of the stations were out, or the antenna of the ancient, beat up, orange and white, Ford pickup truck didn't work. Both were viable possibilities.

They'd commandeered the old truck from the dead man's home they'd ransacked for stale crackers, a couple of cans of chili, and as much water as they could carry in Tupperware, cups, and any vessel available. Ellie switched the stereo off. She'd rather not listen to static. The feeling of being cut off from the rest of the world bothered her, and the buzzing white noise was a reminder. Plus, ever since she'd seen Poltergeist as a child, the sound of static gave her the creeps.

The truck suddenly swerved, jutting Ellie from her thoughts. Mike slowed down and drove around a couple of cars left in the middle of the two-lane highway. It looked as if they'd collided at some point during the night. Both vehicles appeared to be abandoned.

"Should we stop and make sure no one is stranded?"

"No one was in the cars." Mike glanced back at the vehicles in his rearview mirror. "Keep an eye out for anyone wandering in the desert or passed out on the side of the road."

Ellie returned to looking out the window. "What do you think happened to that guy's wife?"

"What guy's wife?"

"The guy in the house, you know…"

"I don't think he had a wife."

"He did," Ellie said, her stomach knotting up. "He had pictures. What if… what if she comes home and finds him like that?"

"I don't think that's likely."

"Why not?"

"The state of the house," Mike explained. "No food. Newspapers and magazines piled up… my guess is that he was a widower."

Ellie thought this over and felt slightly better. She hated the thought of an elderly woman coming home to find her husband's body. What Mike said made sense. Thinking about it, she hadn't noticed anything feminine within the house or the furnishings. No flowers, nothing frilly, and most definitely nothing delicate. She hadn't noticed any women's clothing. Not that she was really looking. But she did remember seeing men's clothing piled on a chair in the corner of the bedroom.

When the truck came to a stop, Ellie opened her eyes. She hadn't realized that she'd fallen asleep. Mike threw open his door and hopped out. They were on the outskirts of Vegas, cars were everywhere, blocking the road. Ellie hopped out of the truck and caught up with Mike who was standing on the edge of the pavement.

"Damn it! There's no way through!"

Ellie frowned staring at the hundreds of abandoned vehicles blocking the highway. It was as if everyone had just decided to leave their vehicles and walk home. Where did they all go? It was so surreal.

"Oh my God, Mike!" Ellie shrieked, upon noticing movement. She pointed across the highway. "There's someone trapped in that SUV! Look!"

Without saying a word, Mike sprinted around the cars, and hopped over the cement middle divider. Ellie followed. As she struggled to get over the cement divider to catch up with Mike, she could hear the person in the backseat of the black SUV banging on the window. Mike was now standing near the SUV, not moving, when Ellie caught up to him. He shook his head.

A little girl with blonde braids, pawed at the window. Her golden eyes were barely visible through her white, puffed up skin. There were other people in the SUV, unmoving. Ellie peered into the driver's side window. The driver's face was unrecognizable. There was nothing left but a bloody pulp. The little girl climbed over the seat following Ellie.

"Do you think she did this?"

Mike shrugged. "Hard to tell." He glanced at the cars backed up on the highway. "Looks like they were probably stuck here for a while. One of them was probably infected... could of have been her, or it began with the other child..."

Ellie averted her eyes. She didn't want to see the other child. "What do we do?"

"Continue walking."

"I mean... about the girl..."

Mike straightened his hat and turned his back to the SUV. The girl's clawing became more erratic. "There's nothing we can do."

"There has to be something. We can't just leave

her!"

Mike began to make his way back toward the truck. "Are you coming?"

Ellie's heart sank. She turned her attention back to the girl. She put her hand on the door handle. She had to do something. What if there was a way to help her? She couldn't just leave her there.

"It's okay," she said to the girl. "I'm going to find help." She tugged at the handle. It was locked. Ellie then tried the driver's side door. Locked. She ran to the other side of the vehicle. Everything was locked. The little girl followed her, springing from seat to seat, climbing over the bodies of her family, snarling and pawing at the windows. Ellie stopped. Tears were streaming down her cheeks as the feeling of helplessness washed over her. If she were to let this little girl out into the world, she'd spread the infection. Mike was right. There was nothing she could do. She stood there watching the girl, feeling completely helpless. She couldn't save her. She hadn't even realized that she was crying until she felt Mike's hand on her shoulder.

"Come on. Let's get out of here."

Ellie spun around and buried her head into his shoulder. Not for the first time, Mike took her into his strong arms, and held her close. He then guided her back to the temporary safety of the truck.

\*\*\*

Bill drove the ambulance as far as he could go. There was no way around the cars blocking the shoulder. He would have to walk the rest of the way to the hospital. At least he was close. Only a couple blocks away.

After scanning the wreckage for signs of the

infected, making sure it was safe, Bill unlatched Benjamin and lifted him from the seat. He began their arduous journey in the direction of the hospital. It seemed an eternity before the building was in sight. He continued to limp, dragging his bad leg. The only thing keeping him going was the hope of finding help for his son. But, step by step, that hope was diminishing. The closer he came to the hospital, the more bodies he came in contact with. By their puffed up skin, and distorted faces, Bill knew they died from the infection. The same infection his son had. He didn't want to jump to conclusions, but he believed this virus was an act of terrorism. It had to be. There was no other logical explanation he could come up with. What else could cause such devastation? Either that or the CDC, Center for Disease Control, screwed up and accidentally let this thing loose in the US. He couldn't imagine that there were any benefits to the government for purposely killing everyone off. Without the little people, there was no one left to govern. Unless, of course, it wasn't meant to kill off this many people.

Shaking his head, Bill told himself again, not to jump to conclusions, and not to waste too much energy thinking about things that he had no answer to. Right now he needed to focus his energy on saving his son.

Upon arrival, Bill had tried the front doors to the hospital. They were locked up tight. Bodies were scattered both inside and outside of the building. Following the signs that were pointing him in the direction of the emergency room, he worked his way around to the back of the building. Above a glass door was a sign in big red letters that read,

EMERGENCY. Bill yanked on the door. It didn't budge. That too was locked up tight. He tried to peer in through the tinted glass, but couldn't see anything.

Setting Benjamin down in the shade near the door, Bill banged on the glass. He looked up at a sign near the door; Gun Shot Wounds, Stab Wounds, Road and Traffic Accidents, Trauma, Asthma, Diabetic Crisis, Hypertensive Crisis, Cardiac in Patient Crisis, Acute Abdominal Pain, so forth and so forth. Bill frowned and banged on the glass some more. "I have an emergency here!" he yelled. When nothing happened, he went in search of something he could use to pry the door open. He came this far and had no plans of going back without finding help. Someone had to be inside.

He wandered around the outside of the building until he came to the ambulance drop off. There were no ambulances. All of the vehicles must've been deployed. Bill stared at the overhead lights of the overhang. They were dim and running off noisy generators. To his dismay, he found more bodies. Many were medical staff. Stepping over them, Bill was able to make it to a door that easily pushed open leading to a long hallway. He made it. He was inside.

Working his way down the hall, past many closed doors, his stomach kept tightening and releasing with anxiety. He stopped walking when he saw the blood, lots of blood. The carnage was everywhere. Bodies were everywhere. The stench of death was overpowering. Bill clutched his stomach, bent over at the waist and began to dry heave. Feeling faint, he leaned against a wall until he was able to regain control over his reflexes.

Upon finding the Emergency Room, waiting room, Bill worked his way to the front desk. He picked up the phone. No dial tone. He could see Benjamin through the front glass door, propped up in the corner, where he'd left him. It took Bill a moment to figure out how to unbolt the door. When he did, he scooped up his son and brought him inside. He laid him across two orange padded chairs in the waiting room before going in search of medical staff, if there were any left alive.

# Chapter 20

Staring at the small black and white TV monitor in the security room, Liam had been surprised to see movement. It'd been hours since he'd last seen any signs of life. However, this was different; this man didn't seem to be infected. Not yet. He watched the man drag one of his legs. He was obviously hurt.

Curious, he watched as the man fumbled with the locks on the Emergency Room door. Once he figured out how to unlock it, he carried in a child and laid him across a couple of chairs. Just then, the door to the small room opened, and a woman entered. "I think we have a problem," he said to her, not taking his eyes off the screen.

The woman joined him in front of the monitor. "Is he infected?"

"Doesn't appear to be."

"Have we been noticed?"

Liam shook his sandy blonde head. "Not to my knowledge."

"Good," she said. "Let's keep it that way."

"He carried in an unconscious child."

The dark-haired, heavy set woman became curious, moving closer to the screen. "If the child was infected, he wouldn't be unconscious," she said. "He'd be losing control…"

"Maybe he's past that stage."

"Then he'd be dead. Zoom in."

Liam did as instructed.

The woman studied the boy's chest and then his face. "I can't tell if he's breathing with the quality of these monitors…"

"The man was careful when he set him down."

"That doesn't mean anything. Humans are sentimental over the dead."

"Yes." Liam tapped his chin. "But perhaps he's what we've been looking for."

"Look. He's infected," the woman stated, tapping on the monitor. The picture quality was grainy, but the tell-tale symptoms were still apparent. "Even with his eyes closed, I can still see the swelling and distortion of the flesh. He's dead."

"I'm not so sure," Liam said. "I think his chest is moving."

The woman stood there, her lips clamped tightly together, quietly thinking this over. "I'd need to get a closer look."

Liam agreed with her assessment. They wouldn't know for sure without a closer look. But the longer they stayed in the hospital, the more chances they took of getting caught. It wouldn't be long before someone realized they'd removed their tracking devices. "We'll have to move quickly. It won't take long before we're noticed. They have eyes everywhere."

The woman nodded. "I understand the risk involved."

"Susan, if we're caught…" Liam swallowed hard. "The consequences…"

"Then we won't get caught." Susan turned on the heel of her shoes and left the room. Liam followed after her.

# Chapter 21

Not wanting to take advantage of their hospitality, Amanda accepted the pair of sandals Jenny had given her, a bottle of spring water and a package of corn tortillas. Jenny had snatched the tortillas and water from the storage room. She'd handed them to Amanda as she ushered her out the back door. Amanda was positive that Jenny would be scolded for the generosity if her mother found out.

The sandals were two sizes too small, and her toes and heels hung over the flimsy rubber sole, but it was still better than not having shoes at all. The bottom of Amanda's foot stung with every step she took, reminding her of the injury. Amanda stood still, putting most of her weight on the opposite leg and scoped out her surroundings. She wasn't sure where to go. She looked through the gate searching for the infected man that'd chased her earlier. Everything was eerily quiet again. There was no sign of him or the hoodlums. After a moment of uneasy silence,

Amanda gathered up her courage and unlatched the gate. The sound of the squeaking metal as the gate swung open rang loudly in her ears. She stood still and waited before closing the gate behind her. Nothing jumped out at her. Nothing moved. Nothing happened at all. With soft, gentle steps, Amanda made her way to the street and stopped. If there were any signs of danger, she'd run back through the gate and beg for Jenny to let her inside. Not that she'd be much safer inside. Since Jenny's grandmother was infected, it probably wouldn't be long before they all came down with it. She hoped Jenny's mother was being careful and knew what she was up against. Maybe she should have said something. Not that anyone would have listened to her anyway.

For a moment, Amanda stood on the street corner, hugging her bottle of water and package of tortillas to her chest. There wasn't a soul about. No signs of the living or the infected. Not even the chirping of birds. Nothing.

She figured she could do one of two things. The first was to keep looking for someone to help her. The second was to head back home on her own. If she could make it home, she'd at least have shelter and her belongings. Right now, she felt she was wasting time. If she'd decided to walk straight home from the hospital this morning, she could've been almost home by now. There was enough food in her pantry to last at least a week. Maybe longer if she rationed. Most of the food in her freezer and refrigerator would need to be tossed out. She'd make sure to use up the perishables first before touching anything in the pantry. At least she'd have time to think about what to do next in the comfort of her own home. And who knows? Maybe life will look better and sort itself out in a week or two. Amanda looked down the vacant street and frowned. Unfortunately, she was a good ten to eleven miles from home. And she'd have to go past the hospital again and then walk down the freeway. She wasn't quite sure how long it'd take to walk that far. *Driving*, took ten minutes with no traffic. *Walking*, she hadn't a clue, especially walking in sandals that were way too small and an injured foot.

Amanda stared up at the sun. She didn't have a watch, and she'd lost her cell phone with her purse. She was guessing it was about noon. She then wondered if she'd make it home with the infected roaming the streets. The thought brought goose bumps to her skin and caused her to shiver. Pushing the negative thoughts from her mind, she focused on her goal. Getting home.

***

The old orange and beige truck bumped and banged as Mike drove at high speeds down a dirt road. A thick cloud of dust followed in their wake. Even with her seatbelt on, Ellie had to brace herself. She had one hand on the dash. Her back was slightly turned so that she could face Mike. Her other hand was gripping the seat. With all the potholes they'd hit at full speed, she'd been surprised the old truck hadn't conked out on them yet.

"They don't make trucks like they used to,"

Mike said, smacking the steering wheel with his hand.

Ellie tried to grin, but was having difficulty pulling it off. She looked out the window at the miles of desert surrounding them. Mike had said he knew back roads to bypass the traffic jam on the freeway. When he'd said *back roads*, Ellie thought he meant *less traveled* paved roads. She hadn't known he'd actually meant *rarely* traveled dirt roads. She worried that the old beat up truck would eventually break down due to the rough terrain, and they'd be left stranded in the middle of nowhere. She wanted to voice her fears to him, but felt it was better not to. She tried to put some faith in the fact that Mike was a sheriff. He probably knew the Nevada desert like the back of his hand. Or at least she hoped that he did. Regardless, if it weren't for him, she'd have been raped and murdered by that man in the motel room last night. Or even worse, she could have become one of the infected.

"Up there!" Mike yelled over the roar of the engine. "You see it?"

Ellie squinted. She didn't see anything but sand, cactus, tumbleweeds, rocks, and boulders. And lots of them.

"There's a road. It'll take us to the left."

Ellie followed Mike's gaze to the left. She could see buildings in the distance. "I see it!" This time she smiled without having to try. Once she was at the sheriff's station, she knew everything would be okay. She'd be able to call her family and also her neighbor whose daughter was dog sitting for her. She hadn't worried about Max because she knew Francesca, and her daughter, Chloe, would take good care of him. However, the thought just occurred to her. *What if they were infected?* Or even if they weren't, would they continue to take care of Max with the current turn of events? He'd starve to death if left locked up in her condo.

Mike smiled back. "I could tell you were getting nervous."

"I wasn't nervous."

"Yeah, okay…" Mike slowed down to take a sharp turn onto a very sandy trail. The truck's tires seemed to be having a difficult time gripping the loose grains. The previous dirt road they'd traveled, the sand had been packed down hard, almost like clay. This one was loose and powdery. Sand puffed up in giant brown clouds all around them, making it difficult to see out the windows.

When they emerged from the sand, pulling up onto a paved parking lot behind some beige stucco buildings, Ellie's nervousness decreased. Mike parked alongside several other vehicles and hopped out of the truck. Ellie undid her seatbelt. When she slid out of the passenger seat, hot and soaked with sweat, her legs felt unsteady. She wasn't used to the Nevada heat and was feeling lightheaded. Mike, unaffected by the climate, was already walking toward the front of the building. Ellie closed the passenger side door, leaned against the truck to steady herself, and then hurried to catch up. Mike was standing in front of the building staring at the destruction. Ellie didn't say anything. She stood next to him in silence. She bit her lower lip to keep it from trembling. There were dead sheriff officers and civilians in the street, on the sidewalks, and locked in cars. Everything was quiet. No sounds of the living.

Without saying a word, Ellie followed Mike to the local sheriff's station. When they entered, Ellie winced at the familiar scent of death.

"Stay here!" Mike pointed to some seats near the

door. Ellie sat down. She watched as he glanced at the front desk while turning to walk down a hall. She could hear him opening and closing doors. Ellie eyed the desk and then decided to look for a phone. She picked up the receiver to an older model multiline telephone. As a receptionist, she was familiar with the outdated model. Her heart sank. No dial tone. She checked the connection. The line was intact, and the phone plugged in. She then hit the number 9, knowing that in some companies, you needed to dial 9 in order to make an outgoing call. Nothing. Knowing that it was useless, but not wanting to believe it, she tried each of the lines. She was punching every button on the phone a second time when Mike reappeared.

"Let's get out of here." Not waiting for Ellie, he left the building with a black backpack slung over one shoulder. Ellie dropped the receiver back into the cradle and scurried after him.

***

Frustrated, Bill punched the wall, and immediately regretted it. His hand throbbed something fierce. The last thing he needed to do was break his hand. So far, there wasn't a soul alive on the entire first floor. He stopped in front of the elevators and tried pushing the button numerous times. He should've known the elevators wouldn't work. The generators probably didn't cover elevators. They'd take too much energy. He'd have to find a staircase and drag his bum leg up the stairs.

Pulling himself down the hall, he noticed a sign suspended from the ceiling. There was an arrow pointing in the direction of the cafeteria. His stomach grumbled. He turned and headed in that direction. Maybe, just maybe, he'd find someone alive in there. He'd grab a bite to eat at the same time. Maybe find some juice or milk for Benjamin. If he could get some nutrients into him, he'd feel better. He worried about Benjamin becoming dehydrated.

Bill pushed open the swinging doors. There was an overhead light on in the back of the room where the food was kept. He figured the generators were running that section of the cafeteria to keep the food from going bad. He worked his way over to a fridge with glass doors. There was a shelf with premade sandwiches, another with different colored Jell-O cups and yogurts, and below that one was a variety of fruit. He grabbed a couple of ham and cheese sandwiches, and two Jell-O cups, one green and one red. He set them on an orange plastic tray that looked like it'd been around since the 1960s. His stomach rumbled.

Clutching his stomach with one hand, he decided he couldn't wait. He was starving, and his hands were beginning to tremble. His blood sugar was dropping, and he needed to eat something before he passed out. He ripped open the plastic wrap over one of the sandwiches and took a huge bite. Nothing had ever tasted so good in his life. He then opened another glass door refrigerator and removed a bottle of water and a carton of chocolate milk.

Unscrewing the lid to the plastic bottle, he took a large gulp of water, when he felt it. A sharp stab in his upper arm. His vision blurred before he could see anything. The room began to spin, and his legs collapsed. Someone caught him before he hit the ground.

# Chapter 22

When Amanda arrived back at the hospital, the sour scent of rotting corpses had worsened, and insects were collecting. Instead of walking past the front of the building, she decided to avoid the mass of dead and walk around to the back where the emergency entrance was located. She supposed, since she was there, she would try one more time to see if anyone was inside. If Jasper was still alive, she believed that he would be inside, being treated for the illness. She wasn't about to give up hope. Not yet. Not until she'd seen him with her own eyes. Finding out that there were still people alive, such as Jenny and her family, gave her hope. Maybe not everyone would, or could, catch this thing. Maybe people could even fight it once infected. She told herself that, even though, deep in her heart, she didn't believe it. She really believed it was only a matter of time before the handful of people still left alive would catch it and become infected themselves. She knew she was one of the lucky few that hadn't caught it yet. It was only a matter of time. And if it wasn't that, it'd be dying from a disease brought on by the millions of rotting bodies.

Pushing the negative thoughts from her mind, Amanda wandered behind the building. She was under an overhang. She found herself over by where the ambulances would normally be kept except there weren't any ambulances around. Apparently, they'd all been dispatched. None had returned. She noticed a black golf cart parked next to the wall with the word, Security, painted in white across the hood. The body, of who she believed was the security guard, was lying in a pool of congealed blood on the ground next to it. There was a dim overhead light flickering that caught Amanda's eye. She frowned upon noticing a paramedic and one of the hospital staff lying on the ground, also in a pool of blood. She watched for a moment from a safe distance, and when she was sure that none of them were moving, she made her way to a door that'd hopefully lead her into the hospital.

Amanda's heart leaped in her chest when the door pushed open. She carefully entered the building and covered her mouth. There was blood smeared all over the walls of the long hallway. Careful not to make any noise, in case there were infected still roaming the building, she crept down the hall to the emergency waiting room. No one was there. She worked her way through the maze of hallways and corridors trying to figure out where to go. To her dismay, there was no one around. Well, no one around that was still alive. Amanda continued her search. She was still optimistic that there'd be a wing or a section of the hospital where doctors were treating the infected. And that'd be where she'd find Jasper.

Grabbing hold of her long, blonde hair, Amanda tucked it behind her ears to keep it out of her face.

Even though she'd cleaned herself up a bit at Jenny's, she knew she still looked like hell. The bottom of her foot began to throb reminding her of her injury. She needed to find somewhere to clean her wound before it got infected. The last thing she needed was to survive the fatal epidemic that was killing everyone off, and then die from something stupid like an infection caused by stepping on glass. She'd have to look for some antiseptic and also some antibiotics. A dose of Erythromycin should do the trick. That's what her doctor always prescribed for her sinus infections since she was allergic to penicillin. A good dose of Erythromycin should kill off any bacteria that'd made its way into her body.

Noticing a sign pointing the way to the restrooms, Amanda decided she'd stop in and wash her wound. Afterward, she'd go in search of a pharmacy. She bet she'd be able to find everything she needed. And hopefully, she'd also stumble across a doctor. Not that she hadn't stumbled across a few already. But she was hoping to stumble across a doctor that was still alive. So far, the odds weren't in her favor.

Amanda ripped off the blood-soaked, makeshift, bandage, that she'd applied at Jenny's with the few things they had in their first aid kit. Her foot stung like frickin' hell and was now oozing, what she believed to be, puss. Biting her lower lip to keep from screaming, Amanda lifted her foot up into the sink and turned on the water. There was barely any light in the otherwise dark bathroom. A small ceiling light, that probably only came on when the electricity was out, buzzed. Amanda wondered how long it would be before the generator stopped running and there was no light at all. She'd better hurry.

Switching on the tap, cold water washed over her foot. The injury was worse than she'd originally thought. The flesh around the cut was now extremely swollen from all the walking. She'd most definitely need to find clean dressing, antiseptic, antibiotics, and maybe even some painkillers. She still had a long walk ahead of her. If she had to, she could probably find an available room in the hospital to take refuge in. Though the thought of staying there for the night, or maybe two, creeped her out. She really wanted to be in the comfort of her own home. Nevertheless, it was an option if her foot was giving her too much trouble. She could easily hide in one of these rooms and would probably never be found. So far, she hadn't seen anyone one alive to oppose of her stay.

Amanda shivered. The thought of all the dead surrounding her, and scattered around inside and outside the hospital, made her feel uneasy. Overall, the hospital staff had done an amazing job of disposing of the bodies inside the building. After the mass of people she'd seen outside, she'd expected to find it just as bad on the inside. However, the bodies she'd been coming in contact with were few and far between. She guessed they were the last to have died.

*That doesn't mean everyone is dead,* she told herself. *There could still be people alive in another wing of the hospital.* She needed to find them.

Amanda switched off the faucet and grabbed a wad of brown recycled paper towels from the wall dispenser. With her foot still propped up on the counter, while balancing on one leg, she carefully patted dry her wound when she heard it. A blood curdling cry for help. She held her breath and listened. The voice had belonged to a man. It was deep, raspy. There was a man, alive, somewhere in the building. He let out another bellowing scream. He sounded like he was being tortured. Her pulse raced. The sound of her heartbeat was throbbing in her ears. She'd been so hopeful to find someone, but not like this. A wave of terror shot up her spine as the man screamed out again.

*** 

Ellie sat quietly in the truck as Mike, tightlipped and angry, raced through deserted back streets. Sand flew in all directions, creating big puffs of brown clouds all around them. She wasn't sure where he was taking her, and she was too terrified to ask. For now, she decided to keep quiet and just go with the flow. She had nowhere else to go. In a way, she felt her life depended on him. She wondered what she would do without him. *Where would she go?* She wasn't sure. She wanted so badly to go home, but was unsure if that was even possible. Her hands were tied. *Would they even be allowed to crossover the border back into California? Were all of the highways congested with abandoned cars?*

Southern California freeways would more than likely be impossible to navigate. Highways might even be worse. Maybe she could find back roads that'd lead her to Oceanside. There had to be other ways to get back home that would bypass the freeways. She'd need to get her hands on a map since GPS was no longer an option. Maybe later, once things settled down a bit, she'd ask Mike to take her to a gas station. Ellie frowned. She'd forgotten all about not having a vehicle. Her poor car had been left on the side of the road. She still had hefty payments to make on it too. Maybe her insurance would cover everything. Ellie shook her head. *Insurance… car payments…* they were hardly something to worry about when the entire world was crumbling apart. It was funny how the things that were once so important were now considered trivial. They didn't fit into this new world that'd been thrust upon them overnight. *Was it weird to feel nostalgic about possibly never making a car payment again?*

Mike entered a residential area with beautiful, earth tone colored, stucco homes and gravel landscaped yards. The streets were barren. No one was about except for a few scattered bodies. There were a couple of abandoned cars in the street. Ellie kept silent, but wondered if there were people still alive hiding in their homes, or if they were all dead, or infected. She looked at Mike. He was visibly upset. His lips were pulled in a tight line, shoulders tense, and his knuckles white from gripping the steering wheel with great force. Ellie wanted to talk to him about it, but felt it was best to keep her thoughts to herself for the time being.

Mike pulled up in front of a one-story, tan, adobe style house with a white quartz front yard, and parked in the street. A black SUV was parked in the short, sloped driveway. Without saying a word, he flung open the driver's side door and jumped out. Ellie wondered if she was supposed to follow or stay put. Instead of heading into the house that he'd parked in front of, he sprinted in the direction of the two-story house next door. That's when Ellie noticed the body. Someone was lying on the front porch. She watched as Mike kneeled next to it. She got out of the truck and began walking across the gravel yard; rocks were grinding and crunching beneath her feet.

"My neighbor," he said, not turning to look at Ellie. With his hand, he closed the golden yellow eyes of the old woman. Her skin was white and distorted with hives. "She was like a second mom to me. Always baking me cookies and casseroles."

"I'm sorry," Ellie said, her voice barely a whisper.

Mike stood up and tried the front door. It was locked. He reached into his pocket and pulled out a keyring. He unlocked the door, then scooped up the woman and carried her inside, gently lying her down on the couch. There was a green and yellow crocheted blanket folded across the top. Grabbing it, he covered the woman's body.

"Does she live here alone?" Ellie asked, looking around the house. It seemed awfully large for one person since it was two stories. She glanced at the carpeted staircase leading upstairs. She guessed the house was maybe three or four bedrooms.

"Widowed. Husband died a couple years back. She has a son in Arkansas. Married with two kids. He didn't visit much."

Ellie nodded. She understood how distance made visiting family difficult. Between lack of time and money, she rarely got to see her family. And she was feeling guilty for not trying to make it more of a priority. She had always thought she had all the time in the world. And now, she realized just how wrong she was. In an instant, everything changed. *What if she never got to see her family again?* Ellie's eyes clouded with tears. With what she'd been seeing in Nevada, the amount of people that'd been infected here, chances were pretty good that she would never see her family again. She swiped at her eyes. Now wasn't the time to cry.

Mike walked toward the front door. He too was swiping at tears. Ellie followed him to his house next door. He unlocked the door, and Ellie followed him inside. "Help yourself to whatever you can find in the kitchen." Mike held out his hand and motioned her toward the kitchen. "This'll take a while. Make yourself comfortable."

Ellie nodded, not asking what he meant. She stepped into the white tiled kitchen with white-washed cabinets. Opening the refrigerator door, she realized she'd better take a quick peek. The air inside was still cool and wouldn't last long without electricity. She really wasn't hungry, nothing sounded good, but her stomach was telling her otherwise. She noticed Mike had quite a few Greek yogurts. Ellie helped herself to a Strawberry Cheesecake one and wondered if it'd still be good. The container felt cool enough to the touch. She felt it was probably better to eat the things that'd spoil first, anyway. From the door, she snatched a diet soda. The caffeine would probably be good for her headache, yet she knew the sodium wasn't the best choice for dehydration. And she'd been feeling dehydrated ever since she woke up this morning. After living near the beach for so many years, she wasn't acclimated to the dry heat of the desert.

The garage door slammed, and Mike walked back into the house with a shovel in one hand. "I'll be next door."

"Are you…"

"Yeah. It's the least I can do…"

"I can help."

Mike shook his head and swiped again at his

bloodshot eyes. It was apparent he'd been crying. "If you need anything…"

"I'll be fine."

"If you'd like to get out of those clothes… I have detergent in the laundry room if you want to hand wash them."

Ellie looked down at the front of her grungy, sweat-soaked tank top, and yanked at the fabric clinging to her damp skin. She wrinkled up her nose. She could only imagine how disgusting she looked, and smelled. Little did she know, Mike thought she looked amazing.

Clearing his throat, Mike tried not to stare at how the thin material clung to her voluptuous curves. When he went to speak, his voice cracked a little. Again, he cleared his throat. "You can help yourself to what you can find in my closet, you know, while your clothes dry."

"Oh, okay. I'll do that, thanks."

Mike gave her a curt nod, leaving Ellie alone in the house.

# Chapter 23

Amanda was in the middle of the hallway trying to figure out which way she should go. After several turns, she stopped and held still, waiting for the man to scream out again. From inside the restroom, she hadn't been able to tell which direction the voice had come from. In all honesty, she wasn't quite sure if she wanted to run toward it or run away from it. Her foot was now throbbing something fierce. She'd need to look for something to wrap it in. She'd rinsed it and patted it dry the best she could. She knew she could've done a better job cleaning her wound, but the man's screaming had interrupted her. She tried to put the sandal back on, but it hurt her foot too bad. She needed to find some gauze to wrap it properly. Besides, if she wandered around the halls with the sandals on, the hard soles made a loud, echoing sound against the tile. With them off, her movements were practically silent.

After a few minutes, Amanda made the decision to look for bandages, antibiotics, and perhaps painkillers. The last thing she needed was to get her foot infected. She followed the hallway to the right instead of back where she'd entered the hospital. She hobbled down the hall, walking on the ball of her right foot to avoid putting too much pressure on the wound.

Regardless of how careful she was with each step, she was leaving a trail of bloody footprints. When she stopped walking, she noticed a sign with an arrow pointing the way to the cafeteria. Her stomach clenched. She had the bag of corn tortillas under her arm that Maria had given her, but needed something a bit more substantial.

Stepping into the dark cafeteria, Amanda shivered. There was a light on in the back of the room where the food was kept. Waiting for her eyes to adjust, Amanda looked around the room, staring hard at the shadows. She couldn't shake the eerie feeling that someone infected may be lurking in the shadows. Or even worse, someone not infected that wished to do her harm. At least when someone was infected, they gave warning with that guttural growl. And they didn't seem to have the capacity to think, just attack. It was as if the fever destroyed all logic, driving them mad. At least, that's how it seemed. Amanda was still on the fence as to what was happening.

One of the things she noticed about the cafeteria was how clean it was. In fact, she realized most of the hospital was clean. She'd expected to find dead bodies everywhere, especially after the bodies piled up outside the hospital and the blood in the hall when she first entered the building. And she knew there were dead bodies in the front lobby of the hospital this morning.

*The staff must've been really working hard at keeping sections of the hospital quarantined,* she thought. They had to have had a decent sized clean-up crew. That thought gave Amanda a tiny glimmer of hope. There still might be a section of the hospital with doctors helping the infected. She might be able to find Jasper. Maybe even get help for herself. That's probably why she heard that man. He's probably in that section being treated.

Even as Amanda thought it, she didn't really believe it. She wanted to, but didn't. Setting down the sandals and bag of tortillas on a round table to free her hands, Amanda went into the area with the refrigerators and greedily gathered all sorts of food items. She piled everything that looked good onto a tray and took it back to the table she'd set her things down on. She looked around the room and wished she had a bag to carry her supplies in. There was a stack of plastic cafeteria trays, but nothing else. A tray wouldn't be of much use to her when walking home. She wandered to the back of the room in search of anything she could use. There had to be bags somewhere. She opened one of the fridges and grabbed a Granny Smith apple and took a bite. The bitterness tingled her tongue. There was a door at the back of the room. She wondered if it led to a storage room. If so, maybe she could find a box. A box wouldn't be as easy to carry, but it'd be better than a tray.

Gripping the door handle, Amanda was relieved to feel it easily turn and click. She pushed it down and yanked open the heavy door. The room was dark. She stepped inside.

*Bam!* The door slammed shut behind her. That's when she heard it. Deep guttural growls. They were close... Too close...

Spinning around, Amanda's hands flew to the cold surface of the door in search of the handle. She patted it up and down. It was too dark. She couldn't see anything. Couldn't find the handle...

*Crash!* Amanda jumped. Her voice caught in her throat, unable to scream. What sounded like a stack of boxes crashed to the floor beside her, hitting her leg as they fell. The growls became louder, more incessant.

Amanda ran her hands up and down the door frame. Her fingers found the handle and yanked down with all her might. She leaned into the heavy door, pushing it open and ran without looking behind her. She could hear the growls and heavy footsteps pounding the ground right behind her. The infected was pursuing her. Grabbing a chair, she glanced over her shoulder for only a second and tossed it, hoping to trip her pursuer. She was too afraid to stand still long enough to get a good look at him. But she did notice that she was being chased by a large, bald man, wearing a blue smock. He easily leaped over the chair.

Hurtling through the swinging cafeteria door, Amanda stumbled out into the hallway and took a sharp left. She could hear the infected man bashing through the door behind her. She needed to find a place to hide. She hoped the infected man hadn't realized she went down the hall to the left. She grabbed a door handle. *Locked.* She stumbled to the next door. *Locked.* There was a sign on the ceiling pointing the way to X-Rays. She grabbed another door handle and turned.

"Arrrrgggghhh…"

Amanda stopped dead in her tracks. Eyes large, she turned her head and made eye contact with her assailant. His golden eyes narrowed in his white, distorted face. Her heart pounded rapidly in her ears. The doorknob slipped beneath her sweaty palms as she tried again to twist it. *Locked.*

She turned to run toward the sign pointing to the X-Ray lab. A ferocious roar bellowed behind her. She ran as fast as she could down the hall when her foot slipped in her own blood. The running had opened the wound and blood was oozing out everywhere. Amanda tried to catch her balance, but couldn't. She landed hard on her right knee, just as the man leaped at her. The man's large body flew over the top of her, overshooting his leap. He hadn't expected her to fall down. His shoulder crashed into the wall at the end of the hall with a loud crunch. Even though the knee Amanda landed on stiffened and didn't want to budge, full of adrenaline, she managed to scramble to her feet, and race toward the X-ray lab. She prayed the door was unlocked. If not, she was at a dead end. The man snarled behind her.

To her surprise, the door to the lab easily swung open. However, there was no way to lock out her assailant. She stumbled through the small waiting room as the man pushed through the swinging door behind her. Ducking down behind the check-in desk, Amanda hoped that he hadn't seen her. On all fours, she squeezed herself beneath the desk, trying to be as quiet as she could. She eyed a rolling chair, not far from the desk opening. Grabbing one of the legs, she slowly pulled the chair in front of her.

Closing her eyes, she concentrated on slowing her breathing as she listened to the man thrashing about the waiting room. He was growling and crashing into things. Her body tensed as a loud thump landed on top of the desk. Amanda opened her eyes and watched as papers flew off the desk, scattering across the floor. A ballpoint pen also landed on the floor and rolled toward her. There was another loud thump above her. Then she watched the chair roll away from her. She wanted to freak out. If the man were to walk behind the desk, there'd be no doubt he'd find her. There was another loud crash and bang above her. A stapler and various other office supplies landed on the floor. Amanda's back tightened. She pushed herself as far under the desk as she could go. There was another loud crash. Amanda squeezed her eyes shut. She didn't want to look. She then felt the breeze of something heavy landing on the floor next to her hiding spot. She'd also heard the wheels of the rolling chair scrape across the floor and then crash as it tipped over.

Trembling, but still keeping her eyes shut, Amanda listened. The growling had ceased. There was no more crashing or banging. As she waited, her breathing slowed. Gathering her courage, she opened her eyes and peeked out from under the desk. The infected man was lying on the floor blocking the opening of the desk. His face was turned away from her. She figured he must've climbed up and fallen over the desk. He wasn't moving, yet Amanda was afraid he was still alive. If he was, she'd have no way to fight him or defend herself if he attacked. She looked around and eyed the ballpoint pen that'd rolled under the desk. Slowly and carefully, she clutched the pen in her hand, gripping it hard. It wasn't much, but at least it was something.

She watched the man's chest to see if he was breathing. It was hard to tell under the bulk of his blue smock. As far as she could tell, he wasn't, but she wasn't sure. She noticed that the back of the man's head and neck were puffed up with what looked like big white welts or blisters. His skin was just like the others, just like Jasper's had been. Amanda scooted herself toward the man, trying to stay as quiet as she could. Her body didn't want to cooperate with her. Her knee was stiff, her foot throbbing, and her arms and legs were cramping up. Grimacing, she scooted a bit closer to the man and stuck her head out from under the desk. If she wanted to stand, she'd need to move the man, lean on him, or somehow straddle him in order to get herself into a position to be able to get up. There was no way around him. She was trapped.

Amanda weighed her options; she could stay under the desk awhile longer to make sure he wasn't alive, or she could make a go of it. Neither option sounded good. If she were to stay put and the man was alive, and he rolled over, there was a good chance he'd attack her, spreading the infection or killing her. But, if she was to get up, and the man was still alive, he could attack her, spreading the infection or killing her. Both would result in fatality. Yet, if she were to get up, and was fast enough, she might be able to get away before the man could attack her. That is, of course, if he was still alive.

She remembered the mass of dead bodies surrounding the police car this morning. They'd all been infected people trying to get at her the night before. At some point, they just keeled over and died. Maybe that's what just happened to this man. She hadn't a clue how long he'd been infected. His blisters, or hives, or whatever the hell they were, were much more pronounced than Jasper's had been. Amanda frowned. Again, for the umpteenth time, she wondered if Jasper was still alive. She hated not knowing.

Eying the back of the infected man's head, Amanda tried to make a decision. She wasn't thrilled with either of her choices and didn't know what to do. She said a little prayer asking for guidance. She wasn't religious, but she did believe that angels were watching over her. She asked for their help.

Regardless of what she should or shouldn't do, Amanda didn't like the odds of her staying put. Plus, her body was cramping up something fierce. She needed to stretch her legs, find some painkillers, antibiotics, and something to bandage her foot with. The way her knee was throbbing, she was again contemplating finding an empty room, and locking herself in for the night. While she was at it, she'd also search for an Ace bandage or a knee brace of some sort. This wasn't the first time she'd injured her knee. There'd be no way she'd be able to walk home without a knee brace. Heck, not that she really should be walking with it this way period. She could feel the familiar swelling around the kneecap. A night of rest might do her good. At least she knew she was in a place where there was food and water in the cafeteria, even though she was afraid to venture back there to get it. It was still a better idea than trying to limp home the ten plus miles. She had absolutely no idea on how long it'd take her to walk home, or the types of danger she may encounter on the way. Not only did she have to worry about the infected attacking her, she had to worry about those still left alive. After her earlier encounter with the hoodlums, she was worried about who was lurking about.

Saying another prayer, this time for strength, Amanda did her best to spring into action. The only way out of her hiding place without shoving the man aside was to straddle him. She held her breath while placing an arm and leg on the other side of the man's body. She studied his face as she crawled over him. His eyes were closed. She could feel heat radiating from his body. He had to have been burning up in order for her to feel it the way she was. She remembered how Jasper had also been afflicted with a high fever. As she got to her feet, trying hard to stay quiet, her darn swollen knee locked into place, and she accidentally kicked the man's side as she stepped over him with her other leg.

"Grrrrr...!"

Amanda shrieked as the man's eyelids popped open. His golden eyes zeroed in on her.

He wasn't dead! The man grabbed hold of her ankle, and she screamed bloody murder. Without thinking, ballpoint pen still clutched in her hand, she leaned forward and jabbed it into the side of the man's neck. She yanked it out and jabbed him again. Letting go of the pen, she screamed again as hot red blood spurted out all over the front of her light pink V-neck shirt. The man's grasp released her ankle, and she watched as his yellow eyes rolled back in his head. Covering her mouth, she tried to stifle another involuntary scream that'd been rising in her throat, in case other infected people were around and could hear her. Amanda ran out of the X-ray lab waiting room, and back into the hallway. She pressed her back against the cool white wall and hyperventilated. Then she heard it again. The man she'd heard earlier when she was in the bathroom. This time his loud bellowing screams were coherent and yelling for help.

*** 

Feeling uneasy, Liam watched the woman run to the X-ray laboratory on one of the security monitors. He was thankful she'd decided to run in there. If she'd made a left turn, instead of a right, she'd have entered the stairwell, that'd lead her upstairs. That'd make their chances of being discovered greater. He didn't want to see the woman hurt by the infected man chasing her, but there was nothing he could do to help her without being seen. Besides, he was not allowed to interfere. All he could do was watch. Then he remembered Susan, who was in the other room, examining the little boy. They were already interfering. However, they were still trying to be discreet.

When Amanda disappeared from the view of the monitor, Liam was feeling a mixture of emotions. He was feeling happy, yet anxious, to see that the woman was still alive. She'd been hiding behind the check-in counter of the X-Ray laboratory. Somehow she'd managed to escape the infected man that'd been chasing her.

Liam glanced again at the clock on the wall. The incessant ticking was a constant reminder of how much time was passing. He was growing more anxious with each passing minute. Susan was taking a lot longer than expected. They needed to move. Quickly. Cloaking their tracking devices, that they'd recently removed, would soon become apparent, and so would their last known location. Time was of the essence. Or at least, that was the saying he'd recently learned, and it seemed to fit the situation.

Susan bustled into the room with a large insulated bag slung over her shoulder, just as Liam watched Amanda on the monitor, enter the hallway, and then press her back against the wall.

"We have another visitor," he said, still staring at the screen.

"Human?" Susan asked, coming up beside him.

"Yes."

"Good," she sighed with relief.

"So far… no signs of…" Liam didn't finish the thought. He was afraid to say it out loud.

Susan pulled off her latex gloves and leaned in to get a better look at the monitor Liam was viewing. "Is she infected?"

"Doesn't seem to be. She just alluded an infected one."

"So, she might be newly infected… is that her blood?" Susan tapped on the screen at Amanda's blood-soaked shirt.

"Doesn't appear to be," Liam said, and then changed the subject. "The boy's guardian is awake…" He glanced at another screen that showed Bill, secured to a bed, struggling against his restraints.

"I know," Susan stated. "He's been making a fuss. The sedative wore off sooner than expected, but at least I already got a genetic sample. It might prove to be useful, especially if the boy pans out. Maybe his resistance to the virus came from the father. I can shut him up… if I administer another dose, but then he'll see me…"

"You can wear a mask," Liam suggested. "His screams have gotten her attention." He tapped on the screen showing Amanda still leaning against a wall. "We can't chance getting caught."

"I don't think she's much of a risk, but you're right, we don't need more complications." Susan thought about it for a moment. "Don't worry about him. Let him holler. She'll find him and undo his restraints."

"You don't need him?"

"No."

"Are you done with the child?"

"Not quite. I need more time and better equipment. The medical equipment here is barbaric. I want to scan his brain. See if the fever has done long-term damage…"

"We haven't got time for that," Liam said. "And we can't go back to the lab. We'll need to make do with human equipment. Ours can be traced."

"I suppose."

"We'll have to release the boy."

"I'm not finished…"

"We can't take him with us."

Susan sighed. "I *need* more time."

"We don't *have* more time. And there's no way to go undetected. You know that."

Susan exhaled loudly. She didn't like the idea of leaving such a superb specimen behind. "I thought you'd say that. As a precaution, I've microchipped him," she explained. "We can monitor the boy… locate him for further study as needed."

"Good." Liam strummed his fingers on the desktop. "If we don't leave soon, we won't be alive to do any further studies."

"It won't be as convenient…"

"Convenience is a luxury we no longer have. Are you ready to go?"

"Almost," she said, setting down the large, silver, insulated bag she'd been carrying, on top of a long rectangular table against the wall. She rummaged through the contents making sure she hadn't forgotten anything. "I've collected blood samples and then hooked the boy up to an IV. He's severely dehydrated," she explained while resealing the insulated bag. "I'll need to unhook the IV before we go… then I should check on him one more time…"

Suddenly the security monitors started to go out, alerting them to danger. Static was taking over each screen, one by one. "Time's up." Liam's grey eyes grew large. "They're on to us. Damn!"

"What about the boy? He's still hooked up…"

"The woman will find him."

"We don't know that. What if *they* find him first?"

"That's a chance we'll have to take."

"We *need* him!"

Liam glared at her. "Not an option! Let's go."

Susan was about to protest but knew that Liam was right. They were out of time. If the boy died, or even worse, fell into *their* hands, she doubted that they'd find another unique specimen to study before the human race became extinct. Not wanting to leave the boy behind, but knowing there was no other choice she reluctantly followed Liam to an emergency exit, to make their escape.

\*\*\*

When Mike returned, he found Ellie wearing one of his T-shirts, a burgundy one. She was sound asleep on the couch, with a book spread open across her chest. He felt bad having left her alone for so long. He stood there staring at her while thinking about how wrong it was to fantasize about how sexy she looked sleeping in his shirt. He couldn't help but wonder if she had anything on underneath.

Shaking his head, he forced the naughty thoughts from his mind and focused on how dark it was in the living room. He'd had all the blinds in the house shut to try to keep out the desert heat. When the sun set in the next couple of hours, he'd be able to open the windows, to try to cool the place down. Even though it was still cooler inside than it was outside, he found the air stifling. He glanced again at Ellie and noticed sweat glistening across her brow.

Tearing himself away from ogling her, Mike headed for the laundry room to retrieve the emergency candles he kept for power outages, a couple of flashlights, and his stash of batteries. Once he gathered the items, he set them down on the kitchen table. He found a lighter in the back of his junk drawer in the kitchen and slipped it into his pocket. He then went around the house strategically setting up candles. He'd wait until the sun was completely set before lighting them, to make them last longer.

He and Ellie were going to have to come up with a plan to figure out what they were going to do. He'd talk to her about it once she awoke, or maybe early in the morning. He didn't want to stress her out because he knew she needed rest. Regardless, they couldn't stay there. Even though his home was well equipped, and he had everything they'd need for survival for quite a while, the summer Nevada heat would kill them. Without electricity, the high temperatures, well into the 100s, would roast them alive. They needed to move to a milder climate. Mike wasn't a Doomsday-Sayer, never had been. In fact, he was a glass half-full kind of guy. But, with what he'd been witnessing, he couldn't imagine life going back to normal anytime soon. The last he'd heard, before the radio stations went out, this crazy epidemic had hit worldwide. There was nowhere to run. They'd need to sit down, do some brainstorming, and come up with a plan for survival.

Mike climbed the staircase, entered his bedroom, and put a candle on the matching walnut nightstands on both sides of his bed. He'd already planned to give Ellie his bed for the night, and he'd crash on the uncomfortable twin bed in the guest room. He then wandered into the master bathroom. Since there was no window in there, he decided to light that candle now, and placed it on the counter while he cleaned up. He turned on the faucet to the shower. He knew it wouldn't be long before he had no hot water. Heck, he wasn't even sure about how long there'd even be running water. He stripped off his sweat-soaked clothes and was about to step into the shower when he heard Ellie.

"Oh," she said, startled, standing in the doorway of the bathroom. "I'm sorry… I should have knocked…" Her eyes examined his body in the flickering candlelight. Once she realized that he'd caught her staring, she averted her gaze. "I'll just let you…"

"Wait," he said before she could leave the room. "It won't be long before we run out of water…" He placed a strong hand on Ellie's shoulder, stopping her from leaving. She turned to face him. When their eyes met, Mike's lips hungrily met hers in a passionate kiss. Before her brain had a chance to register what was happening, Mike was removing her T-shirt and guiding her into the shower. "We need to conserve water," he said, then cleared his throat.

"Oh, really?" she teased, not about to argue with him. For the first time, since the world began to crumble around her, Ellie smiled a genuine smile.

# Chapter 24

Following the man's cries, Amanda crept along the halls. She found a staircase and climbed the stairs. She was beyond frightened at the prospect of what she might find. So frightened in fact, that she no longer felt the stiffness of her knee or the gash in her foot. She *did* feel the coolness of the tile beneath her feet which she was thankful for. It was the only thing keeping her grounded. Her head was swimming, and she had the odd sensation that at any moment she'd float away, as if in a dream.

The man had stopped making sounds. Amanda wanted to call out to him. Let him know she was there and that he wasn't alone. She was there to help him. But the words stuck in her throat, intimidated at the thought of what she might find. What if he was infected? What if he was in the stages of fever and craziness? She decided that it was best to keep quiet until she knew exactly what she was up against.

Barefoot, Amanda's steps were silent; she'd forgotten all about her sandals and had left them behind. She'd make sure to retrieve them later, before her long walk home. The first door she came to, at the top of the stairs, was open. She peeked inside. There were security monitors against one of the walls. All were showing nothing but static. The fluorescent light fixtures above, buzzed and flickered. There was an emergency exit sign to her left. She'd remember that, if needed. With careful footsteps, she continued walking until she came to the next door on the right. Clutching the handle, she said a little prayer for protection, and then lightly pushed down the handle. The door easily clicked open. She peeked inside. A little boy was lying in a bed hooked up to what she believed was an IV.

Forgetting her fears, Amanda rushed to his side. His face was a little puffy, but different than the other infected people she'd come in contact with. It appeared that the welts on his pale hands and face were drying up. Some were scabbed over. *Was he recovering?* No longer hesitating, Amanda touched the boy's forehead and cheeks. He was cool to the touch. No fever. His eyelids flicked open. She took a quick step backwards. His eyes were a cross between yellow and brown. She wondered if he'd attack her.

"Mom?" the boy whispered. Hearing him speak was a relief.

Finding her voice, Amanda approached the bed. "No, sweetie. My name's Amanda." She looked around the hospital room. She hadn't seen any other signs of life in the hospital besides this little boy and hearing the hollering of that man. And the man may or may not be infected. She wondered if the little boy was being treated before the doctors and nurses had disappeared. She knew she couldn't just leave him there alone, unattended. It took her a moment, but she figured out how to undo the IV and other equipment that was hooked up to the child. "How do you feel?"

"Tired," he said. "And my stomach hurts… hungry…"

"Well, let's see if we can find your parents. And then we'll get something to eat," she said, keeping her voice low. "What's your name?"

"Benjamin."

Amanda spied a stuffed bear on the floor next to the bed. "Is that yours?"

Benjamin nodded. Amanda scooped the bear up from the floor and handed it to the boy.

"Okay, Benjamin. We'll have to stay quiet," she instructed, taking his small hand in hers. "There are a lot of sick people. We don't want to disturb them."

"Is that blood?" the boy asked, staring at Amanda's shirt.

Amanda looked down at her blood-soaked T-shirt. She nodded. "We're going to have to stay quiet," she repeated. "Okay?"

The boy nodded his understanding. He was a little wobbly, and leaned into Amanda as they ventured down the hall. Again, she heard the man's voice. It was more of a moan, and then he coughed. She stopped in front of the closed door that she thought the voice had been coming from.

"You stay here," she whispered. "I'm going to have a quick look inside." The handle turned easily. Amanda opened the door a crack and peered in. There was a man strapped to a hospital bed. "I'll be right back."

Amanda stepped into the room and hesitated until Bill turned his head to look at her. His eyes were blue, and there were no signs of hives. He wasn't infected. "What do you want with me?" he asked.

"Um… I don't know what you mean?"

"Why'd you do this to me?" Bill tugged at the restraints, pinning his arms to his side.

"I – I didn't. I heard you…" she said, turning to look at the door, "your voice…"

Registering that Amanda wasn't the one that'd drugged him, and strapped him to the bed, he struggled again against his restraints. "Undo me."

Amanda wasn't sure if she should. *Maybe he's dangerous,* she thought. *Maybe there's a reason why he's restrained.*

"Please," Bill said. "I was looking for someone to help my son…"

"Dad?" Benjamin stood in the doorway.

"Benji?" Tears filled Bill's eyes. "Ben!"

"This is your dad?" Amanda asked. The little boy stumbled to the bedside, dropped his bear on the floor and hugged his father. Amanda quickly worked at the restraints trying to free the man when she heard voices. A lot of voices. Deep voices. And marching. Bill heard them, too.

"Hurry," he said.

The urgency of the situation only made Amanda more nervous. Her fingers fumbled with the restraints. Eventually, she'd managed to unlatch him. Bill sat up and then pressed his fingers to his forehead.

"You okay?" Amanda whispered.

"Dizzy," he said. "Whatever they gave me… I can still feel it."

"Can you get up?"

Bill slid off the bed and almost fell over. He grabbed hold of a bed rail to support himself. "Go hide. Take Ben with you." The room was spinning out of control. "I'll be all right."

Benjamin grabbed hold of his dad's leg and squeezed. He wasn't going to go anywhere without his father.

"Come on," Amanda said, lightly touching his back. "Take my hand."

Benjamin refused to acknowledge her. He hugged his dad's leg tighter.

"Ben, go with the nice woman," Bill said. "I'll catch up."

"No," he sobbed.

Amanda's eyes went to the door. She could hear the voices echoing from downstairs. It wouldn't be long before they came upstairs. The sound of heavy boots clashing against the tile floor frightened her. However, she knew there was a chance that her fears were irrational. *What if they were there to help them?* Then again, what if they weren't there to help them.

Remembering the *Emergency Exit* sign a couple of doors down, Amanda had an idea. "Do you think you'd be able to make it down the hall?"

"I can try," Bill said.

"I saw an *Emergency Exit*."

"Okay," he said. "Ben, I need you to let go of my leg."

Benjamin looked up at his dad and reluctantly let go of his leg. Amanda took hold of the little boy's hand, handed him his bear, and led him into the hallway. Bill stumbled out behind them and leaned against the wall for support against the constant spinning in his head.

Amanda heard the heavy stomping of boots coming up the stairs. There'd be no way they could possibly reach the Emergency Exit before being found. "Change of plans," she whispered, tugging on Bill's sleeve. "This way…"

Amanda practically dragged Benjamin with her, and Bill somehow managed to keep up, as she hurried down the hallway in the opposite direction. She took a sharp left, hoping they'd be completely out of sight by the time the visitors reached the top of the stairs. Breathing hard, Amanda wondered what to do next. Should they try all the doors and find a room to hide in? Or should they keep running down the hallway? What if, whomever, these heavy booted men were, spotted them?

Not knowing what to do, but also not wanting to lock themselves inside of a room with no escape, Amanda rushed down the hall, pulling Benjamin along. He kept glancing over his shoulder to look at his Dad. His constant glances kept Bill focused.

At the end of the hall, they had a choice, left or right. Amanda chose right. As soon as she'd turned the corner, she heard a man's voice yell out. Her eyes widened. She looked over her shoulder at Bill who'd been seen as he stumbled around the corner to catch up.

"Run!" he yelled, waving at Amanda. "Run!"

Yanking hard on Benjamin's hand, she heard his cries for his dad as she dragged him down another hallway. They ran past two elevators. She then spotted a sign for stairs. Just as she reached out to grab the doorknob to enter the stairwell, the door flung open. Amanda froze in her tracks. A man dressed in dark green cammies, aiming a gun that looked like a toy, blocked their escape.

# Day Three

# Chapter 25

Sweating, Ellie awoke feeling overheated. She'd kicked off the sheets at some point in the middle of the night, but was enveloped in Mike's arms. As much as she loved feeling his strong, muscular arms protectively wrapped around her, she was dying of heat. One of Mike's arms was draped over her bare chest. As she carefully lifted his arm, he turned over. She watched as he then hugged a fluffy pillow to his chest.

Ellie scooted out of bed and walked over to the open window. As she approached, she could feel the morning's air seeping through the screen. It was much cooler outside. The sun was beginning to rise, lighting up the world, blanketing her surroundings in a soft orange glow. Closing her eyes, she focused on the coolness of the air, enveloping her damp skin. Normally, she'd have worried about standing there, naked in the window. She wouldn't want anyone to see her. As reality set in, she opened her eyes and frowned at the reason why she wasn't worried. As heavenly as the night had been with Mike, reality was hitting her, hard. Ellie's brown eyes focused in on the few dead bodies lying in the street and on the sidewalk. The acrid scent of decay was beginning to seep in through the screen of the upstairs window. She knew the scent would grow stronger, even unbearable, as the day grew warmer.

"Hey…" Mike's groggy voice startled her. Ellie turned around, suddenly feeling embarrassed and exposed. She crossed her arms over her breasts.

"I needed some air," she answered, wishing she had a robe or something to cover up with.

Mike grinned. "No need to feel shy," he said upon noticing how uncomfortable Ellie was feeling. "You're beautiful."

Ellie shook her head and walked over to the foot of the bed where the sheets had been kicked aside. Grabbing the burgundy colored sheet, she wrapped it around her body, covering herself. "I'm sorry about last night," she said, sitting down next to him.

"Sorry about what?" Mike propped up his head, leaning on his elbow. Ellie tried to keep her eyes from wandering and focused her gaze on his face.

"You know…"

"No," he said. "I don't know."

Ellie gnawed on her bottom lip. "The world is falling apart… There are dead bodies in the street…"

"Yes. I've noticed."

"Well, last night shouldn't have happened."

Mike sat up, thinking this over, and then asked, "Why not?"

Ellie shrugged. "It just shouldn't have."

"Are you attracted to me?" he asked very seriously.

Ellie grinned and let out a nervous laugh. "Well, yes."

"Okay…" he said. "I'm also attracted to you… Would you still be attracted to me if the world wasn't… as you've said… falling apart?"

Ellie felt her cheeks flush. "Yes."

"Then that settles it. I rest my case."

Ellie grinned.

"Now," he said. "On a more serious note, we need to put together a survival plan."

The words, *survival plan*, made Ellie's stomach lurch. She knew he was right; they needed some sort of plan. Regardless, the thought frightened her. "Okay," she said. "What's the plan?"

"That's what I want to discuss with you. We can't stay here."

Ellie scrunched up her forehead. "Why not?"

"The climate," he explained. "It's too hot. Without electricity, the heat will more than likely kill us."

"Oh," she said, knowing that was true. "Then where do we go?"

"You're from San Diego?"

"Yes, San Diego County. I live in Oceanside."

"The climate there would be more habitable without electricity. Do you have any family there?"

"No. They're in Florida… I lost contact with them… I don't even know if…" Ellie hesitated. She didn't like the odds of whether or not they were still alive. "I, I have a dog, Max. My neighbors are watching him for me… or at least, I hope they still are."

"Then we need to retrieve your dog. Unfortunately, I don't think Florida is doable… at least, not at the moment. Once we know exactly what we're dealing with, we'll work on a plan to meet up with your family. Okay?"

Ellie nodded. She prayed her family was okay. However, she did feel relieved that they would go get Max. Her poor little pup had been in the back of her mind. She'd been trying not to think the worst. "Okay… we'll head for Oceanside and go get Max. Then what? Can you imagine the amount of infected people there? The amount of bodies? We won't be able to stay there. Not long anyway."

"I've thought of that," he said. "We'll need to scour the coast for an area with fresh water and a smaller population. Highly populated areas will be riddled with disease from the corpses."

Ellie's stomach leaped into her throat at the thought of all the rotting corpses. "We might be able to get a boat," she suggested. "Do you know how to sail?"

"Um, no. I'm now kicking myself for never having learned," Mike said. "But that's not a bad idea. We'll keep that in mind for a backup plan."

"What about your family?"

"I don't have any family."

"Oh." Ellie wanted to ask him questions about it. Surely Mike had to have family somewhere. She decided that now wasn't the time to pry. If he wanted to elaborate, he would. Right now, she'd focus her questions on their *survival plan*. "How are we going to get to California? I was thinking about that yesterday. I can't imagine the freeways being clear. Do you have a map? Maybe we can stop at a gas station…"

"I know the backroads," he said. "I was stationed in Camp Pendleton, quite a few years back.

We'd take weekend road trips to Vegas. I know all the short cuts."

"I see." Ellie smiled. Since she lived near Camp Pendleton, she'd dated a few Marines in the past and was familiar with the base.

"Let's eat some breakfast, and then pack up supplies. I'd like to get moving before it gets too hot."

"Okay," she said in agreement. "Let me get dressed first."

"I say we eat first, and then get dressed." Mike grabbed hold of Ellie's sheet and pulled her closer to him. "I can use a little dessert."

Ellie had to admit; she liked his idea better.

\*\*\*

Even though Benjamin wasn't Amanda's child, she protectively kept him wrapped up in her arms throughout the night. Bill had been kept separate from them upon capture. The men had locked them in a small waiting room on the first floor. One man stood outside the door. They appeared to be in military gear, but Amanda knew they weren't. Whatever they were wearing, it was foreign. Several times she'd overheard the men speaking in the hallway. She'd pinpointed three distinct voices. They didn't know she was eavesdropping. Or, if they did, they didn't care. She believed the latter to be true.

"We're *not* to interfere."

"Keeping them here is interfering."

"They're not aware of that."

"The traitors were here for a reason."

"I don't like the look of the boy. Maybe we should…?"

"Eradicate the problem? Maybe."

"That's interfering."

"Do nothing until we receive orders."

Sitting in a chair, Amanda had dozed off and on throughout the night. When she awoke in the morning, Benjamin was no longer in her arms. He was sitting in a chair next to her eating a bag of cheese puffs. She noticed two bottles of water, several bags of chips, and what appeared to be chocolate chip cookies, had been left on a chair across from them. She figured that the food must've been brought in while she was sleeping. "Where'd you get those?"

With orange cheese coated fingers, Benjamin offered her a cheese puff.

Amanda shook her head. "Um, no thanks."

"The nice man brought them."

"Nice man?" she asked.

Benjamin nodded. "He said we can go home soon."

"He *did*?" Amanda asked, feeling leery. She got up and walked over to the door. She could hear the murmur of muffled voices but couldn't hear what they were saying. They were purposely keeping their voices down. Earlier, they hadn't seemed to care whether she heard them or not. It made her nervous that everything was suddenly hush, hush. That couldn't be a good sign. Amanda grabbed a bottle of water and a bag of plain potato chips when the door swung open, startling her. She nearly dropped the bottle of water and caught it in midair. Two men pushed Bill through the doorway. He stumbled forwards, trying to catch his balance before hitting the ground. One of the men walked over to Benjamin and grabbed hold of his arm.

"Ow!" he screamed. "You're hurting me!" The man squeezed harder and dragged him into the hallway. "You used to be nice!"

"Orders changed," he replied. "I no longer *need* to be nice."

"Ben!" Bill hollered, getting up from the floor. "Leave my son alone!"

"Where are you taking him?" Amanda screamed. The man stepped in front of her, blocking her view.

An unexpected high pitch whistle, which seemed to come out of nowhere, caught her attention. It also caught the man's attention. He spun around. "What the…" *Zap! Zap!*

There was another high pitch whistle, louder this time. Amanda took a step back. *Zap!* An electric charge encompassed the man's body. He began to convulse right before her eyes and disintegrated into a pile of thick black ash. Benjamin came running back into the room and latched onto his father's leg.

A tall, slim man with sandy blonde hair was standing in the doorway, holding one of those guns that Amanda thought looked like a toy. It obviously wasn't.

"Who are you?" she asked.

"My name's Liam," he said. "We don't have much time."

"How'd… how'd you do that?" Amanda stared at the pile of ashes on the white tiles.

"Do you want a lesson in physics or to get out of here before more come?"

Amanda wrinkled up her forehead with confusion, trying to make sense of what'd just happened.

"We're not going anywhere until you tell us

what's going on!" Bill demanded.

"What are you still doing here?" Susan asked, appearing next to Liam. "We need to move!"

Amanda studied the short, sturdily built woman with dark, shoulder-length hair. She felt the woman looked harmless enough.

"They're refusing to leave," Liam said to her. "I told you this was a bad idea. We should've left them."

"We want answers!" Bill demanded.

"Susan is the one who saved your life," Liam said. "I would've left you. It's not our place to interfere."

"It *is* now," Susan said, pushing past Liam. "There's a lot to explain and very little time."

"How do we know you're here to help us?" Amanda asked. "You just killed, vaporized, or whatever the hell you did, to that guy."

Liam looked down at the pile of ash at Amanda's feet and raised an eyebrow.

"I'll give you the quick version," Susan said. "We're scientists… my name is Susan, and this is Liam. You have contracted a virus that is common amongst our kind, just as a cold virus is to yours. Our reaction to the virus is not fatal. Since we're here only to observe, we have strict orders not to interfere. Interfering is punishable by death under our planetary laws."

"A virus?" Amanda asked, trying to wrap her head around this outlandish explanation. This wasn't at all what she'd expected to hear. "You mean this… this *infection*?"

"Yes."

"I don't understand. Where are you from?"

"Government," Bill said. "The government did this, didn't they? They unleashed this *thing*. Now they're trying to clean up their mess undetected!"

"Not *your* government," Susan explained. "Ours... *The Order*."

"Terrorists!" Bill barked. "I should've..."

"No!" Liam stepped in. "We're scientists, and this virus was an accident."

"And you're not allowed to help us?" Amanda shook her head, baffled. "Why? *You* caused it. You just said you did! People are dying..."

"There are those of us that want to help you. We've formed a resistance," Susan explained. "We know that we're responsible for your demise. We're trying to help you before... before it's too late."

Liam stepped back out into the hall and looked to his left. "I thought I heard something."

"We'd better go," Susan said. "If we're caught, they'll kill us, *all* of us. Your species is no longer under an order of protection."

"Your answer isn't good enough," Bill stated, patting his son's back.

"Our *species*? Planetary law? Who are you?"

"There's no time to explain."

"Why are you helping us?" Amanda asked. "If you're not to interfere... and why do they want to kill us?"

Frustrated, Susan sighed. She knew she'd better give them an answer. However, they were wasting valuable time. "A new instruction was given by *The Order* to wipe out what's left of huma kind if the need arises. This virus has spread too far. An intergalactic war has been declared between our two planets. There are those opposed to aiding in the extinction of a planetary race, and there are those that see the plentiful resources your planet has to offer us since we're struggling for survival on our homeworlds, and there aren't many of you left alive... Now, hurry, follow me!"

"Extinction of the human race?" Amanda's stomach lurched. "Are you telling me...?"

"Yes," Liam said, answering Amanda's unasked question. "We're not from *here*. We're *not* human. Enough questions. Let's go. I *hear* them!"

Amanda didn't hear anything out of the ordinary, but wasn't about to argue with him.

Bill stayed silent, mulling this over while holding onto Benjamin's hand. He was deep in thought. They quickly followed Susan down the hall, Amanda at Bill's side, and Liam trailing behind, making sure they weren't being followed.

Relief washed over Amanda once they exited the building unnoticed. But a new fear replaced the last. "What do we do now?" Amanda asked, thinking of the food and medical supplies inside the hospital. Now she was back outside with no shoes, no antibiotics, no bandages, a swollen knee, no food and no water. Even worse, an alien race wanted to wipe them out.

"Find shelter," Susan said. "As long as you keep your heads down and don't bother anyone, no one will interfere. They'll leave you alone. We're a peaceful race."

"Peaceful race? Aren't they trying to kill us?" Amanda looked nervously over her shoulder. They'd just exited the same way she'd originally entered the hospital.

"Peaceful race my ass!" Bill muttered.

Susan didn't respond. She'd always believed that her race was peaceful. But as of late, she'd been learning otherwise. She'd never gone against the rules before. And as of right now, she and Liam were being hunted by *The Order*, because she'd been running tests on the boy. She didn't want to be the cause of the human races' extinction. She and Liam, along with a select few, had removed their tracking devices. Whether or not *The Order* figured out why or whom she as examining, she wasn't quite sure. She hoped that they had rescued the boy before reports had been made to the homeworld.

Liam stepped in. "Go! Before they see us! Keep to yourself and get as far away from the hospital as possible. More will be coming."

"You're not coming with us?" Amanda asked.

"If we need you," Liam said, aggravated that the humans had so many menial questions with obvious answers, "we'll find you. Go now! Hurry!"

Bill grabbed Amanda's arm and tugged. She allowed him to guide her. "There's got to be an ambulance, a car, or something here. We won't be able to get far on foot."

"We won't be able to get very far by car, either."

When Amanda glanced over her shoulder, Susan and Liam were gone. Bill was spinning around, searching, and trying to figure out what they should do. Then Amanda remembered the golf cart.

# Chapter 26

They'd been driving for a couple of hours now, and it was hotter than hell. To conserve gas, they weren't using the air conditioning. The windows of the SUV were rolled all the way down and scorching hot air, unlike that of an oven, was blasting Ellie in the face. Earlier, she'd tried rolling up her window, but then she felt like she was boiling in her own sweat. She wasn't sure what was worse, being fried to death or boiled alive. Ellie kept her discomfort to herself because she didn't want to bother Mike. He was probably just as uncomfortable even though he hadn't let on that he was. Besides, there was nothing he could do to make their situation any better except for turning on the air conditioning. A part of her was tempted to ask, the other part of her eyed the gas gauge. The last thing they needed was to run out of gas in the middle of the desert.

That morning, after breakfast, they'd filled the SUV with supplies, packing everything from camping gear to batteries to food to water. Mike had a couple of ice chests, and had also obtained one from his neighbor's garage, to fill with perishables from his fridge and freezer that were still good.

To lighten the mood a bit, Mike had slid a CD

into the stereo. Ellie had been surprised when Hip Hop and R&B consumed the speakers. She'd thought Mike would be a Country music sort of guy. She wasn't sure why she pegged him for country music. She just did. She herself liked pretty much everything. Well, everything except Heavy Metal. She'd never been able to get her groove on with Heavy Metal. Ellie closed her eyes, listening to the music. It was nice to be able to feel a little bit of familiarity in this new, strange, nightmarish world, as she listened to the lyrics to one of her favorite songs.

Feeling pain in her neck, Ellie tried to move. Her neck was stiff, and her shoulder blades ached. She hadn't even realized she'd been sleeping. The combination of heat, and the stress of the last couple of days had obviously taken its toll on her. Ellie massaged the knot in her neck while looking around. Mike wasn't in the SUV with her. They were parked in front of an abandoned gas station, somewhere in the desert. Beautiful, desert mountains against crystal blue skies surrounded them.

Flinging open the door, Ellie slid out of the passenger seat. It was hotter than hell outside. Her skin sizzled as the sunlight hit it. There was still no sign of Mike, and she needed to use the restroom. She walked up to the front door of the gas station and gave a tug at the door. It was locked. Ellie cupped her hands and pressed her face to the glass. No one was inside. She was afraid to wander too far from the vehicle in case Mike came back. She didn't want him to worry about her, or even worse, leave her out there, but at the same time, she felt like her bladder was about to explode.

Ellie wearily eyed the SUV. She doubted Mike

would leave her behind. *Would he?* She couldn't imagine that he would. Pushing the negative thoughts from her mind, she decided to walk around to the back of the building. Sometimes gas stations had after hour's bathrooms around the back. Maybe Mike was using the restroom. To her relief, there were two bathroom doors. She grabbed the knob to the woman's bathroom. It was locked. She then tried the men's and was happy to find it unlocked, but a little worried that Mike wasn't there. She peeked inside. It wasn't very clean, it smelled of sulfur, and it was both dark and creepy. No windows. Knowing it was useless, she tried flipping the light switch anyway. Nothing happened.

They'd packed flashlights, but Ellie wasn't about to take the time to go search for them. She could either suck it up and pee in the dark, or find something to prop the door open. It'd only take her a minute or two to go. And it wasn't like anyone was around to see her. From the parking lot, she'd seen small houses dotted all around the gas station, but she figured that if the habitants were still alive, they were probably inside, trying their best to stay cool. She hadn't seen anyone else wandering around the gas station. So it'd probably be okay to leave the door open.

Ellie spied a good sized, rounded, gray rock in the sand, baking in the sun. She picked it up and nearly dropped it. It was so hot that her fingertips were burning. Ellie quickly set the rock down. Using her foot, she scooted it in place to keep the heavy door propped open.

A couple of minutes later, Ellie emerged from the bathroom feeling a hundred times better. She was about to round the building when she heard the familiar guttural growl of an infected person. She froze in her tracks. A man with a bushy black beard stumbled around the building obstructing her view of the SUV. Golden eyes glared at her through puffed up white skin.

Her mind racing, Ellie stood completely still, trying to figure out her next move. *Run past the infected man to the SUV?* She'd probably never make it. The infected seemed to take on extraordinary speed and agility. *Run into the desert and hope that he didn't follow?* Again, he'd be too fast for her if he pursued her. *Bathroom?*

The man lifted one side of his upper lip exposing brown, tobacco-stained teeth. Ellie nailed him as a chain smoker. Shifting her eyes left to the right, she knew she needed to do something fast, before he added the color of her blood to his stained teeth.

Without so much as a blink of an eye, Ellie sprinted to the bathroom. The rock was still in place, propping the door open. She grabbed the handle and tried to slam the door closed, but the stupid rock was in the way. The man's arm reached in and grabbed the side of her shirt. Ellie screamed, while leaning into the door. The damn rock was keeping it from closing. With her foot, she kicked at the rock, but she was also leaning her full weight into the door, to try to keep the man out. The rock wouldn't budge. He was clawing at her shirt, snarling wildly. Ellie could hear the stitches go as the material ripped apart. The man managed to shove his other arm through the gap and grabbed hold of her hair.

Screaming, Ellie swung at his hand with her fist,

trying to get him to let go of her. In the process, she'd accidentally shifted her body weight, and the man came stumbling into the bathroom nearly taking them both down to the floor. He still had a hold of Ellie and slammed her up against the bathroom wall, one hand tangled in her hair.

The rotten stench of his putrid breath penetrated her senses. The rock had moved in the struggle, and the door slammed shut, bathing them in darkness. Ellie screamed out again and fought with all her might. She wasn't going to go down without a fight. Her knee connected with the man's genitals but it didn't seem to affect him. Her hands came in contact with the man's face, and she dug her fingernails into his flesh as he tried to chomp down on her neck. She could feel her thumb push into one of the man's eye sockets, with a horrible squishing sensation. She continued to push until the man released her, bellowing out in pain, before his teeth were able to make contact with her skin.

At that moment, sunlight blinded Ellie when the bathroom door flung open. Mike was standing just outside the restroom. The infected man, with one good eye, turned toward the light like a magnet and charged at him. The door slammed shut again. This time Ellie was alone in the dark. *Bang!* Chills coursed through Ellie's body at the deafening sound of a gunshot. Her knees suddenly felt weak. She could feel sticky blood on her hands. Her back slid down the wall until her rear-end made contact with the cement ground.

"You okay?" Mike asked, after propping the bathroom door open.

Ellie didn't answer. She couldn't seem to find

her voice. Her body was shaking, and tears were rolling down her cheeks.

Mike crouched down in front of her. He placed a hand to her cheek, and gently wiped away a tear. "It's okay now."

Ellie nodded. That's all she could manage to do. And even that, seemed like a challenge.

"Did he hurt you?"

Ellie shook her head, *no*, even though she wasn't sure. She didn't think he had hurt her. At the moment she was too numb to know. She wasn't feeling any pain. Not physical pain, anyway. Was she in shock? Maybe.

Mike looked at her bloody hands, torn shirt, and disheveled hair. "Let's get you cleaned up."

Ellie let him help her to her feet and lead her over to the sink. He turned on the tap, and in stunned silence, Ellie stood there as he began to wash the blood off her hands.

***

The golf cart was working out better than Amanda had hoped. Her nerves were beginning to settle the farther away they got from the hospital. She kept looking behind her expecting to see them being followed by people with crazy sci-fi ray guns, but so far no one was.

The golf cart had been useful with the traffic jams and crashed cars. A few times, she'd worried that they'd have to get out and walk, but somehow, Bill had managed to get them through tight spots. And so far, they hadn't come across any infected people on the road. Well, not ones still alive anyway. Most of the cars had been abandoned or the owners dead.

Amanda tried not to dwell on the death around her. She tried not to think of Jasper being amongst the dead. She tried to focus her thoughts on getting away from the hospital, and getting away from the people, or aliens, or whatever the hell they were that wanted to kill them. She still couldn't wrap her head around what Liam and Susan had told them.

*Could it be true? Was this infection brought to Earth by aliens? Was the human race truly dying out? How many people were still alive?*

Maybe Susan and Liam were delusional. Maybe not. Maybe she was the one that was delusional. She didn't know anymore. She felt as though she didn't know anything. And she didn't really care at this point either. Thinking about it was distracting her. Right now, she needed to concentrate on finding shelter. She just wanted to get home. Once she was home, she'd be able to think more clearly, and figure out what to do next.

"Hey," Bill said, snapping Amanda out of her thoughts. "Where do you live?"

"Just a few more miles down the road. How 'bout you?"

"Same," Bill answered, remembering his wife. He couldn't go back home. He couldn't take Benjamin there. Not until after he'd taken care of things. He'd have to go back alone and… He didn't want to think about it. It didn't seem real. And he didn't know if he had the strength to see Joanna that way. He wondered if Benjamin remembered what he'd done. Bill prayed that he didn't, but he found it odd that Benjamin hadn't been asking for her. Bill prayed that Benjamin would never learn the truth.

Amanda gave Bill directions. When her

apartment building was finally in sight, her heart thumped in her chest. She couldn't believe they'd actually made it. She made it home.

Even though she was excited to be home, the street was vacant. No one was around. Everything around them was abnormally quiet which really bothered Amanda. She kept expecting someone to jump out and attack them. Bill turned into the parking lot of the apartment buildings. They were spread out amongst rolling hills, trees and grass.

"I'm in the G building," Amanda said, pointing in the direction of her home. She noticed that the golf cart was now moving at a snail's pace.

"Needs to be charged," Bill said. "I'm surprised the battery lasted as long as it did."

Amanda frowned because she doubted her building had electricity since it seemed to be out everywhere else. She was hoping to be able to use the golf cart to get around town when needed. There was too much traffic congestion in spots for a regular sized vehicle. However, she was more than thankful to have made it home before it died. "I didn't realize it was electric."

"Not sure if we'll be able to charge it…"

"We're almost there." Amanda pointed to her building, next to a fenced-in grassy area with bright red benches and obstacles for dogs. "It's the one near the dog park."

"Nice complex," Bill said, pulling into a vacant parking space.

"Yeah, it's okay," Amanda said. "Expensive as hell. But what isn't out here?"

"You won't have to worry 'bout that anymore." Bill got out of the cart and grunted, straightening his back. He then looked at Benjamin who was sound asleep in the backseat. He gently shook the boy's shoulder.

Amanda watched as Bill then touched his son's forehead. She knew he was checking for signs of a fever. He looked up at her and grinned. She returned the smile, knowing that was a good sign. Bill was stiff in his movements and Amanda could tell he was in a lot of pain. She wondered what'd happened to him, but hadn't the nerve to ask. When things settled down, she'd start asking questions.

"Why don't you and Benjamin stay with me for a while? I have a spare bedroom," she offered, nodding at the building. She didn't want to be alone in her apartment. She also worried about how Bill and Benjamin would make it home now that the battery had died in the golf cart. Bill had stated he didn't live far from there, but regardless, he'd have to walk.

Bill glanced down at his son and then up at Amanda. He hadn't been sure where they were going to go since home wasn't an option. "We won't be putting you out?"

"Of course not," she said. "Besides, I think it's better for us to stick together for a while. You know, until we know what's going on."

"Thanks."

"Um, my place is 'round the back," Amanda said, staring at the apartments. She was feeling a little anxious about walking around the back of the building. Everything was too quiet. "That window up there," she said pointing to the side of the building, "is my room." She then forced her swollen knee to bend as she slid out of the passenger seat.

She tried to stand on the outside of her foot to avoid putting the wound flat against the asphalt. She was still worried about getting the wound infected, if it wasn't already. Under her bathroom sink, she had hydrogen peroxide, and in her medicine cabinet, she had a few antibiotics that she'd never finished from her last sinus infection. Once they were inside, she'd make sure to clean her foot, bandage it with whatever she might have, and take a dose of Erythromycin. She hated the stuff because it killed her stomach, but it was better than the alternative. "I don't have my key…"

Bill stared down at Benjamin and then at the building. He was debating on letting his son sleep, since the place seemed safe enough, while they found a way into the apartment. But then again, maybe he should wake him. "Do you think it's okay to leave him here for a bit?"

Amanda looked around. Her eyes noticed something on the other side of a red painted bench within the dog park. Bill followed her gaze. It was a body of a woman. There was no sign of the dog.

"I wouldn't leave him," she said, still eyeing the body. "Just in case…"

Bill agreed. The body was all he needed to sway his decision. He grunted as he hoisted Benjamin onto his shoulder. He limped behind Amanda, following her around the building. She stopped at the bottom of the first set of stairs. "The one on the left is mine." She looked at Benjamin, his eyes still closed. "Has he always been a sound sleeper?"

"No," Bill said. "I think it's…" He was afraid to say too much. He didn't want to frighten Amanda by bringing up the infection. He had nowhere to go and didn't want her to turn them away.

With her swollen knee and injured foot, Amanda awkwardly climbed the steps to the door. Bill stayed at the bottom, holding Benjamin, watching her. She tried the door. Just as she'd thought, it was locked. There were no accessible windows without a ladder.

"It's locked," she muttered. "We could try the office. They have keys to let themselves in for repairs and stuff."

Bill eyed the balcony. "Is the sliding door unlocked?"

Amanda hopped down the stairs on one leg and stared up at the balcony above. "I doubt it. But maybe…" She'd been in such a hurry to get Jasper to the hospital that she may have left the door unlocked. It was doubtful, but worth a try. "I'm not sure I can get up there." She was afraid of heights, but was desperate to get inside. She didn't like being out in the open where an infected person could get at them. Not that she was seeing or hearing anyone, or anything, except for some birds in the trees behind the complex. There was a small canyon of trees, grass, and hills directly behind her building. Late at night, yipping of coyotes could be heard roaming the canyon.

"If you can take Benji," he said. "I can…"

Amanda could see that Bill was struggling with his pain. He didn't let on, but she could see it in his eyes and his stiff movements. Even with her injuries, she was in better shape. "Let me give it a try first. If this doesn't work, I'll see if anyone is in the office." Even as the words tumbled from her lips, she doubted anyone would be working in the office. She wondered how many people were even in the apartment buildings. And just how many were still alive? It freaked her out to think about it. She'd noticed that the parking lot wasn't as full as normal. She bet a lot of people tried fleeing from the area when the virus hit.

Hoisting herself over the fenced-in patio of her downstairs neighbor, Amanda wondered if anyone was home. She'd never really spoken to her neighbors except for a quick *hello* or *good morning* from time to time. The woman that lived downstairs was a single mom with two school-aged children and a very loud baby that cried all the time. She'd often see the woman wearing green scrubs. Her guess was that she was a nurse, but she wasn't sure. There was also an older Hispanic woman that didn't speak much English staying there a good portion of the time, watching the children. Amanda believed she was the nanny.

Standing on the patio, Amanda's curiosity got the better of her. She walked up to the sliding glass door. The beige plastic vertical blinds were pulled closed, but there was a gap where one of them was turned and hadn't shut properly. Amanda cupped her face with her hands, shielding her eyes from the sun, and leaned against the cool glass. She couldn't see anything. Without electricity, it was dark inside. The only light coming into the room was through that small gap in the blinds.

Amanda then turned and made eye contact with Bill who was watching her.

"Anyone home?"

Amanda shrugged. "Can't tell."

"I'm going to sit on the steps," he said, walking over to the staircase. "Ben's getting heavy."

"Okay." Amanda then eyed the door to the outside storage unit. Each apartment had a small storage room off the patio and balcony. It also housed the air conditioning. Amanda kept her Christmas decorations, fake tree, bins of files, a few tools and a dolly in hers. Maybe the neighbors had a stepladder. Amanda grasped the handle and was surprised when the door opened. She kept her storage room unlocked, too, but being that this unit was on ground level and hers was upstairs, she figured it'd be locked up tight. Opening the door, she peeked inside. There were a lot of beach toys, shovels, pails, etc., a few unmarked storage boxes, and two folding chairs. No ladder.

Amanda grabbed one of the folding chairs, tucked in the back of the unit. Unfortunately, when she yanked it, she'd caused an avalanche of toys to come clattering out of the room and onto the pavement.

"You okay?" Bill called to her from the stairs.

"Yup!" Amanda said, unfolding the chair. "Knocked over a few things." Carefully, Amanda stepped up onto the chair, using her good knee, while holding onto the patio wall.

*Bang! Bang! Crash!* A loud thrashing from inside the downstairs apartment startled her. Frightened, she grabbed hold of the wall to steady herself. The blinds inside of the downstairs neighbors' unit moved all over. Someone was banging against the glass door.

"Oh my God!" she shrieked.

"What the hell?" Bill rushed to the patio, peering over the wall at the sliding glass doors. "Someone's in there!"

Amanda watched as the blinds were being ripped

away from the glass door. A puffed up white face with golden eyes and dark hair stared at her from inside. The infected woman began to bang and paw at the glass trying to get at Amanda. It was the woman Amanda believed to be the nanny. "Oh my God!" she screeched, forcing her swollen knee to bend. She scrambled up onto the wall and was now gripping the bottom edge of her upstairs balcony. She wasn't sure how she was going to get the strength to pull herself up.

"Amanda! Get out of there!"

"No! I've got it!"

Benjamin began to awaken due to the commotion and squirmed in Bill's arms. Bill set the boy down. With rapid movements, the woman began to pound on the glass trying to get outside. "Amanda," he warned. "If she gets through that glass… I don't want…"

"I know…" Amanda clutched hold of the balcony and tried to pull herself up. She was balancing on her tiptoes. She was able to grab the wooden slats. If she could only pull herself up a little more, she'd be able to swing her foot up there and climb up. "I'm almost…"

There was a loud cracking sound. Amanda's stomach leaped into her chest as the woman came barreling through the broken glass. She looked down in horror as the woman, cut and bleeding from her wounds inflicted by the glass, came after her.

"Amanda!" Bill yelled, drawing the attention of the infected woman to himself. "Run, Benji," he said to his son while nudging his back. "Now! Up the stairs!" Benjamin clutched hold of his dad's leg, refusing to let go. "Now, Benji! Up the stairs! *Now!*"

Benjamin let go of his father and ran up the stairs. He crouched down near the door at the top of the landing and buried his face in his hands, crying.

Amanda kicked her feet. She'd accidentally knocked over the chair and was hanging from the upstairs balcony. She reached up, grabbed the next wooden slat and somehow managed to pull herself up a little higher, but not high enough to be out of reach. Kicking hard, her foot accidentally came in contact with the side of the woman's head which drew the woman's attention away from Bill and back to Amanda.

Without thinking, Amanda's foot pushed with her full weight against the top of the woman's head, giving herself just enough oomph, to propel herself upwards to another rung in the wooden balcony. The woman then clawed at Amanda's foot, fingernails raking her skin. Amanda shrieked. Bill grabbed the largest tree branch he could find and swung it at the infected woman, whacking her in the back of the head.

*Smack!* He whacked the woman once more, drawing her attention away from Amanda, and again back to him. The woman snarled exposing her teeth while thick saliva dripped from the corners of her mouth.

Scrambling over the top of the wooden railing, Amanda made it to safety. She quickly flung open the door to her storage room and looked for the heaviest thing she could find. Her eyes zeroed in on the large plastic bin full of old bills and tax returns in files. Grunting, she hoisted the large bin onto the railing.

"Hey!" she yelled, looking down at the woman. "Yeah! You! Up here!" Drawn to her voice, the infected woman's head snapped to the side in an unnatural way. "Look! Up here!" The woman looked up. A set of golden eyes zeroed in on Amanda. The woman growled while crouching as if getting ready to leap.

"Don't even think about it, lady," Amanda warned as she pushed the large bin over the side of the balcony. To her amazement and relief, the infected woman didn't have the sense to move out of the way. The heavy bin crashed on top of the woman's face, snapping her neck with a loud crunching sound. The orange lid popped off the bin, and papers scattered across the concrete.

Bill raced to the neighbor's patio wall and peered over the side. "She's not moving." He then looked up at Amanda with concern in his crystal blue eyes. Amanda could tell he was worried about her. "You okay?"

Amanda pressed her hand to her racing heart. She could feel it pounding through her ribcage. She nodded while trying to catch her breath. "Yeah, I'm okay. I knew I kept all those stupid files for a reason. I'd always thought my taxes would be the death of me... didn't realize they'd save my life." She then remembered the sliding glass door. Closing her eyes, she prayed to her angels, and yanked on the handle. Her angels had been working overtime. It slid open.

***

"Damn it!" Mike swore, smacking the steering wheel. He came to a screeching halt, and then threw the SUV into reverse, tires squealing. He couldn't find a way around the blocked freeway. They were only a few miles from Ellie's condo. They'd come to several standstills during the trip, but Mike had always found a way around the collisions. Ellie has been surprised at how far they'd been able to go. Mike had stuck to backstreets most of the way. It was a longer trip, but they were able to bypass the freeways until now. They were at a point where the freeway had no longer been an option, and now they couldn't find a way off of it. Mike had turned around several times.

He was now driving down the freeway in the opposite direction. It made Ellie feel uncomfortable even though there wasn't anyone on the road. More than anything, it just felt odd. "Right there," Ellie said excitedly, pointing at the exit on the opposite side of the freeway. "I live off Mission!" The only issue was getting to the exit. There was a barrier blocking them from crossing the lanes. The only way off the freeway was to go up the on-ramp. However, there was a Big Rig lying on its side, blocking the ramp.

Frustrated, Mike smacked the steering wheel again.

"It's okay," Ellie said. "Let's try Highway 76. I live in between the 76 and Mission. We're almost there."

Mike frowned. "I don't think we're going to make it."

Ellie glanced at the console. For the first time, she noticed the little red light warning them that the gas tank was on empty.

"We're only a few miles away."

"We don't have a few miles," Mike said. "The light's been on for a while."

"Oh." Ellie nervously gnawed on her lower lip. The SUV slowed and came to a stop about a quarter mile from the 76 exit, or in their case, since they were driving the wrong direction, the 76 on-ramp.

Mike flung open the driver's side door and got out. Ellie wasn't sure what the plan was now. Surely, they weren't going to leave the SUV and all of their supplies on the freeway. She opened her door and joined Mike at the back of the SUV. He opened the back hatch and pulled out an empty gas can and a hose.

"You're gonna siphon gas?"

"That's the plan."

Mike pulled out his pocket knife and hacked at the hose, shortening it.

"Have you ever done it before?"

"Once."

"You really come prepared," she stated, watching him gather what he needed. Again, she wondered where she would be right now if she were alone. Probably dead.

"Years of training for an emergency, I guess." Mike shut the back hatch, walked to the cement center divider and hopped over. There were two abandoned cars on the other side of the road. Ellie followed him, scrambling to get over the divider. Mike had hopped over it so easily, making her realize how out of shape she was.

Pulling out his pocket knife, Mike pried open the gas tank door of a silver Camry. The windows had dark tint.

"What if someone is inside?" she asked, trying to see through the glass.

"They'll let us know."

Ellie wandered to the front of the car where the tint was a lighter shade. The front seats were empty. She then tugged at the door. Locked. The owners probably planned to come back for it.

Ellie glanced at the other car, a red Mercedes. She didn't realize how much farther away it was until she started walking in that direction. It was several car lengths down the road. A part of her was a little worried about wandering too far from Mike's side after what had happened at the gas station. However, the freeway was abnormally quiet. No one was around. She shielded her eyes against the sun, eyeing her target. Curiosity had gotten the better of her, and she wanted to see what was inside. Besides, she'd feel awful if there was a person inside needing her help.

Walking up to the car, she glanced through the back windshield. The tinted windows were too dark to see through. Ellie walked along the side of the car and gasped. The front end was completely dented in. Whomever or whatever the Mercedes had crashed into was no longer around. There was glass from the headlights on the ground, and the front bumper was mangled. The front windshield had been shattered creating an intricate spider web effect. *What if there is someone injured inside the car?* She couldn't tell.

Ellie tried to peer in through the driver's side window, but still couldn't see inside. She wrestled with the idea of trying to open the door, but couldn't seem to gather up the courage to do it. *What if an infected person was inside?* She then tried peering into the backseat. It was still too dark to see anything. Talking herself out of opening the doors, Ellie decided to wait for Mike. She'd feel more comfortable having him by her side. As soon as she began to walk back to the silver Camry, she heard it. She stopped walking and listened. She heard it again. *Scraping.* It was coming from inside the car. Ellie's pulse quickened. Someone was in the car. She turned back around and stopped by the driver's side back window. "Hello?" she called and peered through the glass. "Do you need help?" There was no answer. Ellie tapped on the window. "Hello?" There was more scraping. It became more fervent. She took a few steps back. It could be an infected person. But it could also be a child.

"Ellie?" she heard Mike call to her. "You okay?"

"Yeah!" she called back. She placed her hand on the door handle, heart drumming in her ears. The scraping stopped. She couldn't make up her mind. Should she try the handle? What if a child needed her help? What if the child was infected like the little girl she'd seen in Vegas?

"Ellie!" Mike called her again. "You ready?"

Ellie let go of the handle. Mike was heading toward the center divider, gas can and hose in hand.

"I think someone is trapped inside!" she called to him.

Mike stopped walking and set the gas can down next to the divider. "Wait for me!"

Ellie did as he said. Mike sprinted toward her.

"The backseat," she said, "someone's inside." The scraping continued.

"Stand back," he instructed.

Ellie did as he said without argument.

Mike lifted the handle. The door was unlocked. He opened it just a crack. He peeked inside and then flung it open. A little gray and black dog with long straggly fur, hopped out of the car, and ran into the street looking confused. Mike took a better look inside the car while Ellie tried to calm the dog.

Kneeling, she held her hand out to him. "It's okay, sweetheart. Come here, sweetie. Come here…

I'm not going to hurt you."

The dog watched her, obviously frightened. He kept a safe distance, hind legs trembling. His tail slowly wagged from side to side.

Ellie stayed in a crouching position with her hand held out to him. "It's okay, honey." She made a couple of kissing sounds that she always did with her own dog. "Poor baby, being trapped in a car."

Mike scooted out of the backseat and closed the door, startling the dog.

"It's okay," Ellie cooed. Nervous, the dog took off running down the street. "Oh no!" She jumped to her feet.

"Let him go," Mike said, putting a hand on her shoulder.

"I can't just let him go," she said. "The poor little guy. Why would the owner leave him locked in a car? That's horrible!"

Mike sighed. "She's dead."

Ellie eyed the car. "Oh."

"We should get going."

"I can't just leave him." Ellie watched the dog. His pace slowed down, and he was sniffing the ground, lost.

Mike sighed, again. "Okay. Let's go get him."

"Walk," Ellie said. "If you look aggressive, he's going to run."

"Are you sure it's a dog? Looks more like a rat."

"I'm sure," Ellie snapped.

The dog looked back at them and continued forward.

"I think this might be a lost cause," Mike said.

Ellie stopped walking. "Why don't you put gas in the SUV? I'll see if I can get him. If it's just me, he might not be as scared."

Looking up and down the freeway, Mike thought it over. He didn't like the idea of Ellie being on her own, but everything seemed quiet enough. He nodded his agreement. "If you don't catch him by the time I'm done, we'll have to leave him behind."

Ellie gave him a sour look. Mike couldn't help but smile. The evil look she threw at him didn't fit her personality. But he had to admit that he liked her determination and her big heart, caring about this animal's well-being.

"I'll get him," she said, and took off after the dog. Mike didn't doubt her.

Picking up the gas can and hose from where he left them, he hopped over the center divider, heading for the SUV.

Ellie followed the dog. She tried to keep her footsteps quiet and non-threatening. He kept stopping to sniff around, and then would look over his shoulder at her, and begin walking again.

"It's okay, sweetie." Ellie noticed the little dog was heading for the 76 off ramp. Her condo was just over a mile down the road. If only they could get the SUV over the center divider. From here, she'd easily be able to walk home. Being so close, it was tempting. She'd feel a hundred times safer, in the comfort of her own home. She thought of her dog, Max, and prayed that he was okay. She prayed that her neighbors were okay. As much as she wanted to go home, she was just as afraid of what she'd find there. She wondered how many of her neighbors were still alive. Were they hiding in their homes? Or would she find them all dead or infected?

Ellie started walking down the off-ramp

wondering if Mike was right. Maybe going after the dog was a lost cause. Maybe she was being plain stupid thinking she could help the little guy. Ellie glanced over her shoulder in the direction of the SUV. Being this far away from Mike was beginning to worry her. But she couldn't go back now. Not without the dog. She had to at least try.

Ellie had an idea and stopped walking. She began to smack the tops of her thighs in a playful manner while calling the dog. Max always became excited when she did that and wanted to play. Maybe this dog would be the same. "Come here, sweetie! Come on. Here little guy…" She smacked her legs again. "You're such a cute doggy."

The dog looked at her for a second, and then broke into a full-blown run down the off-ramp.

"You've got to be kidding me," she breathed, then took off after him. She stopped running when she noticed a pile-up of cars, up ahead, blocking the ramp's exit. One car had gone off the side of the road, and three others were crashed into each other. The dog had stopped running and was staring at the cars.

Ellie crept up closer to the dog. He was sniffing at a back tire of a white Honda. He walked over to the back door and stood on his hind legs. While he was distracted, Ellie moved a bit faster, hoping to snatch him. The dog sat down and perked up his ears, staring at the car.

Taking this opportunity, Ellie ran up behind him and clutched him in her hands. "Gotcha!" she said, and pressed him to her chest. She tried to calm him by petting his head with her other hand. "It's okay, sweetie." Then she stopped moving. She heard what had distracted the dog. *Moaning.* A man's voice.

The dog squirmed trying to break free of Ellie's grasp. She held him tight to her chest until he settled down. The deep moaning started up again. It was coming from inside the car. Ellie walked up to the driver's side door. A man was in the driver's seat, blood was all over his face and splattered on the window. She tugged at the door handle. To her surprise, it opened.

"Are you okay?" she asked, knowing full well the man was far from okay.

He moaned again, not turning his head to look at her. The side of his face was painted red with blood from a head wound. Ellie peered into the car, but didn't see any passengers. The dog squirmed again. Ellie tightened her grip. "I'm going to get you help. Okay? I'll be right back." When she turned to leave, the man snatched hold of her shirt and growled.

Ellie screamed. She could feel his fingers tighten in the material. The dog jumped from her arms and took off running.

Without thinking, Ellie smacked at the man's arm and pulled away. Luckily, the man's fingers lost their grip on her shirt. He growled the familiar guttural growl of the infected. Yellow eyes gleamed through a swollen, bloody face. His arms flailed wildly as he tried to get at her. His seatbelt kept him restrained. Ellie was just out of reach. Quickly, she scanned the area around her. The little dog was long gone.

Having heard her screams, Mike was running up the off-ramp in her direction. "Ellie!"

Ellie ran toward him, hoping the infected man couldn't break free of the seatbelt. She could see the SUV on the other side of the divider. "He's infected!"

Mike took her into his arms. "You okay?"

Ellie nodded.

He didn't ask about the dog. "Let's get you home."

Not even ten minutes later, Ellie was looking at her condominiums. As luck would have it, the 76 on-ramp, which became their off-ramp was unobstructed. There were a few cars blocking the intersection before Canyon Drive, but they were easily able to maneuver around them, bypassing the accident.

Mike followed Ellie's directions. "I have a garage," she said. "Oh, wait. The remote is in my car. I also have a parking space."

"Doubtful it matters where you park anymore."

"Oh, yeah," Ellie said. "We should still park in my space. We don't know…" She couldn't get herself to finish her thought out loud. *We don't know how many people were still alive.*

Mike parked where instructed. Ellie hopped out of the SUV, excited to be home. She walked hurriedly through the complex. Mike followed her, noticing a body sprawled out on the balcony of a unit across from the building Ellie was heading to. He didn't say anything to her about it. He didn't want to make her more anxious than she already was. He wanted her to have this moment of happiness of returning home. Ellie climbed steps to a second floor. She stopped outside a door and tried the knob. Locked.

"I don't have my keys," she said, turning around. "My neighbors, the one's checking in on Max, have my spare."

A dog started barking excitedly on the other side of Ellie's door. Her eyes grew wide. "Oh my God! It's Max! Hi Max!" she called to him through the door. Mike could hear him jumping up and down, claws raking the other side of the door.

Ellie knocked on her neighbor's front door. No answer. She rang the doorbell and waited. Still no answer. She tried the doorknob. Locked. Cupping her hands, she peered in through the window next to the door. The blinds were open. The place appeared vacant.

"No one's there. I can't believe they'd just leave Max."

Mike was studying the window next to Ellie's front door. She watched as he pulled a pocket knife from his pocket and easily pried open the window. "You know," he said. "You really should put locks on your windows."

"I hope Francesca and Chloe are alright." Ellie eyed her neighbor's door.

Max barked at the window. "Probably a good idea if you go in first," Mike said, not wanting to get bit.

Ellie laughed. "He's a little dog with a big bark who's afraid of his own shadow." Ellie reached in and pulled the cords, lifting the blinds before crawling through the window. She was greeted by loud barks and squeals of excitement. She unlocked the front door, letting Mike inside. "Watch your step," she instructed. Her condo smelt pretty ripe. Max had obviously been locked inside for quite a while, confirming the fact that something horrible had happened to her neighbors. There were several piles on the tile floor near the front door where he'd relieved himself. Ellie opened the sliding glass door of her balcony to air out her condo. She was immediately greeted with a gust of fresh ocean breeze. Her condo was only a mile from the beach. The temperature was in the low seventies. It felt heavenly after being stuck in the desert. Ellie was thinking of how fortunate she was to have made it home when she noticed the body of an elderly man, sprawled out on the balcony across from her.

Max raced around the condo, thrilled to have her home. He then ran out the door, relieved himself, and then raced back up the stairs and into the condo. Ellie noticed that a large bag of dog food, that she'd bought before she'd left for Vegas, was torn open in the middle of the kitchen. Kibble was scattered all over the floor. Max had shredded open the bag himself.

Ellie took in the sight of her home and suddenly felt both emotionally and physically exhausted. Even though she was surrounded by death, she felt like a huge weight had been lifted from her shoulders. She walked over to the kitchen, grabbed the paper towels from the counter, and began to clean up Max's mess by the front door.

"I'll go unload our stuff," Mike said. "Go get yourself cleaned up and relax a bit."

"Unload?" Ellie asked. "Are we staying?"

"For now," Mike said.

Tension released from Ellie's shoulders as relief washed over her.

# Day 10

# Chapter 27

A week had passed since returning home. Amanda was saddened by the turn of events, but also happy that the week had been pretty much uneventful except for the car with the loud base she'd heard a couple of times driving up and down Mission Avenue in the middle of the night. Hearing the booming base of rap music gave her the chills. Whoever was driving the car was up to no good. It was obvious the person, or persons, wanted that to be made known to those still alive. Bill had told her not to worry about it. If they kept to themselves, they'd be alright.

Other than that, everything was still eerily quiet. So far, they hadn't come across anyone else alive or infected in the apartment complex, but they also stayed close to their own building. The complex was quite large, and Amanda couldn't fathom that everyone was dead. She was sure that those still alive were doing what they were doing; keeping to themselves and hoping everything would go back to normal. Eventually, they'd come out of hiding when they ran out of food.

They had scavenged all of Amanda's neighboring apartments in her building for food and supplies. The bodies Bill had come across, he'd dragged over to the dog run, doused them with lighter fluid and burned them. Amanda worried that the smoke would draw attention. But so far, the car with the loud base hadn't made an appearance during the day. She prayed it stayed that way.

Amanda had wanted to be strong enough to help Bill with the bodies, but couldn't get herself to do it. The smell alone made her throw up. She hated herself for being such a wimp.

Bill had explained that if they left them to rot, it would become a health hazard. If they were planning to continue to stay in her apartment, they needed to clear the dead around them to keep from spreading disease, which made perfect sense to Amanda. The last thing she wanted to do was have to look for a new place to live. She'd been burning incense in her apartment to help cover up the smell of death, and spraying Lysol to hopefully kill off any germs. While Bill worked on clearing the neighboring apartments of bodies, Amanda went in after him and removed food items and other useful items. She felt bad taking other people's things. It felt like she was stealing from them, or stealing from those that had vacated their residence. *What if they came back home?* Every time she entered an apartment, she said a silent prayer for the person that lived there. She'd realized that she'd been saying a lot of prayers lately.

Benjamin had fully recovered from the virus. There was no sign that he'd ever been sick except for a slight hint of golden yellow outlining his irises. He stayed inside the apartment, only coming out onto the balcony from time to time to sit in a lawn chair. She and Bill were doing their best to shield him from the atrocities of the new world. Amanda had supplied Benjamin with books, coloring books, crayons, and toys that she'd found in other apartments to help to entertain him. Recently, she'd overheard him asking his dad about his mother. She didn't mean to eavesdrop. Bill had explained to Benjamin that his mother was in heaven. Amanda wanted to ask Bill what had happened to his wife but didn't. She could tell it was a sore subject. Bill had never mentioned whether she'd become infected, and Amanda didn't feel it was her place to press him for answers when he was grieving. Instead, out of respect, she kept her questions regarding his wife's death to herself and did the best she could to comfort Benjamin.

That afternoon while standing in the kitchen making peanut butter sandwiches for lunch, Amanda was thinking about the hospital. "Do you think that this virus… or infection… is from aliens?" she asked Bill who was sitting on the couch in the living room, taking a break from clearing apartments. He was thumbing through an old Newsweek magazine he'd found. The loaf of bread she'd been using to make their lunch was stale, but still edible. Being that she couldn't eat wheat, she smeared peanut butter on a rice cake for herself.

Bill chuckled at Amanda's question. They hadn't discussed the cause of the infection since leaving the hospital. "Don't tell me you believed that bunch of bull shit?"

Amanda scowled at him. She didn't appreciate being laughed at or talked down to. "You have a better explanation?"

"Yeah," he said, tossing the magazine onto the coffee table. "Something much more believable, like an act of terrorism or government conspiracy."

Amanda didn't reply. Instead, she changed the

subject by calling Benjamin into the room. "Ben, your sandwich is ready!"

Benjamin opened the door to the guest bedroom that he and his dad were sharing. Amanda set the sandwich down on the small wooden table in her eat-in kitchen. Bill joined Benjamin at the table. Amanda handed him a sandwich.

"I'm thinking of checking out the grocery store on the corner," Bill said.

Amanda gnawed on her bottom lip. She worried about leaving the safety of the complex. "You think it's safe?"

"Probably," Bill said, taking a bite of the sandwich. "I'm thinking of picking up some charcoal. Put that grill to use that I found."

"We don't have any meat. I'm sure everything at the store is spoiled."

"We can grill veggies and some canned goods."

"If there are any vegetables not growing mold."

"Won't know, if we don't try. Plus everything tastes better on the grill. We'll stock up on water, too."

Amanda nodded. So far the water was still running, but who knew when that would come to an end. She also worried about the safety of drinking the tap water. "There's a hardware store over there too."

Bill raised an eyebrow. "That should be useful."

When they finished their lunch, Benjamin went back to his room to continue building with the large bin of Legos Amanda had found for him. Bill went back to work on the apartments. Amanda was clearing the kitchen table when it happened. The lights began to flicker on and off, there was a buzzing noise, the air conditioning unit kicked on, the

Television set clicked on, and her microwave beeped.

"Oh my God!" she screamed.

Benjamin came running out of the bedroom. "The lights are on!"

Amanda smiled at him. Excitement coursed through her veins. If the electricity was up and running, that meant things were going back to normal. She ran to the front door to go find Bill. Bill was bounding up the stairs in her direction.

"Electricity!" he said, grabbing hold of Amanda at the top of the landing and giving her a great big bear hug. They were both laughing. Benjamin came running and joined in the group hug.

"I can't believe it!" Amanda shrieked. She'd never felt more excited in her life. Then everything grew dark; it was as if a big storm suddenly moved in out of nowhere, blocking out the sun.

"What the hell?" Bill ran down the stairs and looked up at the sky. He stood there in stunned silence staring upwards.

"What is it?" Amanda asked.

Frightened by the sudden darkness, Benjamin grabbed hold of her hand.

"Bill? Bill… what is it?"

Not taking his eyes off the sky, Bill muttered, "Maybe I was wrong."

***

Ellie was walking Max around the complex while Mike showered. The water was cold, but they were both thankful for still having running water. So far Ellie had only found one of her neighbors alive. Throughout the week, she and Mike had knocked on all of the doors in the complex. Still, that didn't mean they were all dead. A lot of people had vacated the premises when the virus hit. Ellie knew this by how empty the parking lot was. Generally there wasn't enough parking for everyone that lived there, and people ended up having to park on the street. Also, she wouldn't be surprised, if there were survivors hiding in their homes, too afraid to answer their doors. Would she answer her door to a stranger and risk becoming infected? Probably not. If Mike hadn't been there with her, she'd probably stay hidden, too.

Knocking on Mrs. Marshall's door, she and Max waited on the doorstep. When the door opened, Mrs. Marshall peered out at them. She'd been completely oblivious to the virus infecting people and what was happening around her. Mrs. Marshall was in her eighties and lived alone. Ellie believed that she might have been suffering from some sort of dementia. "Are you here to clean?" the older woman asked.

"No," Ellie said. "I'm your neighbor, Ellie. I live around the corner from you." She'd had this same conversation with Mrs. Marshall yesterday.

"My phone's not working," the woman complained. "And my electricity is out."

"I know," Ellie said. "That's why I'm checking on you. I brought you something to eat." Ellie carried in a plastic grocery bag filled with food.

"A bad storm is coming. I can feel it in my bones. Electricity can go out with a storm."

"Yes, it can," Ellie said, not arguing with her. Yesterday, she'd spent a long time explaining the situation. However, it didn't do much good. Mrs. Marshall obviously didn't remember their conversation.

"When are you going to start cleaning?" she asked. "This place needs a good scrub."

"I've only dropped by to check on you." Ellie smiled and put the items she'd brought with her on the kitchen counter. She opened a bag of chips and poured some onto a plate next to a Nutella sandwich she'd made with stale bread. "Here, I brought you lunch."

Mrs. Marshall eyed the sandwich and the chips. "The other lady is a much better cook. That looks like crap."

"Well, I'm not your cleaning lady or your cook," Ellie explained, ignoring the old woman's harness. "I'm your neighbor."

Mrs. Marshall sat down at the table and noticed Max for the first time. He was sitting by her chair, staring up at her plate, and then at Mrs. Marshall with big brown eyes. "Whose dog is that?"

"He's mine," Ellie said, opening a bottle of spring water and setting it down on the table. "Max, stop begging for food."

"I'm allergic," Mrs. Marshall snapped, glaring at the dog. "Get him out of here! You can't bring a dog to work with you. I'll have a word with your agency as soon as the phone lines are up."

"You ready to go home, Max?" Ellie patted the little Corgi-Terrier mix on the head, ignoring the useless threat. "I'll check on you again later."

Mrs. Marshall huffed and complained under her breath. As Ellie was walking to the front door, Max following close behind, the lights began to flicker. Max growled, spooked by the sudden onset of electricity.

Ellie looked around the room, startled. She hadn't expected the electricity ever to come back on. That had to be a good sign, right? Excitement coursed through her veins. Maybe things were beginning to look up. When Ellie opened the front door, Max raced down the stairs, into the sunshine and began to bark. He looked upwards toward the sky. Mrs. Marshall got up from the table and peered out the front door after them. The sky suddenly grew dark, encompassing them in shadow. Ellie ran over to Max who was still looking upwards, growling and barking. She'd never seen him act like that before. She looked upwards. An enormous spacecraft, unlike those she'd seen in movies, hovered over them, blocking out the sunlight. Ellie couldn't believe her eyes.

"See?" Mrs. Marshall said, looking up at the sky, her vision not what it used to be. "I told you. A bad storm. I can always sense when something bad is going to happen. I feel it deep within my bones."

Ellie gnawed on her lower lip. She felt it too. And this was only the beginning.

# About the Author

M.A. Hollstein resides in Southern California with her two wonderful children and her spoiled kitties. Under the name, Michelle Ann Hollstein, she's the author of the paranormal mystery series *A Vienna Rossi Paranormal Mystery,* the quirky and comical *Aggie Underhill Mysteries*, the Fantasy Trilogy, *The Niberia Chronicles,* and the new nonfiction series, *Who Says You Can't Paint?*

You can visit her website at
www.MichelleHollstein.com
to learn more about her books and to view book trailers.

**Fatal Reaction**
The Beginning
Survival
Battle of the Hunted
Nightfall

**When Darkness Falls**
Awakened
Metamorphosis

**The Niburu Chronicles**
Book of Dreams
Ashes to Diamonds
Hidden Identity

**Ms. Aggie Underhill Mysteries**
Deadly Withdrawal
Something's Fishy in Palm Springs
Maid in Heaven
A Hardboiled Murder
One Hell of a Cruise
A Prickly Situation
Vegas or Bust
Dead Ringer
The Case of the Haunted Address
The Mystery of the Beautiful Old Friend
All I Wanted was a Drink
Love is Murder
End of the Rainbow

**A Vienna Rossi Paranormal Mystery**
Awakened Within
Beautiful Beginnings
Cheating Heart
Ghostly Gig, A Vienna Rossi Halloween Short Story

Made in the USA
Monee, IL
25 February 2023

28693973R00164